D1706247

CODE NAME: LIBERTY

a novel of romantic suspense

MARSHALL THORNTON

Published by Kenmore Books

Edited by Joan Martinelli

Cover design by Marshall Thornton

Images by 123rf stock

ISBN: 9781688743410

First Edition

 Created with Vellum

"A hair divides what is false and true." – Omar Khayyam

MAADI MILITARY HOSPITAL

Cairo

July 27, 1980

The terrible night had gone on so long. She watched as the king hemorrhaged, receiving bag after bag of blood, falling into a coma for much of the night, and then, for three short, precious hours, woke and spoke to them. Spoke to her, to their children. Now he was quiet again, seeming to float between life and death.

The heavy drapes were drawn; somewhere behind them the sun had risen. Why? Why must it continue to rise? She was sure they would lose him today. She wished the day would not begin.

In the dim light of the room, in his face she could see a shadow of the distinguished man she'd met at the embassy in Paris, the man she'd married as in a fairy tale, the man she'd fought with over his excesses, and at last followed into exile. She saw all of those men there in the sunken shadows of his cheeks.

Her daughter stood on the other side of the bed murmuring, "Baba, Baba."

Taking the king's hand in hers, she watched his eyes, open but not seeing. Whispering his name, she waited for a response, but none came. Suddenly, he took two short breaths and a final long one. And was gone.

Though it was happening in front of her, it seemed impossible. He had been so strong, so capable, so much the king. They stood by the bed, uncertain. Already adrift.

A voice behind her said, "Close his eyes."

Leaning over the bed, she brushed her hand gently across his face to close his eyes. Then, she reached under his pillow and took out a small cloth bag of prayers and Iranian soil. The small bag had traveled everywhere with them: Egypt, Mexico, New York, Panama and then, finally, back to Egypt. It, and they, had traveled thousands of miles. Their homeland had been with them always.

The doctor bent over the king and carefully removed his wedding ring. He held it out to her. She took it and put it onto her finger next to her own wedding band. She promised herself she would never take it off.

CHAPTER ONE

"Now you may tell your friends you have kissed a prince."

"What if I'm not the kind of guy to kiss and tell?"

He gifted me a smile.

"Then you may get to kiss a prince again."

The club was called Exile and it had just opened, giving the night an extra feverish charge. Silver streamers hung from the ceiling, trading flashy winks with the mirror balls. Pink and blue beams slashed the dance floor like light sabers. The floor was crowded with people—mostly men, young, attractive—bouncing, jumping, writhing, eyes flirting, smiles flashing, hands in the air, T-shirts off, sweating. Streisand and Summers warbled together through the sound system, refusing to cry. The club smelled of expensive colognes, sweat and poppers. A heady mix.

I wanted to lean into the prince and kiss him again. We'd seen each other on the dance floor. I was dancing with my friend, Wendi. I had no idea who he was dancing with—a friend, a boyfriend, I didn't care. I hustled toward him, abandoning Wendi to her private dance: eyes shut, floating on the music, hips wiggling. Now, as though watching, The Village People were sending me west. And then I was in front of him, our eyes locked, bodies falling into a matching rhythm. Before the song ended he was kissing me, pulling me close, hips pressing into me with the beat.

Two songs later he pulled away, saying good-bye. Telling me I'd kissed a prince.

"I came with my friends. I'm sorry, but I have to go."

Digging an expensive gold-plated pen out of his jeans, he handed it to me saying, "Give me your number." He stretched out his arm for me to write on. There was nothing to do but write my name and a phone number on his arm. Another smile, beautiful white teeth and those lips calling me to press myself against them one more time. But he turned and disappeared into the crowd.

Finding Wendi at the bar, I took her drink from her and sipped it. Gin and tonic, tart and tasting of pine forests. She was a small girl with brown hair she'd cut into a pixie, a gap in the center of her smile, and a very long menthol cigarette floating in one hand. She wore a black dress with white polka dots she'd found in a vintage store on Rhode Island Avenue. She called it her Audrey Hepburn dress. Over her heart she wore a large Carter/Mondale pin.

"Who was that?"

"Cigarette," I demanded. She kept my Salems in her clutch. My Calvins were too tight; they'd crush the pack so she carried them for me. If she left earlier than I did, I'd slip them into my boot. She handed them to me along with a red Bic lighter.

"He said his name is David. He's a prince."

"A prince of where?"

I shrugged. "I don't know. I didn't ask. He has a British accent, though."

She rolled her eyes. "There's no Prince David in the royal family."

"Yeah. He doesn't look British either," I said. And he didn't. He looked exotic. His hair black, curling in waves over his forehead and ears; eyebrows thick and wide over cloudy gray eyes; skin like warm sand; and his lips, red, bowed, delicious—

"Patrick?"

"Huh?"

"Are you going to see him again?"

I shrugged. "He had me write my name and number on his arm."

"That's romantic," she shouted in my ear. "Too bad you don't have a phone."

———

Of course, when it comes to lineage I, Patrick Henry Burke, am no slouch. My mother was a Henry, a direct descendant of one of the founding fathers, Patrick Henry. You know, "Give me liberty or give me death!" That Patrick Henry.

When I was a child, Mom was DAR, spending her weekdays driving up and down the New England coast attending luncheons to give presentations on her ancestor's accomplishments. They were many, including attendance at the First Congressional Congress, being the first governor of Virginia and a brilliant orator. The talks would last forty-five minutes. I know; she rehearsed in front of me once a week.

Henry, though a slave-owner himself, wrote against slavery and fought to end the importation of slaves. My mother's branch of the family was full of far more rigid abolitionists, which in time caused them to move north to Massachusetts, and that is how I came to grow up just outside of Boston two centuries later.

As a kid, I was duly impressed by our connection to a founding father, until I reached junior high school and my biology teacher explained—in order to demonstrate some aspect of genetics, I think—that there were probably ten million Americans who could trace their families back to the tiny group of colonists who arrived on the Mayflower. While I was related to just one man, seven or eight generations ago, I still probably had hundreds of thousands of cousins once, twice, three times removed who could claim the same line.

And then there was my father. Burke, which sounds very British but is actually an Americanization of some Slavic name given to the family when my grandfather arrived at Ellis Island five years into the twentieth century. Grandfather Burke met an Irish serving girl while delivering coal to one of the better neighborhoods in Boston. That union resulted in ten children, my father being the sixth and final boy.

So, when my parents met at a chowder restaurant in Boston's North End while my dad was home on leave from Korea, their union was a disaster in the making. They eloped, which so enraged my maternal grandfather that when he died he left several hundred thousand dollars in trust to my mother. In trust, meaning it was money she could have *after* the death of my father.

The money was left with a financial firm that mismanaged it— Wall Street's way of saying the money had been systematically stolen through a series of self-dealing trades that left my mother the loser and her broker the winner. By the time my father died of an aneurism shortly before my tenth birthday and their sixteenth wedding anniversary, there was barely enough money for a decent funeral.

My father's death belied another of my biology teacher's lessons. We'd been told that long lines of breeding the same gene pool back onto itself led to weakness, and by that logic it should have been my mother, with her rarified genes, who kicked the bucket early and not my mutt of a father.

All of which meant that, when it was time for me to go to college, some other eighteen-year-old, whose investment broker father was inept in only the cleverest ways, was already receiving my Harvard education. So instead, I did a year at Massachusetts Bay Community College and signed up for my second year only to drop all my classes a few weeks later. After the 1978 election, as a dewy-eyed nineteen-year-old, I followed our new senator to Washington. Well, I followed a twenty-two-year-old junior staff assistant in our new senator's office. The junior staff assistant wore tightly tailored rayon slacks that held his ass—

Never mind. The relationship lasted only a few weeks due to the junior staff assistant's political ambitions. He suddenly—and I have no idea why he hadn't thought of this before I moved—recognized that a live-in boyfriend was a political liability. And so, I had to go.

That left me adrift in our nation's capital. I found a job as a busboy, and later a waiter, at Le Marquis, the four-star restaurant atop the Hotel Continental. I also found a Dupont Circle apartment to share with my new friend, Wendi, who worked with me at Le Marquis, and settled in. I could have gone back to Massachusetts, I suppose, but I was still only nineteen and they'd just raised the drinking age there to twenty. I'd already discovered the Fruit Loop—a nickname for the gay bars located near Dupont Circle—and I could drink in Washington. There were clubs to be explored and princes to be kissed.

The Hotel Continental was a ten-story building sitting across from Lafayette Park that was wider than it was tall. It had been built during the first Roosevelt administration, the first *Teddy* Roosevelt administration. I wasn't ever sure what architectural period the building fell into, but if you told me it was called The Wedding Cake Period wedged between Rococo and Victorian, I wouldn't have been at all surprised. Le Marquis was the French restaurant that sat on the very top of the cake, I mean building, and boasted a view of the White House.

The restaurant was paneled in walnut, had a blue carpet with white stars—eight-pointed stars, not to be confused with the five-pointed stars of our flag—and Colonial furnishings, many of which were original and not at all like the cornucopia-patterned Colonial sofa my mother bought during my last year of high school. The dinner service was gold-trimmed white china and thick pewter flatware. The décor at Le Marquis was all-American, but the food and the name of the restaurant—after the Marquis de Lafayette—were very French.

Le Marquis was one of *the* places to eat in D.C. and we hosted many politicians, celebrities and the just plain rich. Walter Cronkite came in from time to time, Gore Vidal ate there when in town, as did Jackie O—she never ordered from the menu, but instead would request a baked potato with sour cream, chives and caviar.

The politicians, I seldom recognized. I mean, they're all the same anyway, right? I did learn to recognize the type: older men shoveled into expensive suits, suits that were all shades of gray and, very occasionally, brown. Black and blue having been banished; black being too morbid and blue too frivolous.

I'd begun as a busboy for the first eight months, before I was taught French service and allowed to wait tables. That meant I had little seniority and my regular schedule was Tuesday through Thursday. These were the least profitable nights. The waiters and waitresses who'd been there a long time, some of them fifteen or twenty years, worked Friday, Saturday and Sunday. Several worked only one of those nights and had full-time jobs as realtors or teachers or librarians during the week.

Keeping their one shift at Le Marquis, a shift in which they often made as much or more than they made during the week, allowed them the luxury of pursuing more interesting work. My three nights a week, in which I never got the best stations, rarely added up to what could be made on a single Friday or Saturday night.

Most of the staff, whether they worked during the week or weekends, were there so they could do something else. Wendi, for instance, was a serial volunteer. During the day, she worked for Planned Parenthood, the ERA, the NAACP, and, most recently, the Carter/Mondale campaign. And I, well, I wasn't really into anything yet, so I spent my off-time reading or sleeping or dancing in nightclubs.

The Tuesday after I kissed the prince, I was working in the Madison Room, a small square room off the main dining room with five four-tops, which were almost never filled at the same time. I had only one party: four men in gray suits; congressmen or some such. They were smoking cigars, meaning the hostess was unlikely to seat anyone else in the room until they were finished and gone. Their dinner polished off, they settled in with their coffee and cognac and cigars—the three C's dear to a congressman's heart. I checked on them, filled up their coffees and, when I was sure they were okay, went back to the employee lounge to smoke. A cigarette; cigars are disgusting.

Lounge was hardly an accurate word for the space they gave us. Beyond the pick-up line and the grill and the salad station, and even the patisserie where two French (though actually Canadian) pastry chefs argued for eight hours a day while making wonderful pastries, the so-called employee lounge was a space only big enough for a table, three chairs, a pay phone and an overflowing ashtray. The freight elevator was right there, and we sometimes had to stand up and move out of the way when there was a late delivery.

I had just passed the salad station, when a smirking Wendi ran up to me. "You have a phone call. Someone with a British accent."

Despite my pounding heart, I casually walked back to the employee lounge, lit a cigarette, and then, feigning as though I couldn't care less, picked up the receiver from atop the pay phone where Wendi had left it.

"Hello?"

"Patrick, this is David. We met—"

"Yes, I remember you. You're one of the two or three princes I met last week. I didn't think you'd call me."

"Why didn't you think I'd call you?"

"Oh, I don't know," I said, honestly. I hadn't thought about it, I just assumed he'd never call. "I guess I thought you'd have better things to do."

"If I had better things to do, I'd be doing them."

What did that mean? There was an awkward beat before I said, "Okay. I guess you were bored today."

I wished I'd thought of something clever to say back to him, but my mouth had gone dry and my mind blank. Wendi had come back and was making a face at me. David said something I didn't hear.

"I'm sorry, what did you say?"

"This isn't your phone number, is it?"

"Not really," I admitted. I imagined he could hear the sound of the restaurant in the background, plates clanging together, orders being screamed out. "I'm a waiter at Le Marquis. This is the employee pay phone."

Wendi started passionately making out with the back of her hand. I gave her the finger and turned away.

"Oh, yes. I've been to Le Marquis many times," David said. "I've never seen you, though."

"Do you come on the weekend?"

"Yes, of course."

"I work during the week."

"I see. Are you going to give me your real phone number?"

"We don't have a phone. Neither one of us have good credit and they want a huge deposit."

"Who is 'we?' Do you have a boyfriend?"

"No. I meant, me and my roommate. I think you saw her. She was with me at Exile. The polka-dots?"

"Ah, yes."

"Is he really a prince?" Wendi whispered.

I was afraid he might have heard, so I asked quickly, "Hey, where are you from?"

"Persia."

"Persia?" I repeated for Wendi's benefit. She raised an eyebrow. Then I said to the prince, "But there's no such place. Except in history books."

"Don't you think I know that?" His voice sounded hurt.

"Sorry."

"It's Iran now, of course. But you see, my family went into exile when it was still Persia, so that's what we call it."

"So, you're not related to the shah?" I knew they'd kicked him out and I had the feeling he'd died recently, but wasn't entirely—

"You mean Reza Pahlavi," he said, coldly.

"I guess."

"No, we are not related. He was nothing but a commoner. It is my family that is royal. But it doesn't matter anymore. He's dead. And will never return."

"Oh yeah, I think I heard that."

"When can I see you?"

"You want to see me?"

"Of course I do. Tell me when you have a day off."

"I'm off on Friday."

"Then I shall see you Friday."

We made arrangements to meet and said good-bye. Wendi lit a cigarette and held it near her face.

"So?" she asked. "You're seeing him Friday?"

"You shouldn't listen to private conversations. Or make faces at people having private conversations. Or make out with your hand."

"Where are you meeting him?"

"Why do you care? You're not coming."

"I'm curious. I'd like to know what a prince does on a first date."

"None of your business."

And then Maxim, the headwaiter, was screaming my name in the kitchen in his fake French accent, "Pat*rick*, where is Pat*rick*?"

My congressmen wanted their check.

CHAPTER TWO

Wendi and I shared a two-bedroom apartment on P Street, a few blocks east of Dupont Circle. The building was a red brick row house, four floors, chopped up into apartments. Ours was the English basement once used by servants when the house was still in one piece. The front door was three steps down from the street and there were two square windows at the front, another window next to the back door, and a couple of equally small windows along one side of the apartment. It was dark, often damp—and expensive. But, we could walk to work—eight blocks south—and to the Fruit Loop—three blocks east.

Of course, we had almost nothing. A Salvation Army couch covered in an Indian bedspread from Pier 1, a portable record player, a stack of albums, a portable TV from the late '50s with controls at the top corners like insect eyes, and some old plastic milk crates serving as end tables. Wendi's bedroom was right after the kitchen and was the most furnished room in the apartment, since her father had moved the French provincial bedroom set that had been her teenaged fantasy from their home in North Bethesda.

My room was all the way in the back and held only a full-sized mattress and a snaking row of paperbacks lined up around the floorboards. I kept my socks and underwear in the suitcase I'd brought when I came to Washington on a train and never left. All my other clothes hung in the closet.

That Friday, I'd showered, shaved and dowsed myself in leathery cologne. Then, towel wrapped around me, I stood in front of my closet unable to decide what to wear. I didn't want to wear much; it was well over ninety degrees outside. Of course, the trick would be staying cool while not looking like a complete slut.

I could wear white shorts and a black tank, but the shorts were very short and the tank very tight. Cut-offs and a white tank? The cut-offs were ripped up the sides, though. I could make a new pair. I had an extra pair of jeans. Well, I had two pairs of jeans. I guess one could be called extra. Maybe it wasn't such a good idea to cut it up, though. I had a pair of soccer shorts I could wear with a Key West T-shirt—I'd never been, though. The shirt had been given to me by a guy I saw for about two weeks who might have taken me there if we'd made it to week three.

I couldn't decide.

"Wendi!" I yelled. "Help!"

A moment late she stood in my doorway, wearing a peach-colored kimono and bunny slippers, and cooling herself with an opera fan. One nice thing about an English basement was that it didn't get too hot, which didn't mean it wasn't still over eighty.

"I need to decide what to wear," I said. Then I laid out the possible outfits on my bed.

"No, no, and no," Wendi said. Then she went to my closet and picked out a simple white Oxford shirt and a pair of jeans.

"Wendi, it's hot out."

"Don't wear socks," she suggested.

"I'm going to sweat."

"Make the prince buy you an ice cream."

"Can I borrow your fan, at least?"

"Absolutely not. You'd look like a geisha," said the girl who looked like a geisha.

In the end, I went with her suggestion, and wore the jeans, the white shirt—buttoned only mid-way up my hairless chest—and a pair of penny loafers without socks.

We met at seven in front of Lambda Rising on S Street. If it had been cooler, I would have walked. Instead, I took a bus. It wasn't air-conditioned, but the windows were open and the air seemed cooler when the bus moved. It was only three stops anyway. I stood in front of the bookstore there, looking in the window. There were stacks of books artfully displayed: *Faggots*; *The Joy of Gay Sex*; *States of Desire*; *Gaywyck*. The books seemed random, but then maybe that was the point. Whatever you wanted was inside.

I knew better than to go in, even though I wanted to. But every time I went I stayed for at least an hour and spent every penny in my pocket. Neither of which I wanted to do just then.

I was so absorbed in trying not to go into the bookstore that I didn't notice David coming out of it. He wore a very dark pair of Sergio Valente jeans and a pinstriped collarless shirt that was unbuttoned halfway down his chest. I could see the dark hair growing between his pectorals. In one hand, he grasped a paper bag that held a book.

"I'm sorry," he said. "Did you want to go inside?"

"Oh God, no."

"You don't like books? Why is it good-looking men never like to read?"

"No, I love books. If I go inside I won't say a word to you for at least an hour."

"Oh, I see," he said, as though he didn't.

"What did you buy?" I asked.

"*The Persian Boy.*"

I smiled. He did have a sense of humor. That was nice to know since he hadn't shown it much.

"You haven't read it?"

"I read it years ago. I bought it for you. A gift."

"Oh, um, thank you."

"You've read it already, haven't you?"

"My mother read it when it came out in paperback. I was about sixteen and I asked if I could read it when she was done. She said that I could, but explained there were sex scenes between Alexander the Great and the eunuch. She told me when I got to them I should pretend the eunuch was a woman. That's what she did."

"And did you follow her advice?"

"Not at all." I smiled.

"Since you've read the book, should I return it? I could get you something else. I'm sure they have books you haven't read."

"No, I want it. I'd like to have my own copy. My mother insisted on having hers back."

He smiled. "Sometimes it's enough to own a book, isn't it? You know you may never read it again, but you still want it."

"It's a terrible vice," I admitted.

"Nonsense. There's an Oscar Wilde quote, I think it goes 'he hadn't a single redeeming vice.' That's not true of you, is it though? You have many redeeming vices."

I was giddy. I was with a very attractive prince who quoted Oscar Wilde to flirt with me. What more could I want? I felt like the luckiest boy in the world.

We walked around the corner to Connecticut Avenue and began heading south. The street was made up of small storefronts at the bottom of two- and three-story brick buildings from the turn of the century. Trendy businesses popped up every month and either thrived or withered. There was always something new to look at.

"So, if you're from Persia, why do you have a British accent?"

"My family is Persian, but I was born in England. I went to school there. I travel on a British passport."

"Isn't that the same thing as being British?" I asked.

"That's so American. Thinking you can be something simply because you choose it."

There was something slightly offensive about his saying that. I had the feeling he'd find me very rude if I made a similar kind of generalized comment about Persians. Though I could hardly make one since I didn't know enough about them. I decided to ignore it.

"What are you doing in Washington?"

"My father has business here."

"What kind of business?"

He was silent. The sky was thick with dark clouds that made it seem later than it was.

"Have you eaten dinner?" he asked, changing the subject. "I'm sorry, I should have said dinner when I called."

"I haven't eaten," I said. I'd been too nervous to eat. I was still too nervous, but I could pretend to eat if that's what he wanted to do.

"What kind of food do you like?"

I tried to think what was nearby. Rascals had food. Did I really want to take my prince to a gay bar? Not on a first date. And I didn't want to spend a whole lot of money. Did princes go Dutch? Or did they always pay? Or did they ever pay?

"I think there's a pizza place. Do you like pizza?"

"Everyone likes pizza. What do you like on yours?" he asked.

I'd worked at a pizza place when I was seventeen, which meant I'd gotten pretty bored with pizza and had begun to experiment with some exotic combinations.

"I like ham, onions, black olives and mushrooms," I said.

"Ham, interesting."

There was something wrong with ham and it took me a moment to remember exactly what. "Oh, so I guess you're a Muslim?"

"Yes, of course."

"Do you go to chu—mosque? It is mosque, right?"

"I go very seldom. My father considers religiosity to be vulgar. You're a Christian, aren't you?"

"No, I'm not. I don't really believe."

"But you were born to a Christian family?"

"Well, yeah, my mother's a Methodist."

"Then you're a Christian. What you believe has little to do with religion. You can't escape your birth."

I wasn't sure I believed that, but I didn't say so because it was a first date and I did really want him to like me. After a moment, he asked, "Do you like Chinese food?"

"Yes, I think so."

"You think so? Aren't you sure?"

"I like sweet and—" I almost said sweet and sour pork, but it felt rude to mention that after the ham thing. "Lemon chicken. I like lemon chicken."

"Why don't we eat here then," David said, gesturing toward a Chinese restaurant called Imperial Palace. We went in and it was hardly a palace, despite the presumably royal decor.

The restaurant, which took up only a single storefront, was red. The walls, the floors, the booths, everything was red, and anything that wasn't red was gold.

We were led to a booth in the back by a small Chinese woman. Before we ordered, we were brought a teapot and a couple of handle-less teacups. We talked about the restaurant for a few minutes—the food was good, he'd eaten there before—and then we fell into staring at each other. Stares that made my heart quiver.

Another Chinese woman, younger than the first, came to our table and said, half command/half question, "You order now."

I began to order lemon chicken, but David wouldn't let me. "No, don't order what you always have, be more adventurous. Order something you've never had before."

"You go first then," I said, to give myself another few minutes to decide.

He ordered General Tso's Chicken while I scrambled to decide on something, finally ordering broccoli in oyster sauce with beef. I dreaded finding out what oyster sauce really was, but I did like beef. Maybe it wouldn't be so bad.

When the waitress left, he smiled at me and then said, "Tell me your dreams, Patrick."

"My dreams? Sometimes I dream I'm back in school and it's time for the final and I didn't go to any of the classes and haven't studied at all for the test."

"I didn't mean that kind of dream and I think you knew that. What do you like to do?"

"I like to read."

"Do you want to be a writer?"

I shook my head. "I don't know what I'd write about. I don't think I have anything to say."

"Maybe you will one day."

"I hope not. If you think about it, books are always about terrible things."

"Yes, they often are. In that case, I hope you're lucky enough that you never have anything to write about."

When he said that, it seemed like he was sure no one was that lucky. Since I didn't want to think about that too much, I turned the question around on him and asked, "What are *your* dreams?"

"I have a simple dream. I would like someday to go home."

I wanted to tease him, but he looked lost and hurt and proud at the same time. The sadness in his voice made me want to buy him a ticket home right then, except I think the home he meant did not exist.

When our dinners came we shared them, so I ended up trying two dishes I'd never had before. I liked them both, but I liked the beef with oyster sauce more. We said little as we ate, other than 'try this' and 'this is good.' Between bites we smiled at each other as though we shared a secret that only we knew. And perhaps we did.

Taking my last bite, I said, "I'm dying to get you into my bed."

"I'm sorry, I don't have sex on a first date. Should I call you an ambulance now? Or later?"

"Ambulance?" I asked, then I got it. "Oh, because I'm dying. I tried to smile as I wondered why he didn't want to have sex. At the club he'd seemed so forward, so confident, so—

"You kissed me seconds after you met me. Actually, you hadn't yet met me when you kissed me."

"That was a bit out of character. I don't know what it was, your eyes perhaps, or the way you smiled at me. Whatever it was, it was impossible for me not to kiss you."

I wondered if I had a smile that would make it impossible for him not to have sex with me. I tried one out. He smiled back at me, looking amused, as though he knew exactly what I was trying to do.

"You're not a very patient person, are you?"

"No. Not at all.

After the dinner dishes were bused, we read our fortune cookies: I would be 'traveling soon and should pack wisely,' while David would be 'betrayed by a fair-weather friend.' He brushed off the bad news and shrugged, "It's a very easy fortune to give. Everyone suffers betrayals big and small every day."

Then he walked me back to my apartment. I asked him again to come in, but he shook his head and then there, in the dark of my doorway, he kissed me deeply, passionately, saying, "There's nothing wrong with waiting for something you want."

"And there's nothing wrong with having what you want right now."

"How very American. You live in a world of instant coffee and microwave ovens and TV dinners ready in minutes."

I was pretty sure they had all those things in England and possibly even Tehran, but I didn't say anything. Instead, I asked, "Did you just compare me to a TV dinner?"

"I don't think you're a TV dinner. I think there's much more to you than that. Perhaps a full, sit-down, gourmet meal."

I smiled at him. "Like at Le Marquis?"

"Better. And I'm making a reservation."

And then he kissed me again. I grabbed him by the front of his shirt and thought about pulling him inside my apartment against his will. But I had the feeling he meant what he said, and that he'd be upset if I tried to get him to do something he didn't want to do.

Eventually he stopped kissing me and said a very formal, "Good night, Patrick."

"Good night."

Floating on a cloud made of every silly, romantic movie I'd ever seen, I drifted into my apartment only to come face to face with my roommate lurking on the sofa.

"I'm so sorry," she said, as soon as she saw I was alone.

"What are you sorry about?" I asked, too distracted by the feel of David on my lips to figure it out.

"The prince. It didn't work out."

"It worked out just fine."

"Did he fuck you in the alley?"

"Of course not. He just kissed me. He wants to wait for the rest."

She frowned. "Is he gay?"

"Of course he's gay."

"Are you sure?"

"He kisses like a gay guy."

She shrugged. "Every gay guy I've ever known was all fuck now, talk later. Including you."

"Well, now you know one who's not like that."

"Okay…" she said, giving up the point. I started to walk toward my bedroom. "Hey, did you see you got some mail? A catalog for Georgetown. Are you going back to college?"

"My mother probably asked them to send it. She wants me to go back to college."

"Is she going to pay for it?"

"No."

"Do you have the grades for Georgetown?"

"No."

"So, your mom's delusional?"

"Something like that. Night."

CHAPTER THREE

For our second date, David double-parked in front of my building in the most amazing car: a white Lincoln Continental Mark V. The sun glinted off its sharp elegant angles, the sunroof opened to the beautiful evening, while the tinted windows promised an intimacy that can only be purchased. When he climbed out of it, he looked like an ad for the sunglasses he wore, or his pleated gray slacks, or maybe the Lincoln itself.

I ran out of my apartment and jumped into the gorgeous vehicle. The inside was white leather and butterscotch-colored carpet. The dashboard had all sorts of gages and dials, and a built-in 8-track player. In the back seat was a leather case with all of David's tapes. I picked out Fleetwood Mac's *Rumours* album and we listened to it as David drove me to a crab restaurant in Maryland. We ordered one of those steamed dinners where they bring everything in one pot and dump it on the paper-covered table in front of you.

Somehow, as we ate mussels and clams and lobster claws all drenched in butter, David managed to stay completely clean while I ended up dipped in melted butter.

"So, I was wondering, have you ever had a boyfriend?" I asked, licking my fingers.

"I suppose, yes."

"More than one?"

"Yes."

"Tell me about them?"

"The first was my friend, Ebrahim. We went to public school together at Uppingham. You've probably never heard of it. It's in the middle part of England. I suppose that's not important, though. Ebrahim was my first."

"You said 'friend.' You still see him when you're in England?"

"Oh no, no, he's here. Our fathers are constantly hatching plans. He was with me at Exile. You didn't see him?"

"I didn't see anyone but you. Tell me, who were your other boyfriends?"

"Just one other. That was last year, right after we came to Washington. He worked for a nonprofit that does charity work in Africa. It was very intense."

"How did it end?"

"He went to Africa. What about you? Have you had a boyfriend?"

"Not exactly. I mean, there have been guys." I suddenly realized if I told him too much I might sound like a slut. There had been guys, a lot of guys, just very few who were even close to being boyfriends. "There was a guy at school. And then, I came to Washington with another guy who I thought was going to be my boyfriend, but it turned out he wasn't."

"And girls?" he asked.

"Me? Never. What about you?"

"Oh yes, of course." He smiled vaguely. "It's pleasant enough."

"Pleasant?"

"Yes." He studied me a moment and considered. Then he shrugged and said, "A woman is like black-and-white television. But who wants to watch black-and-white television after they've seen color?"

I decided I probably shouldn't share that opinion with Wendi. She was likely to get offended, and she could be offended for days.

"I've never been in love," I said.

"Sometimes, I think I have but then I wonder. If you've been in love you don't wonder."

Two more dates and David came inside. There was something about his wanting to wait I'd begun to find charming. No one had ever made me do that before. The guys I'd known had all wanted sex right away, and often did not come back. Really, they were little more than tricks. David was different. He kept coming back, even without sex.

When he said he wanted to come in, I said, "Finally."

That made him laugh. He often laughed at me, though I wasn't always trying to make him laugh.

We went back to my room and took off our clothes. That first touch, I expected a spark to go off, to ignite us. But there was nothing out of the ordinary, just his lovely skin; his body like a foreign land, exotic and undiscovered. My tongue mapping the hills and dells, the dips and turns; my fingers exploring him, uncovering him, exposing the landscape of him. I touched as much of him as I could, like an animal rubbing in his scent.

Under him, legs hooked over his shoulders, his hair teasing my face, sweat running off him in tiny rivers, I wanted him, even in the midst of having him. I wanted him, ached for him, could not quench my thirst for him. We arched and shivered, shook and began to giggle. He crushed me to him and for me, unschooled and untraveled, he was Persia. A mysterious, mythical land, my own Persia.

It was too hot to sleep entwined, but we found ways to touch one another without causing massive puddles of sweat. Our fingertips brushed through the night, fluttering against each other and when he turned on his side, I took a finger and ran it gently down his spine until he purred.

I fell asleep imagining what our lives would be like. Would he make me a prince someday? The queen of England did that, made the man she loved a prince, a prince consort. That's what they called it when you married royalty. The consort part let people know you were only royalty by marriage. I wouldn't mind being a prince consort. I wasn't very interested in power, but living in a palace with people to wait on me and bring me whatever I could think up—that part was appealing.

Of course, David might want my opinion on things. Should he kill his political opponents or just exile them? God, I hoped he'd never ask me something like that. I didn't know the right answer. Sparing them seemed much kinder and might make David more popular, but what if they came back and killed him—and possibly me? No, off with their heads! That really seemed the way to go.

On the other hand, David might never get his country back. So instead of ruling we'd be floating around the world with the jet set. We'd be invited to cruise the Mediterranean on a friend's yacht, but first we'd stop in Monte Carlo to gamble. We'd know people who said funny things and were terribly, terribly…famous. I drifted off to sleep with visions of caviar and champagne filling my head.

That next morning, David took a shower while I went into the kitchen to make coffee in the small, dented metal drip pot we had and tried to figure out something we could eat for breakfast. Wendi heard me in the kitchen and slipped out of her room.

"Have you gone through his wallet yet?" she asked in a whisper.

"Why would I do that?"

"The minute a guy hits the shower you always go through his wallet."

"You are *so* jaded," I said, nosing around in the refrigerator.

"Everything's in a guy's wallet. You find out if he's lying about his name from his driver's license, or maybe there are pictures in there of him and his wife, or maybe he doesn't actually work where he says he works."

"I'm not going through his wallet."

"What if he's not really a prince? Don't you want to know that?"

"I didn't have sex with him because he's a prince. I actually like him. A lot. Besides, I doubt it says prince on his driver's license."

"Will you still like him when you find out he's a liar?"

"Wendi, that's terrible."

She shrugged. "They're all liars in the end."

That was hard to argue with, so I said, "Yes, but some of them are worth forgiving."

"You're such an innocent. Leave me half a bagel."

August was a scalding month. David and I spent much of it in my room naked. I loved that we were opposites. My hair light, his dark. My eyes dark while his were light. I was almost twenty-one, he was twenty-three. I had almost no hair on my body while he had hair on his chest, thick dark hair on his legs and even some hair springing up in the small of his back.

I watched him standing naked in front of the fan he'd bought me, thinking that as the years went by he'd have more and more hair on him. Hair would grow on his back and his shoulders and his upper arms—there were faint shadows of it beginning already. He would lose the hair on his head, but he'd make up for it with hair everywhere else. I tried to think whether I might be repulsed by him some day, but I didn't believe it. I was eager to watch him get old. I wanted to notice each new hair as it grew. I was ready to love the hairy, pot-bellied old man he would one day be.

My ideas about relationships were somewhat fractured. When I was just hitting puberty, there was a report about homosexuals on television that said we were sex-crazed freaks who'd never have a stable relationship. I was a child, so I did what children do and simply accepted the idea. The part about never having a relationship, at least. If that's who I was going to be, I thought, I would make the best of it. At the time, I didn't feel particularly sex-crazed. I assumed that came later.

It was only recently, once I'd gotten out of high school, that I'd begun to realize gays could have relationships, could have boyfriends. There had been a couple at the community college I went to, I think they were in the art department. They boldly went everywhere together, dressed in Qiana shirts and rayon slacks, identical mustaches, hair cut long and perfectly styled. I watched them and they knew it. Occasionally, one or the other would catch my eye and smile, knowing looks that were both teasing and smug. They knew I wanted what they had, though I didn't know how to get it.

My attempts at finding a boyfriend were fumbling, bumbling and misguided. There was a boy named Andrew in my English class I helped with homework, but that ended badly. And then, shortly afterward, there was the junior senatorial assistant. By the time I met David, my prince, I'd nearly given up hope.

"David, are you my boyfriend?" I asked one naked afternoon as we lay on my mattress.

"Well, I am your friend. And I am a boy."

"That's not what I mean, and you know it."

"Then I don't know what you're asking me."

"Yes, you do."

"You're right. I do." He was quiet a moment, then he said, "My father expects that I will one day marry a woman and give him grandchildren. And I will. It is my duty."

"So—" I barely knew how to talk about this, barely knew what I wanted, what was reasonable to want even.

"There is no reason we cannot find joy with each other until it is time to do my duty," he said. He'd rolled over and was looking me in the eye, hopeful, pleading almost.

"Don't you have a duty to yourself?" I asked.

He smirked, like he had before and said, "That's such an American—"

"Don't. Don't tell me I'm ridiculous because I'm an American. If you think I'm ridiculous it should be because that's who I am. Don't blame it on my country."

"You're not ridiculous, Patrick. You just don't understand—"

"Never mind. Sorry I asked."

THE DARKENING CLOUD:

Themes and Factions in the Iranian Hostage Crisis

by Phillip Klpplinger
Senior Fellow Middle Eastern Affairs
The Madison Association

September 15, 1980

The seizing of the American Embassy in Tehran on November 4, 1979, and subsequent capture of American diplomatic personnel has been the defining factor of American-Iranian relations for nearly a year, as well as redirecting the course of the Iranian revolution, the aims of the United States in the Persian Gulf and relations between the United States and its allies.

The taking of the embassy occurred at the height of the anti-American demonstrations, which erupted after the admittance of Shah Mohammed Reza Pahlavi into the United States for medical treatment. A group of approximately 500 Iranian students stormed the embassy compound, taking 63 of the embassy employees hostage. Following this event, the government of Premier Mehdi Bazargan, after suffering months of interference from Ayatollah Khomeini, collapsed as the seizure of the embassy was seen as usurping his authority.

The Iranian political landscape became increasingly polarized following the embassy takeover with Islamic Socialists, Pro-Soviet and Islamic Fundamentalists factions struggling for control of the government. Rather than soothe various factions, Khomeini has remained unwilling to compromise, and through harsh rhetoric and periodic crackdowns has inflamed discontent within the country.

Inflation in the country reached nearly fifty percent during the early part of this year and more than a third of the country is now unemployed. A week after the invasion of the American embassy, hundreds of unemployed workers, spurred on by leftists, occupied the Ministry of Labor demanding jobs, unemployment benefits and health insurance.

While the overall mood of the country is bleak, the state-run media (IRIB) has assured the Iranian people that the world supports them in their conflict with the United States even though the United Nations condemned Iran in Resolution 461…

CHAPTER FOUR

That night at Le Marquis, I was picking up an order for a four-top: two stuffed filets of sole, a boeuf Bourguignon and a chicken Provencal. At the pickup line, Wendi stood next to me, garnishing her order.

"He's going to marry a woman someday," I said.

"Do you get to help pick her out?"

"Don't joke about it."

"Oh honey, there's nothing to do but joke about it. We all think Cinderella married Prince Charming and they lived happily ever after. But chances are she was stuck in the palace with three royal brats while he was out boning Snow White."

"Screw you," I said, then lifted the large oval tray over my shoulder.

Weaving my way out of the kitchen, I was quickly gliding through the dining room. I was working the Madison Room again and had just three parties. If I could move them along fast enough I could be home by eleven o'clock and in bed reading *A Confederacy of Dunces*—a book I was finding annoying and hysterical in equal measure.

I strode into the Madison room, tray in the air. I'd grabbed a stand from outside the room and set it up quickly next to the table in the corner. At the table were four men in wrinkled gray suits. Politicians.

"There has to be a way to stop him. He can't win again. It's just absurd."

"Calm down. A handful of polls have put Carter ahead, but there's nothing to worry about."

"Of course, there's something to worry about. What if there's an October surprise? I mean, we all know the hillbilly's working on that."

In the corner, sat an older man of about fifty not saying a word. He still had most of his hair, was relatively thin, and his skin hadn't begun to slide off the bone the way it can with older people. He wore a pair of round, tortoise-shell glasses and looked intently at everyone at the table. Including me.

I decided I'd serve him first, based simply on the fact that he somehow seemed the most important man at the table. He was having the boeuf Bourguignon. At Le Marquis, we served the dish over the homemade egg noodles the pastry chefs deigned to make. I brought the noodles and stew separately in covered metal pots. Folding a napkin around the pot of noodles, I took off the lid and, using a serving spoon and a fork that I'd arranged between the index finger on my right hand, scooped the noodles out of the pot. I used my thumb to press the fork down on them holding them in place until I dropped them onto the gentleman's plate.

When I'd served all of the noodles, I asked, "Would you like your stew on your noodles or next to them, sir?"

"On top, please." Then, as I served his dinner, he began responding to the others, "Listen, it's Carter's job to continue to work on getting the hostages back. It's unlikely he'll succeed. They're demanding an apology from the U.S. just to come to the table, and he can't give them that. It would look weak."

I moved around the table to the next gentleman and served his stuffed sole with a creamy sauce in much the same way I'd served the beef.

"Can't we do something to guarantee Carter fails?" one of the others asked.

"Hussein is rattling his sword again. There's fighting on the border—"

The gentleman with the boeuf Bourguignon cleared his throat. The others grew quiet. I realized he wanted them to be quiet around me. Quickly, I finished serving the table and scurried away. The moment I walked away they began talking again.

Whatever. I didn't think they'd said anything terribly interesting or even important. My two other tables were fine and in no hurry, so it was time for a cigarette back in the employee's lounge. Wendi was sitting back there, halfway through her own cigarette.

"So, are you going to break up with him?"

"I guess."

That seemed like the right thing to do. It wasn't so much that the prince would one day marry a woman, it was that I knew one day I would become as inconvenient to David as I had been to my senatorial assistant with aspirations. I'd had a couple of really rough weeks after my aspiring politician threw me out. Did I want to go through that again?

"Just as well," Wendi said. "You're not really the princess type."

"Stop making jokes. This is my life."

"How do you think he'll take it?"

"Probably not well. He's is a prince, after all. He's used to getting his way."

"Make him think it's his idea."

"It's not an episode of *Laverne & Shirley*."

"No? Wasn't there one where Shirley breaks up with a prince?"

I gave her a nasty look.

"Just don't do it in the apartment. I don't want to listen to it."

"I'll keep that in mind. After all, the most important thing about my breaking up with my boyfriend is how it affects you."

She shrugged. "At least we're clear on that much."

I stubbed out my cigarette and went back out to the floor. One table was ready for their check, so I added it up, put it on a silver tray with chocolates, and set it near the boisterous gentleman who seemed to be treating.

The gray suits looked to be finished with their dinner, so I went over and began to clear their dinner plates. I arranged the dishes as neatly as possible on a tray stand against the wall. The busboy, a high school senior from Maryland, would take them away in a few minutes.

"Would you gentlemen care for coffee or dessert?" I asked after I'd cleared their dishes.

They ordered coffee and cognac. I had the feeling the cigars would come out soon and my night would be at an end. Maxim might try to seat a party, but when they smelled the cigar smoke the table would most likely be refused.

I smiled anyway and went off to the bar to get their drinks. On the way, I asked the busboy to prep a coffee set up for four. I ordered the three Remys and one Courvoisier VSOP. The bar was all dark, wood panels and soft lighting. Mounted over the cash register, a television was set to the brand-new Cable News Network.

While I was waiting, Wendi came up behind me. "Honestly, how do you think he'll take it?"

"I'm sure it will be fine. We've only been seeing each other for six weeks."

"Are you sad?"

"Of course I'm sad. I liked him. I still like him."

"You just don't want to share."

"Would you want to share?"

"How can you even ask a question like that? Women are good at sharing their dinners, their outfits, their tampons and their opinions. What they're not good at sharing is men."

The bartender, Pete, who could have been my grandfather, set the last cognac on the round tray I was using. The old man had worked at the State Department during the fifties, but had been chased out for being queer. Now, he was full of old-timey stories I did my best to avoid.

Giving Wendi a look, I picked up the tray and walked back through the restaurant to the Madison Room. As I was setting down the last of the cognacs, the gentleman with the round glasses tugged the sleeve of my blue jacket and said, "Bring the check to me."

"Yes, sir."

As I served the coffee, carefully holding a saucer over the cup to make sure no steam got into the customer's face, the cigars came out. Before I poured the last cup, another party was asking for their check as well. And the first party was ready to pay. It was an exodus.

In the kitchen, an adding machine sat on a specially built shelf. I waited in line to add up my two checks. I could have done it in my head, but Maxim insisted that we all use the adding machine to cut down on errors. We had to attach the tape to show our work.

What was I doing? Was I really going to break up with a prince? Honestly, a part of me was exhilarated by the idea. The opportunity to break up with a prince happened even less often than the opportunity to date one. But then, I thought about David, the David who was separate from simply being a prince, and I liked that David. I mean, yeah, he could be kind of arrogant —but what prince wasn't?

Glancing at my watch, it was ten forty-five. There was a chance I would make it home by eleven-fifteen. I took the checks out to the dining room, set them down, dropped off the change to the first party, and then stood near the entrance to the room acting like I wasn't watching each and every one of them.

The non-cigar smokers almost immediately put down a Diner's Card. I picked it up and went back to the kitchen to run it through the credit card machine that sat on the same shelf with the adding machine. The machine rubbed the card number through three layers of carbon paper, then I wrote in the amount making sure not to total it so they could add my tip. Then I had to skim through the newsprint booklet the credit card companies sent every month to see if the card number was there, in case the card was stolen. I didn't know anyone at Le Marquis who'd ever found a bad card, but we still had to look. The number wasn't there, so I went back out and had the customer sign the slip. After he did, I ripped his carbon out of the center and told everyone at the table to, "Enjoy the rest of your evening." They'd left a below average ten percent tip. Nine bucks.

I'd had two seatings, totaling seven tables. Tips had run between seven and ten dollars. I was going to gross about sixty dollars. I'd have to tip out to the bartender and the busboy, so I'd be going home with about fifty-two or fifty-three dollars. I got paid, too, but that was only about a buck eight-something an hour. My bi-weekly checks were less than twenty-bucks.

The busboy was cleaning the recently vacated table. Rather than just stand there, I started over to pitch in, when the guy with the round glasses got up and came over to me.

"Here you go," he said, pushing the check at me. There were several large bills pressed against it. "The rest is for you."

"Thank you," I said, though I couldn't count out the money in front of him, so I had no idea what exactly I was thanking him for.

He continued, "I know you're not deaf, so I appreciate your discretion. It wouldn't do to repeat the things we say."

"Oh, yes, of course. Um, I didn't actually hear very much anyway. My mind was elsewhere," I said, because it was mostly true. I remembered a little of what they said, it hadn't been all that interesting.

"Well, I just wanted to show my appreciation," he said and went back to his table.

I tried not to run out of the room to see how much of a tip he'd just given me. Instead, I walked slowly, casually, out of the room. When I got into the kitchen, I looked at what he'd given me. Their bill was just shy of a hundred dollars. He'd given me a fifty and a hundred-dollar bill. A fifty-dollar tip.

I began spending it in my head immediately.

CHAPTER FIVE

That next afternoon, David arrived at my door with tears streaming down his face. He said something I couldn't understand.

"What? What is it? What's the matter?"

He inhaled deeply and steadied himself. "Iraq has invaded my country."

"I'm sorry," I said, I had no idea what he must feel. Nothing like that had ever happened to America in my lifetime. "Why did they do that?"

He sniffed and rubbed his nose. Then said, "Like many things in the Middle East, it depends on who you ask. Some would say it's Khomeini. He's called for religious war in Iraq. Saddam Hussein wants to make sure that doesn't happen. Others would say it's oil. Iraq has wanted Khuzestan for some time."

"Will Iraq win?"

"No. I don't think so."

"Then it's not so bad."

"You don't understand. This will strengthen Khomeini's hold on the country. It will make it almost impossible to overthrow him."

I stood there awkwardly, not inviting him in.

"Did I come at a bad time?"

Since I was planning to break up with him, yes, he had come at a bad time. "No, come on in," I said, stepping back to let him into the apartment. "But Wendi and I have to leave for work an hour early. Employee meeting."

She popped out of her bedroom wearing her navy-blue waitress uniform. "They're changing the menu again, so we have to learn new dishes."

"I will give you a ride," David offered.

"No, we'll just take the Metro. It's easier—"

"Sure," Wendi said over my refusal. I gave her a nasty look. "I wouldn't mind a ride. Why so glum your princely-ness?"

"Iraq has invaded Iran."

"Oh, yeah, I heard about that. Bummer."

He frowned at her casualness. I made a face at her that David couldn't see.

"Shouldn't you be with your family?" I asked.

"I was with my father all day. The telephone has been ringing off the hook. Everyone wants to speak to him, wants to know if there's anything he can do. But what can he do? We're exiles. Still, they want him to do something. Some of them are bold enough to say we should seize the moment, that we should get the British and Americans to put us back in power."

"What about the shah's son? Why wouldn't they put him in power?" Wendi asked.

I cringed.

"He's a boy and has many enemies. My father is a man and has few enemies."

Wendi opened her mouth to say something else, but I glared at her. Instead, she said, "We should really go. We don't want to be late."

As David drove us to the Hotel Continental we didn't say much; it wasn't far, so there was barely any time to say anything anyway. David dropped us at the employee entrance in the back. As we were getting out of the car I kissed him quickly on the cheek and said, "I'm sorry about your country."

He tried to smile, but sort of screwed it up. "Thank you."

Wendi and I ran into the building. As we were going up to the top floor in the freight elevator, Wendi said, "I thought you were breaking up with him?"

"I am. But they just invaded his country, so it's going to take a few days."

"No, you shouldn't do it that way. He's already having a bad day. You should have done it now, he'd hardly notice."

"I'm going to give him a few days."

"So, he has a sucky day now and in a couple of days he has another sucky day? You think you're being kind, but you're not."

No matter what she said, though, I couldn't help myself. I was an asshole and waited a few more days to break up with David. I had him meet me at the fountain at the top of the Spanish Steps. I sat on the lip of the fountain, water running out of a lion's mouth behind me, for a good twenty minutes before David showed up. While I had nothing to do, I counted the days we'd known each other: fifty-seven. That was hardly anything, though it felt like a lot. They'd been lovely days.

A sexy guy came up the steps and cruised me heavily. See, everything would be fine. I didn't need David. There were other guys. Guys who weren't destined to marry whatever girl their father chose for them. I shouldn't feel bad but somehow I did.

The reason I'd wanted to meet at the fountain was that I wanted to spend at least part of my fifty-dollar tip on books and the Spanish Steps were about three blocks west of Lambda Rising. I'd gone to the bookstore first and bought *Kiss of the Spiderwoman*, *The Boys in the Band* (the play) and the latest *Blueboy*, which—in addition to the hot naked guys—promised to tell me all about San Francisco. I wondered if I should move to San Francisco. It seemed like the kind of thing someone who'd break up with a prince might do.

Also, I thought it would be easier to end things in public. But now I realized that might not have been such a good idea. What if David couldn't keep it together? What if *I* couldn't keep it together? *What if we both*—?

The afternoon was hot, dark and a bit windy. The sort of day that makes you pray for rain. David ran up the steps wearing a pair of gym shorts, a tank top, running shoes and a glistening layer of sweat.

"I hope you don't mind. I decided to kill two birds with one stone," he said, panting.

"I don't even know where you live," I said, stupidly. But it was something I'd just realized. Well, not just realized, remembered I suppose.

"I live with my father, you know that."

"Yes, but I don't know where."

"He rents a house on 20th and Q. Is that important?"

"No, no, it isn't." It might have been, if we weren't about to break up.

"Your message was very cloak-and-dagger. Why are we meeting here? I could have just come to your apartment."

"It's a nice place. Quiet."

"I have to have dinner with my father and some of his friends. But I can get away later. We'll go dancing."

"No, no. David, this isn't working out."

"This? What this?"

"Us. We're not working out."

"Don't be ridiculous. We get on well. We don't fight. I thought we liked each other quite a lot."

"I do like you. Quite a lot."

"And we've been having fun, haven't we?"

"Yes, but I think I want more. I think I want a future."

"A future? You're talking like a girl."

"What's wrong about wanting a future?"

"Are you going to stay home and keep my house and take care of my babies while I see to the affairs of the world?"

"No, of course not. That's stupid."

"Then what future are you talking about?"

"I don't know. A life we could have together."

He sighed and sat down next to me. "I'm only twenty-three. My father won't pressure me to settle down for another five or six years. Isn't that enough future for you?"

It was tempting. It seemed easy enough to say that it was. Could I live with that, though? With knowing it would all end in a few years? I wasn't in love with him. Not really. But I would be at the end of five years. It would be hard to give him up. Harder than it was now. So much harder.

"No. It isn't enough."

He flinched. He'd been sure I would agree, sure I'd take those five lovely years of fun and sex and him.

"You're telling me goodbye? That's why you wanted to meet here?"

"Yes, it's time to say goodbye."

"You're being a child."

"That should make this easier, then. You don't want to be with a child, do you?"

"What if I say no?"
"It's not a question, David."
"There's nothing I can say?"
"No. Nothing."

KOMITEH PRISON

Tehran

September 23, 1980

The room was relatively large with walls painted a sickly pale green, a concrete floor, a metal door and two high, barred windows. There were three plastic chairs, three thin foam mattresses, light bulbs hanging from the high ceiling, and a small end table which had once had a drawer. When the three men were brought there a bit more than two months ago, they had been told it was for their protection, that they were not prisoners but instead guests. That is how they knew they were in a prison.

The walls were not thick. They could often hear the prison around them. The bathroom was just down the hallway and they could hear other prisoners being led there. They caught snippets of English, American English. The guards were casual, even friendly and would often answer back pleasantly. Much of what they heard was not pleasant though. Sometimes there were screams; men, women. The screams always ended in begging and murmured sounds of assent. Somewhere in the prison a woman sang Persian songs and talked to herself.

They played cards, pulling the plastic chairs around an end table. A game called "Oh, Hell." It was a game with convoluted rules that included a declining and increasing number of cards, a trump, bidding and scoring. The night they heard the bombs, they were playing cards. Trump was clubs.

Suddenly, there was the growing sound of a jet flying low above them. It passed over them. Seconds later the sound of an explosion far away followed almost immediately by one closer. Close enough to shake the walls.

The men looked at each other and lay down their cards.

"American?"

The light bulbs above them went out. They sat in the half-dark. They heard more explosions, smaller and closer.

The smallest man nodded toward the windows. They knew what to do, they'd done it before. Walking over to the wall, two of the men squatted and laced their fingers into a step. The third man stepped up with one foot in each set of hands. They raised him up, so he could see out the window.

A moment later, he was saying, "Tracers. Antiaircraft. Someone is attacking."

"Who?"

"It's not us."

"Are you sure?"

"If Carter was going to level Tehran it would have already happened."

"Russia?"

"No reason. Iraq probably. Iran is weak. They have few allies. This would be the time."

The men left the window and sat on their mattresses in the dark. They listened to the sounds of jets flying nearby, the occasional explosion, the popping sound of the antiaircraft guns, citizens firing rifles at the sky.

The loudspeakers that hung on the mosques to broadcast adhan five times a day crackled on in anxious fury. A man spoke frantically in Persian.

One of the men translated, "It is Iraq. They've just invaded. Thirty-five have been killed at the National Works. He's asking that people near the airport not shoot at planes. Their own planes have been shot at. He's urging people not to go to the hospital unless it's an emergency."

"What about us? What does this mean to us?"

The two others shrugged.

"Who knows."

CHAPTER SIX

The look on David's face right before he walked away from me would haunt me for a very long time. I didn't think my reasons for breaking up with him were terrible, but somehow I hadn't imagined I might be hurting him. Inconveniencing him, angering him, insulting him, those were possibilities I'd considered. But I hadn't thought I might hurt him. And he was hurt. The look in his lovely, silver-gray eyes was enough to crush me. How could I have done that to him?

I limped through the rest of that week, trying not to think about David, trying to read the books I'd bought. Not getting far. Working my shifts at Le Marquis. Wondering if I should go to a movie that Friday. I didn't really want to; something about sitting in the dark was unappealing just then.

And yet, that was pretty much what I did every night that week. I sat in the darkened living room listening to some of Wendi's records. Her favorite breakup album was the self-titled *Eric Carmen*. It had two near perfect songs back-to-back: "Never Gonna Fall in Love Again" and "All by Myself." The great thing was that the album version of "All by Myself" was seven minutes long, which meant between the two songs you only had to get up every eleven minutes to move the stylus back to start again. By the time you'd listened to the songs ten times you were either cured or dripping blood from both wrists. By Thursday Wendi had hidden the album somewhere in her room.

Saturday, I stayed in bed most of the day. I did a better job of concentrating on my books—especially the *Blueboy*, repeatedly—but decided, as much as I wanted to, I couldn't stay at home reading all day long. That meant I had to do something, anything.

Around nine o'clock, I threw on my white shorts and black tank, slipped into a pair of Converse high tops and walked over to The Fraternity House. The bar was only a few blocks away. It was just down an alley in an old, brick, carriage house. The street in front was cobblestone. Though they had tried to pave over it, the pavement had worn off so the cobblestone showed through, the city's history refusing to go unnoticed.

I made myself comfortable at the downstairs bar and began ordering Stoli salty dogs, one after another—spending the last of my fifty-dollar tip. I'd had three drinks when a skinny guy around thirty sat down next to me and said, "Smile. It's not the end of the world."

"You don't know that for sure."

"Trust me, the sun will come out tomorrow."

"That seems like a pretty low bar."

Taking a good look at him, his polyester pants, disco shirt and gold chain—he obviously hadn't bought any new clothes in the last few years—I decided I wanted him to go away.

"I like you. You're clever," he said.

"That happens when I drink."

"Then let me buy you another."

Before he could wave down the bartender, I leaned in close and asked, "If I kissed you, would you turn into a prince?"

It took him a moment to figure that out. "Did you just call me a frog?"

"If the amphibian fits."

"Hey, that's not very nice."

"It wasn't meant to be."

"Why are you being such an asshole? I'm just trying to be friendly, get to know you. You don't even know me and you're shitting all over me." He was beginning to talk a bit too loud, and I had the feeling this might go on for a while.

The words, "Beat it" were on the tip of my tongue, when I noticed another guy hovering nearby. This one was also in his early thirties but much more interesting. He had shaved most of his blond hair off and had deep, dark blue eyes. He wore a green flight jacket, a very tight BVD T-shirt, jeans and work boots.

"There you are, I've been looking for you," he said.

"Hey, who are you?" Polyester wanted to know. I was curious myself.

"We had a date. I'm a few minutes late." He leaned over and pulled me into a kiss, my heart jumped from the surprise of it. The stubble at the very edges of his mouth raked over my lips. The kiss was awkward and breathtaking all at once. He leaned back and asked, "Can you forgive me?"

"Yeah, I think so," I said. Looking into his eyes, his body pressed to mine, I had the feeling I could forgive him a lot of things.

"Now wait a minute, he didn't say anything about a date."

Ignoring the guy, he said, "Why don't we get out of here?"

I guzzled the last of my drink and jumped off the stool. Getting laid was exactly what I needed. The best way to get over one guy was to jump into bed with another. We walked out of the bar while Polyester yelled a few profanities after us.

"Thanks. I guess you rescued me," I said when we got to the alley outside.

"I'm sure you would have gotten rid of him eventually," the guy said. "Why don't we go this way," He led me out to P Street and then turned east toward Dupont Circle.

"Do you live around here?" I asked, my hip accidentally bumping his as we walked.

"No, I don't," he said, not bothering to tell me where he did live. "Let's go over to the Circle."

That was odd. Did he want to have sex in the Circle? That was not a good idea. I'd heard some heavy cruising went on late at night, but it was an open space. There were trees and small shrubs, but nothing big enough that you could hide behind and have sex. Anything you did in the Circle was on full view to whomever happened to be passing. All that happened there was cruising.

We jaywalked into the Circle and found a spot on the park bench, the continuous park bench that curved around the entire park. I had no idea what we were doing, so when we sat down I pulled my cigarettes out of my tube sock and lit up.

"May I have one of those?"

"Sure," I said, flipping one out of the pack and then lighting it for him.

He inhaled deeply and exhaled. Then he made a face and said, "Menthol."

"Beggars can't be choosers."

"I'm trying to quit."

"You're not doing a very good job."

Then he was quiet. I was afraid I'd insulted him. Things felt like they were veering off track, so I suggested, "My place is a few blocks from here." And when he didn't respond, I added, "I feel like we started something in the bar. Something I'd like to finish."

"I think we should cut to the chase," he said, then took another deep drag.

"That's what I was thinking," I moved a tiny bit closer to him. "I really do live a couple blocks from here. Two and a half to be exact."

"I know where you live."

"You know where I live? Are you a psychic? We just met five minutes ago."

"I know a lot about you. I'm a CIA agent."

I laughed. "You know, you're not the first guy in D.C. to try that as a pick-up line."

"I'm not trying to pick you up."

"You don't have to try. You already have."

Something finally clicked. He wasn't acting like a guy who wanted to have sex with me. Well, not much. I gave him the once over, saying, "You look the part, though. You look like a faggot on the make. Is this just a costume? Something you had lying around?"

His lip almost turned up into a smile, but then he ignored the question. "I'm a case officer. I recruit people to help us out and then they report to me. Good, patriotic people."

I giggled, still not sure if he was serious. It was entirely possible this was just a very elaborate sex game.

"Do you love your country, Patrick?"

"Um, yeah, I guess. I mean, sure, I'm patriotic guy. What do you want me to do? Can I do it on my knees?"

"I want to talk to you about Prince Davoud al-din Qajar."

For a second, I couldn't breathe. This wasn't a game. He wasn't playing. He did know things about me. He knew my name. He knew about—

"David?"

"Yes, he goes by David."

"You want to talk about David?"

"That's what I said."

"Do you have identification? Show me your badge."

He gave me the kind of sympathetic look you give the village idiot. "We don't carry badges. We're spies. You can see how that would be a bad idea, can't you?" He reached into his inside jacket pocket and pulled out a small silver box meant for carrying business cards. He handed me one. The card said, GARY WALKER, THE PUBLIUS SOCIETY. There was an address at 1313 NW K Street and a phone number.

"Publius is a not-for-profit group that provides cover for many of our agents." I started to hand the card back to him, but he said, "Keep it. It's how you'll reach me if you need to."

"Is Gary Walker your real name?"

"Would you believe me if I said it was?"

"How do I know you're really CIA?"

"You're Patrick Henry Burke, you grew up outside of Boston, you went to Massachusetts Bay Community College for two semesters but didn't do well. You're smart enough; you just don't apply yourself. You had to leave two years ago when you were caught cheating."

"That wasn't my fault," I said quickly. It embarrassed me that he knew about that. I didn't talk about it I didn't talk about it with anyone.

"You moved to Washington in seventy-eight with Ronald Haywood. The two of you broke up shortly after you got here due to his political ambitions, I believe." He ended by giving me my social security number. Rattling it off quickly, clearly memorized, better than me since I tended to flip the last two numbers.

"You're a descendant of Patrick Henry, aren't you? I'm hoping love of country flows in your veins."

I struggled to understand what was happening. Part of me was still in the midst of a pick-up, expecting the conversation to end in a moment or two and then we'd go back to my place and screw all night long. Looking at him didn't help much. He was exactly the kind of guy I'd seen around, a clone, that's what they called them. They oozed sex. I'd never gotten my hands on—

"What do you want from me?" I asked.

"Davoud's father and his associates are attempting to manipulate our presidential election by interfering with the administration's attempts to free the hostages in Tehran."

I began to say, *No, they wouldn't do that*, but then I didn't know why I thought that. I didn't know much about the hostages, but I did know that the people who took them hated the shah. One of the demands they made was that the shah be returned to Iran to face punishment for his crimes—I think Wendi had told me that. And then I remembered that David's family didn't like the shah either. It seemed possible they'd know someone in the new government. Or someone who was with the students who took the hostages. Maybe they *were* on the same side.

"David's not involved with any of this," I said, more to reassure myself than to convince Agent Walker.

"He's a loyal son," was all he'd say. "It's day 327, Patrick. Can you imagine what it's been like for them?"

Honestly, I tried not to think about it much.

Walker continued, "We need you to track Nasim al-din Qajar's associations and movements. Nasim is Davoud's father. He calls himself the Crown Prince."

"I don't know how I could help you."

"Get Davoud to invite you to their home. There will be—"

"I broke up with him."

"You what?" He gave me a look suggesting I'd done it knowing it could affect national security. "Can you get back with him? Can you say you're sorry and get back with him?"

"No, I won't do that."

"It's important, Patrick."

"I don't think David will take me back. I dumped him. He's too proud."

I just stared at him. Whether or not I went back to a guy was important? To the CIA? It barely made sense.

He stared right back at me. Seeming to make a decision, he leaned forward and pressed his lips against mine and slipped his tongue between them. The kiss was as electric as our first.

When he leaned back, I asked, "What was that for?"

"I want you to remember me. You have my card."

CHAPTER SEVEN

It had to be fate, right? One thing leading to the next. I mean, if I hadn't met David, I'd never have met Agent Walker. Obviously, I knew it couldn't be my destiny just to end up as some prince's throwaway boyfriend. Was it my destiny to end up with a CIA agent? A spy? Who asked me to be, well, a spy just like him. Or, sort of like him.

Of course, that posed a problem. Getting back with David wasn't going to work. I was pretty sure he never wanted to hear from me again.

It did mean I could stop feeling bad about breaking up with him. I mean, the CIA wanted to spy on him so maybe he wasn't the right kind of boyfriend to have, you know?

It was weird that Walker knew so much about me. Especially the cheating thing. I didn't tell anyone about that, not even Wendi. It was about a boy, of course. It's always about a boy with me. I needed to grow out of that.

Anyway, this particular boy was twenty-one. A whole two years older than I was at the time. His name was Andrew and we were in Introduction to Literature together. It was a large class, almost a hundred students. The professor had two teaching assistants to help with passing out papers and grading. The midterm was an essay test and the final was a ten-page paper with three footnotes that would count for half our grade.

I noticed Andrew the first day of class. He had dark hair, pale skin and wore his high school letterman jacket even before it got cold. It was worn and frayed at the edges, which somehow only added to its appeal. At every class, I tried to sit near him. Four seats away, three, two. I dared not get closer than two. Finally, about a month into the semester, he said, "So, this William Blake guy was nuts, right?" as he was slipping his notebook into a backpack.

I wondered if he'd been sleeping through the lecture. This had been covered. "Um, yeah, they thought he was crazy at the time. But that just might be because he was a genius and kind of weird."

"He's no genius. Geniuses invent shit."

"Poetic genius," I said.

He rolled his eyes. Obviously, poetry was not important to him.

At midterm, he met me at the library and I coached him through everything we'd covered. He managed a C-plus on the test and was thrilled. I suggested he buy us a bottle of wine so we could celebrate.

"Oh yeah, we'll have to do that sometime," he said. But even though I brought it up several more times, it never happened.

The semester was going to be over in a couple of weeks and he asked to talk to me after class. He was in a panic about the final paper. The teacher wanted us to go in depth about one poem or story we'd read during the semester. I was doing Blake's "The Tyger." My thesis was that the poem was really about good and evil, and the way the tiger encompasses both. Andrew hadn't even picked a poem or story to work on. I was weak. I offered him a copy of my paper, so he could see how it was supposed to be done. It didn't occur to me that he was going to retype the paper and turn it in as his own. But that's what he did.

The first I heard of it was the following fall, when I received a letter asking me to appear in the dean of students' office a week after the semester began. Appear; it actually said that. I should have known I was in deep trouble. The dean's office was rather antiseptic: walls of painted concrete blocks, linoleum floor, metal furniture, diplomas on the wall. The dean was a pallid man of around sixty. When his secretary showed me into the office, I found Andrew sitting there with our literature professor. I had the sinking feeling this wasn't going to be good. Our professor began speaking, "Patrick, it's come to my attention that you and Andrew turned in what is basically the same term paper."

Before I could say anything, Andrew said, "I gave him my

paper to look at, you know, for how it should be done, and I guess he copied it. I didn't think he was going to. I thought he was going to do his own paper and, you know, copy how you do the footnotes and sh— stuff."

"That's not true," I said. "It was the other way around."

"It really makes no difference," the dean said. "Our plagiarism policy covers both the plagiarist and anyone who facilitates plagiarism. One of you gave the other their work and allowed them to copy it. That makes you both guilty."

I didn't pay close attention to the rest of what he said. Basically, we were both being expelled immediately, and the incident was going on our permanent record, which meant transferring to another school was out of the question.

I was nineteen and my college career was over.

———

That Sunday, the day after a very attractive CIA agent attempted to recruit me, Wendi and I went to the Circle Uptown Theatre for a matinee of *Ordinary People*. I'd read the book and liked it, so I wanted to see the movie. Wendi had crammed an old purse with cookies and candy we got at a funky supermarket practically across the street from the theater. We munched our way through the movie, eating Pepperidge Farm Chessmen and Twix. The movie was good and affecting.

While we waited for a bus to take us back down Connecticut Avenue, Wendi said, "I'm so mad at Mary Tyler Moore right now."

"She was good, wasn't she?"

"It's like she lied to us all those years on TV. Do you think she would have walked out on Dick Van Dyke like that?"

"Wendi, she was acting."

"Oh, that's what they all say. I think she finally let us know who she really is. Do you want some jelly beans? I forgot about them while she was throwing away her son's breakfast. Who would do something like that?"

"I think I've had enough sweets," I said. After the cookies and candy bars I was afraid I'd puke.

Our bus came and we got on. I was itching to tell her about Agent Walker. What would she think? Would she tell me to go back with David just to spy on him?

"So, do you think they'll release the hostages before the election?" I asked.

"Where did that come from?"

"I don't know, I just wondered."

"I think Carter's going to get them out and win the election and everything will be fine."

"And if he doesn't?"

"Then Iran will have picked our president for us." She didn't stop looking at me, though. "You already broke up with the prince, what do you care what happens in his country?"

"I *don't* care. I was just making conversation. You're the one who's campaigning for Carter."

"I don't want to talk about it. The whole thing makes me nauseous."

"Nauseated."

"Whatever. You read too much."

That settled it. I couldn't tell her I'd been approached by a CIA agent to stop David's father from preventing the hostages from being released. She'd want me to do something no matter what. And I really did not want to get involved.

We got off the bus at Dupont Circle and walked home. As soon as we turned onto P Street, I saw the white Lincoln parked across the street from our apartment.

"David's here."

"Oh God, is he going to turn into one of *those* boyfriends?" Wendi asked.

"I don't know. It's going to be okay. I'll just talk to him."

When we got to our building, David was sitting on the stoop leading up to the first floor. I wasn't sure our neighbors would be too happy about that, but it didn't look like they were home. He looked awful: dark splotches under his eyes, his brows seeming to slump over his eyes, his beautiful mouth turned down.

"Patrick, may I speak with you?"

I glanced at Wendi and nodded toward the apartment to let her know she should go in. She looked like she might argue, so I whispered, "I'm fine." Reluctantly, she went into the apartment. David came over and stood a few inches away from me.

"I'm sorry," he said. "I didn't think things through. I was arrogant and thoughtless. I made decisions alone, I didn't consider you, my friend, my lover, when I made them. I don't know what I want the future to be, but I want you to be there. I want you to help me choose what the future is."

"That sounds like a maybe. Maybe you won't up and marry a woman on our fifth anniversary."

"If I marry a woman on our fifth anniversary it will be because we've both decided it is best. Together. Isn't that enough?"

I started to ask why he thought I'd *ever* agree to a maybe—and then I remembered Agent Walker. He wanted me to get back with David. Not to build a life with him, but to help my country. When that was over, David and I would be done. There wouldn't be any fifth anniversary; there wouldn't be any first anniversary even. There would just be me reporting his and his father's every move to the CIA.

Could I really do it? Could I spy on David and his family? Yes, I could. It would be simple—right?

"All right."

"All right? You mean, we're back together?" he asked, his face breaking into a tremulous smile. "Oh Patrick—"

There on the street, in the light of day, he kissed me. I couldn't believe it. He was usually so self-conscious—and then, for a moment I was lost in the kiss. When he stopped, he held my face in his hands saying something in Persian.

"What was that? What did you just say?"

"'Be happy for this moment. This moment is your life.' It's from an old Persian poem."

Pulling him into my arms, I buried my face into his neck, I didn't want him to see me, sure that if he could he'd see the duplicitous scoundrel I'd become.

CHAPTER EIGHT

From a drug store on Dupont Circle, I called the number for The Publius Society that Agent Walker had given me. He wasn't there. I suspected he almost never was, so I left a message that he should meet me that afternoon at the same spot we'd met before. Whether I was talking to an answering service or a real secretary, she didn't react at all to my vague message. I imagined Walker got vague messages all the time.

The drugstore sold newspapers from all over the world. They were stacked on the floor in front of the magazines. *The New York Times*, *The Los Angeles Times*, *The Times* from London and, of course, *The Washington Post*. I browsed the front pages. Several of them had an article about the plan to rehabilitate the hostages whenever they got released. That seemed weird. They couldn't get them out of Iran, but they had a plan to help them when they did?

I fantasized for a while about what the headlines would say when I foiled David's father's plot to prevent the hostages' release. It was a hard thing to fantasize about though. For one, I suspected it would always be secret. And if it wasn't, if it *did* ever come out, the CIA would get the credit. Not some waiter from a French restaurant. I left the drugstore and spent the rest of the morning trying not to think about what I was about to do.

Arriving early at the Circle, I tried to read *A Confederacy of Dunces*. I figured I'd look more normal sitting on a bench reading a book. It was a nice enough afternoon. Besides, I was close to the end and the characters were running every which way. I kind of wanted to know what happened next, mainly so I could decide whether I loved the book or hated it. I was leaning toward loving it but still wasn't sure.

David had spent the night after we made up. He'd been sweet and kind, and after we made love he said, "I can't believe how much you mean to me after so short a time."

There wasn't anything I could think to say to that, so I kissed him again and thought, 'I can't believe how pleasant it is to have sex with someone I'm spying on for my country.'

And the sex had been pleasant, more than pleasant, surprisingly good. David seemed different than he'd been before, more vulnerable, more compliant. He was gentle and considerate, but he'd been that before. Mostly. No, it was his looking at me that I noticed. He stopped every so often and simply looked at me, baring his soul, seeking out mine. But my soul remained closed to him. As it had to. As it would always have to.

What was I doing? I thought. I should never have agreed to this. I should break up with David immediately and never see Walker again. It was none of my business. I wasn't even that patriotic. I mean, it did all seem kind of glamorous—spying on a prince, kissing CIA agents. I couldn't just spend my whole life reading books in my room—

Too late. Agent Walker sat down next to me. I sat up straight and tried to gather my thoughts. Today he wore a business suit, a gray, lumpy business suit. He could have been working undercover as a politician, except there was still something sexy about him even in the badly tailored suit.

"Hi," I said, giving him a nervous smile.

"It's nice to see you again. I'm glad you changed your mind."

"It's nice to see you too," I said, staring at his lips. They were pink and full and I wanted to—God, this was confusing.

I'd just been thinking about how nice it had been with David and now I was thinking about Walker's lips. And then I felt bad for having any nice thoughts about David at all. He was an enemy of my country. I needed to remember that.

"—when you call him you should be apologetic, contrite. You may need to win him over."

"David showed up at my apartment yesterday and wanted to get back together. It seemed easy to say yes. I mean, it's for my country, right?"

And for you, I thought, quickly deciding to keep that to myself.

Walker was momentarily flustered. "Oh, um, yes, it is. It is for your country. And it's good that he came to you. That way he won't suspect anything."

I lit a cigarette and right away Walker bummed one off me. "Thanks. I really am trying to quit."

I shrugged. His strategy seemed to be bumming cigarettes from people until all the smokers he knew hated his guts. It might eventually work.

"What kind of things do you need to know?" I asked, getting down to business. "We spent last night together and I didn't even try to find anything out. I mean, I don't know what you're looking for."

"We want to learn anything we can about his father. Where he goes. Who he sees. What deals he makes."

"It's going to be hard for me to find those things out. Those aren't the kind of things you talk about in bed."

"I'm well aware of that. The Qajars are having a party on Friday night. You need to get yourself invited. That will make it easier to talk about his father."

"I don't know if I can do that," I said, quickly. "David didn't say anything about the party. I'm seeing him tonight but I can't exactly bring it up. If I say, 'Hey, I heard you're having a party on Friday,' he'll get suspicious."

"Come on, Patrick, you're smarter than that. Ask him to do something special on Friday. Dinner. The Tabard Inn, that's a fancy place. Tell him you won a dinner for two in a raffle and you want to treat him. Tell him you want to celebrate getting back together."

"What if he decides to have dinner with me instead of going to the party?"

"He won't."

"But what if he does?"

"Then I'll make a reservation for you and pay in advance."

"I don't know."

"It's day 329, Patrick. Think about what that means to our people in Iran."

I didn't think about it, though, I thought about his plan. I was dubious. I might get David to tell me about the party, but it wouldn't necessarily get me invited. Still, Walker thought I was smart enough to figure it out. Maybe I was. Maybe I wanted to find out if I was.

"All right, I'll try."

"You do understand that this is all very secret. You can't tell anyone what you're doing. You can't tell anyone about me. Are you good at secrets, Patrick?"

"I spent a lot of time in the closet. That's a secret."

"You're not old enough to have spent a lot of time in the closet," he pointed out correctly.

"It seemed like a long time to me."

"And now you're *not* in the closet?"

"Well, my mother doesn't know. Or at least we pretend she doesn't. And I don't walk around telling strangers on the street. But my friends all know and the people at work."

"Why tell anyone?"

"I don't know that I'd want to live an entirely secret—" I stopped. I imagined that Agent Gary Walker lived a nearly secret life. No one knew he was in the CIA, and I'll bet no one knew he was gay either. Especially his buddies in the CIA. "You have a lot of secrets don't you?"

"As a matter of fact, I do. But we're not here to talk about me."

"You know you could come to my apartment. My roommate would just think you were a trick."

"She knows you're back with David?"

"She does. She wouldn't tell him though."

He smiled blandly. "I'm flattered, Patrick, but you're an asset now. It's not a good idea to have sex with an asset. No matter how cute they are."

He'd just called me cute. My skin went all tingly when he said it. And it gave me enough courage to ask. "Why not? We don't have to tell anyone, do we?"

"Best not muddy the water." He smiled again, this time raising his eyebrows in a kind of 'what can you do?' sort of look.

"Well, do I at least get a code name?"

"How about Patrick?" he suggested dryly.

"That's not a code name."

"What do you want it to be?"

"I don't know." And at first I didn't know. Then I thought about my super-great grandfather, Patrick Henry, who famously said, 'Give me liberty or give me death.'

So I said, "How about Liberty?" I mean, the other choice was death and I didn't think I'd like that as a code name.

"Sure," Walker said. "Your code name is Liberty."

"Thanks."

"Do you have any other demands?"

"No, that's it."

Relaxing his face, he asked, "You need to give me your telephone number."

"I don't have a telephone. I thought you'd know that."

"I assumed your phone number was unlisted."

"You got my social security number, you can't get an unlisted number?"

He scowled at me. "You're right. I've been sloppy. I hope you won't tell my boss." The last was almost flirtatious.

"I don't know who your boss is."

He smiled. "No, you don't. Tell me, why don't you have a telephone?"

"I can't afford the two hundred and fifty dollars for the security deposit."

"I thought Le Marquis was a good place to work?"

"It is if you work Friday, Saturday or Sunday. I don't have seniority yet so I work during the week. Does it really matter why I don't have a phone? I just don't."

He stared at me for a moment and then took a wallet out of his inside jacket pocket. It was the kind of wallet that didn't fold. Flipping it open with his thumb, he took out two one hundred dollar bills, then a fifty and handed them to me.

"Get a phone."

"Um, all right."

After my meeting with Agent Walker, I didn't go home. Instead, I took the Metro downtown and walked over to the main library. Named after Martin Luther King, the building was a long, low, black steel building that covered most of a block. Open and cold, my footsteps echoed on the marble floor. I walked up to the card catalog and looked up Persia. What I found was a strange collection of books: biographies of people who'd fled, retellings of thousand-year-old wars, and a book by Winston Churchill. I tried looking up

Iran, but that wasn't much more useful. I was looking for a book that would show me the royal families of Iran. I wanted to read about the Qajar line. I looked up Qajar and found a book on 18th-century painting. There wasn't even a general book about Iran's history. I wasn't getting very far; then I had an idea.

Encyclopedias. Yes, they were my primary source when writing a high school report, so I was pretty sure I'd find exactly what I wanted in an encyclopedia. I went over to the circulation desk and asked where I could find them. They were on the second floor.

Pulling out the Encyclopedia Britannica volume labeled "I," my search ended with an article entitled "Dynasties of Iran." From that article, I learned that David's grandfather was overthrown in a military coup and sent into exile, traveling Europe for most of the rest of his life. He had five wives, to whom he seemed to have been married at the same time. There were five children: three girls and two boys—no reference as to which child belonged to which wife. The youngest boy was Nasim el-din Qajar, David's father.

I sat back from reading the entry. I wasn't sure what exactly I'd learned. David wasn't lying to me, he really was a prince. But I hadn't thought he was lying. It certainly didn't make any sense for the CIA to be interested in someone who was lying about being a prince.

After that I was at a loss, so I went to the reference desk and asked for some help. A librarian showed me how to look through the *Washington Post* index and write down which issues referenced what I was looking for. When I had what I wanted, the librarian gave me the microfiche containing the editions I was looking for.

I was led to a small, darkened room with six fiche machines. I slid the blue sheet of plastic onto the glass platform and pushed. The machine clamped down on it and then the tiny photos of the newspaper were blown up into something actually readable.

The only article that was at all valuable was titled "EX-PATS INFLUENCE U.S. POLICY ON IRAN. The article contained just a few sentences that made sense to me: "Nasim el-din Qajar seeks Western aid in restoring the Qajar dynasty's rule of Iran, promising a government aligned with Western interests, while also more acceptable to the Iranian people than restoration of the Pahlavi dynasty."

I tried to decipher what that meant. If Nasim was using his contacts to keep the hostages in Iran until after the election, then he must feel it more likely that the Qajar dynasty would be restored by Reagan rather than by Carter. Well, President Carter did allow the shah into the United States for cancer treatment. Maybe Carter supported the Pahlavi dynasty?

On the way home, I stopped at the C&P telephone office on R Street and, after waiting twenty minutes, gave them two hundred and fifty dollars cash. They promised to send out an installer within the next three days. As soon as the phone was installed I was supposed to call The Publius Society and leave the number for Agent Walker.

"You know, my roommate might get suspicious if you're calling me all the time," I'd said after he gave me the money.

"If she answers I'll ask for Sylvia. If she tells you about a wrong number for Sylvia, you'll know to call me."

I didn't know why he thought she'd tell me about wrong numbers, but I agreed anyway.

After the library and the phone company, I went home. I only had a couple of hours before I was supposed to see David. Walking in the door, I asked Wendi what was going on with the hostages.

In the midst of giving herself a manicure, she looked at me like I was crazy. "They're not even talking right now. Why do you keep asking about them? You don't care."

"I care. I just care quietly. Why aren't they talking?"

"Because the ayatollah is demanding the United States apologize and all this other shit. Money and stuff."

"Apologize for what?"

"The fact that the U.S. exists, I guess."

"Okay."

I flopped onto the sofa next to her.

"Hey, be careful. I don't want to spill the polish. I'd never get it out of this bedspread."

"I got a phone. It's being installed sometime in the next three days."

"I thought you didn't want to spend the money on the deposit," she said.

In all honesty, the phone had been the only problem we'd ever had as roommates. She'd suggested we get the phone in my name and split the security deposit. I didn't want to. The fact that she couldn't have it in her name wasn't my fault. I had no credit—which made the deposit big enough, but Wendi had bad credit and that made the deposit ginormous. She'd gone a little crazy with an American Express card and still owed them a lot of money. From Wendi, they wanted almost twice the deposit and several body parts.

"I changed my mind," I said, lamely.

"Does this have anything to do with the prince?" she asked. She was right, of course, but not in the way she thought.

"I guess."

"Where did you get the money?"

"I've been saving for a while."

"No, you haven't. You don't know how to save money." That was the kettle calling the pot black. "David gave you the money, didn't he?"

"Don't mention it to him, okay?"

"Why would I talk about the phone bill with your boyfriend?" She frowned. "I suppose now you want my half of the deposit."

"Don't worry about it."

She looked at me suspiciously for a moment. "Really?"

"I shouldn't have been such a dick about it in the first place."

"That's okay. My parents offered to pay for it, but I said no because you pissed me off."

I laughed. We'd both been a little vindictive and had ended up not having a phone for a very long time. We'd done fine, though, with the phone at work and the drugstore nearby.

"Of course, it also gave me an excuse to call my parents collect," she said. "And keep the conversation short."

"Well, you don't have to tell them you have a phone if you don't want to."

HUNT & WERNER ENCYCLOPEDIA

The Qajar Dynasty

A family dynasty ruling Persia from 1789 to 1925. Of Turkic origins (see entry), the Qajar family deposed Lotf 'Ali Khan, last shah of the Zand dynasty seizing power. Initially, Mohammad Khan Qajar (1742-1797) reunited the country and restored territories in Georgia and the Caucasus. These territories were lost by later generations in the Russo-Persian wars of the early 19th centuries. The territories of modern Georgia, Dagestan and Azerbaijan were permanently lost from the Persian empire.

Naser-e-Din (1831-1896) who became shah in 1848 proved to the most successful of the dynasty, bringing Western culture and modernization into the region. In 1851 Dar ul-Funun was built, the first university in the region, importing French and Russian professors. Naser-e-Din was assassinated in 1896.

Despite remaining neutral in World War I, Persia was occupied by the Russians, the British and the Ottoman Empire. The final shah, Ahmad Qajar (1898-1930), was but a teenager and unable to protect his country. In 1921, military leader Reza Khan staged a coup d'état overthrowing Ahmad Qajar and sending him into exile.

The head of the Imperial family and heir presumptive is Prince Sultan Nasim el-din Qajar (1922-present).

CHAPTER NINE

When he arrived that night, David suggested we go to a movie. He wanted to see *Dressed to Kill*, but I didn't think I'd learn very much if we sat in the dark, and the last thing I needed to do was go to a movie that might make me feel edgy.

My idea was that we order a pizza, drink a bottle of Riunite Lambrusco and hang out with my roommate. David didn't seem exactly thrilled with the idea, but, since I'd broken up with him a few days before, he had a vested interest in giving me my way. Of course, I'm not too sure Wendi was exactly thrilled with our hanging out with her either.

It was still in the low eighties outside, but David had worn a pair of jeans and a dress shirt—probably anticipating he'd spend the evening in an air-conditioned movie theater. Instead, he was wedged between Wendi and me, both wearing cut-offs and tank tops and not much more. She put the B-52s on the stereo. David seemed faintly annoyed with them by the time "Planet Claire" ended.

I got up and poured us all a glass of wine, bringing them back to the couch, I said, "Wendi doesn't believe you're a prince."

Her eyes opened wide. She'd never said exactly that.

"It doesn't matter what she believes," David replied.

"Gee, thanks," she said.

"I'm sorry, what I mean is I'm a prince whether you believe it or not. It is simply a fact."

"Explain to her exactly how you're a prince," I said.

"For more than a century my family ruled Persia. Until we were deposed by the despot Reza Khan, a commoner, a nobody. It was his son you called the Shah of Iran, as though there had only ever been one."

"My mother has been having a feud with her next-door neighbor for twenty years," Wendi said. "It's over a rose bush. But honestly I can't remember whether it was my mother's rose bush and our neighbor killed it or if it's the other way around."

"Are you making fun of me?"

"No. I'm telling you how far removed from me, from us, your family's experience is."

That seemed to mollify him, but I knew she was also making fun of him.

"Are you a Muslim?" Wendi asked. I blushed when she asked him. I'd asked the same question, but now it seemed like it was the only question Americans wanted to ask.

He hesitated. "That's a tricky question."

"Your religion is a tricky question?"

"Americans hear Muslim and they think the ayatollah, which is unfortunate. The ayatollah is not a Muslim, he's a fanatic."

"So, you're a Muslim. And Americans don't know what that means."

"If you want to understand what has happened to my country, imagine what America would be like if Pat Robertson suddenly became president."

"Shit. That would suck."

"Exactly."

"What brings you to Washington?" she asked.

David sipped his wine and then said, "My father has business here."

"I've got a little extra cash," I lied. "I was thinking I could take you out to dinner. How about Friday?"

He shook his head. "I'm busy Friday."

"Oh? What are you doing Friday?"

"My father is having a party. He expects me to come."

"I love parties," I said.

"Not this kind of party, I'm sure."

"If it's a party, it can't be that bad."

"It wouldn't be appropriate."

"Appropriate. You mean, people will know I'm your boyfriend?"

"Not people. My father. He's the only one I care about."

"I'll bring Wendi," I suggested.

"Oh, now wait a minute," she said. "Don't drag me into this."

"You'd just have to stand next to me and let people assume you're my girlfriend."

"What's the party for?" Wendi asked David.

"It's for my father's associates."

"See," she said, "we don't belong there."

"Why is your father giving a party for his associates?"

"It's to see what we can do about the war. But we don't say that, or no one would come."

"You're having a party but not telling people why?" I asked.

David shrugged. "People in Washington are always giving parties. They want to gossip and make deals. No one asks why."

"What about your mother?" Wendi asked. "What's she like?"

"She's dead. She died when I was a child."

"Oh. Sorry." She frowned at me, pissed I'd involved her in this. And that I'd never mentioned his dead mother. Not that I remember asking David about her.

"I really don't remember her," he said.

"So, it's just you and your dad."

David smiled. "He's not the kind of man you call dad."

"Well, I'm going to order the pizza, what do you want on it?" I asked.

After we negotiated that we'd have a large pizza with mushrooms and onions—I wanted pepperoni but that had pork in it, a surprise to me—Wendi left to go down to the drugstore on the other side of Dupont Circle and make the call. Normally, she'd have fought tooth and nail not to be the one to go, but I think she didn't want to be left alone with David.

As soon as she was gone, he moved closer and kissed me. When he finally pulled away, he said, "We are horribly rude to make Wendi order the pizza. A gentleman would not have allowed that."

"She deserves it. She never goes."

"I'm going to get you a telephone," David said imperially. I was so glad he didn't say that in front of Wendi.

"Oh, you don't have to. I ordered one this afternoon. It'll be installed by the end of the week." As soon as the words were out of my mouth I realized I had a problem. I'd told him I couldn't afford a telephone and suddenly I could. And on top of inviting him to dinner, no less. I scrambled a bit. "My tips have been really good for the last couple of weeks. One guy gave me fifty dollars for my discretion."

I'd spent the money immediately, but David didn't know that. And the story was still true, so I figured it was better to lie with the truth than to simply make something up. Or at least it always had been in my experience.

"Who was this guy? What did he want you to be discreet about?"

"Oh, they were politicians talking about the election, that's all."

"And what did they say?"

Oh my God, I was terrible at spying! I was being grilled by the guy I was meant to be grilling.

"I can't remember what they were saying exactly." Except I did remember, it had something to do with the hostages and whether Carter would get them out in time. "Maybe it was about some new tax bill."

"There's no new tax bill."

"How would you know? You're not even American."

"Are you suggesting Americans know what bills are before their congress?" He teased. They didn't, of course.

I shrugged. "Maybe they were talking about after the election. Didn't Reagan promise something like that?"

He looked at me suspiciously for a moment and then kissed me. Into my ear he whispered, "You're beautiful. A beautiful boy."

"I'm not a boy. I'm just a couple of years younger than you are."

"Some men will always boys," he teased.

"About the party—"

"Do we have time to have sex before your roommate returns?"

"Probably not," I said. "Are you really not going to invite me to your party?"

He sighed heavily. "You can come to the party."

I kissed him and then we raced into the bedroom.

"What was all that about?" Wendi asked, the next morning, cereal bowl in hand. David had showered quickly and slipped out of the apartment.

"All what?" I asked, groggy. He'd kept me up most of the night. I had painful whisker burn all over my face and I was sore in places I didn't know could get sore.

"'Wendi doesn't believe you're a prince?' Roping me into being your beard for a night."

"I want to go to the party."

"Why? It doesn't sound like it's going to be much fun."

"I want to see where David lives. I want to meet his father. He's not going to just invite me home to meet the family, you know. This is probably the only chance I'll ever get."

"I'm still not understanding why you went back with him. Did anything really change? Did he say he's not going to marry a woman some day?"

"His apology was very sweet." And, it was. I might have accepted it even if the CIA didn't want me to spy on him. Well, no, I wouldn't have.

"There's something about this that doesn't ring true," she said, clearly suspicious. But then she gave up and said, "I need to buy a dress."

"You don't need to do that. You can wear the one you wore to Exile."

"Oh God no. It smells like poppers. I'll never be able to get that out. I need a new one. Or at least a new old one. You need to take me shopping."

"Me! I can't afford to buy you a dress."

"You should have thought of that before you insisted I pretend to be your girlfriend."

"You can't wear anything you have? Nothing?"

"Fine, I'll buy it myself. But you have to go with me. Get ready."

"Now? We have all week."

"It may take all week; get ready."

Forty minutes later we were in a consignment store on Rhode Island called Second Chances. All the Washington socialites sent their old dresses there to be sold on consignment. The clerk at the front said, "Hello Wendi, how are you?"

Wendi chatted with her for a moment then pushed me deeper into the store.

"I can never remember her name," she said under her breath. "Now, what's new?"

We went through the racks and every time she liked something, she hung it over my extended arm.

"Do I need to wear a hijab?"

"I don't know what that is."

"A scarf on my head."

"Then why not say scarf?"

"Because when you wear it for religious reasons it's not a scarf, it's a hijab."

"I don't think you have to wear one. I mean, you're not Muslim, so why would you?"

"To show respect for their religious tradition. David doesn't seem very Muslim, though. I mean, other than not eating pork."

"I don't know. How Muslim does he have to be?"

"Does he pray six times a day?"

"Not that I've noticed."

She shrugged and said, "Of course, a *good* Muslim wouldn't be banging you silly every night."

"I guess he's a bad Muslim then."

"At least for now."

"Why do they make women wear hijabs?" I asked.

"Because just looking at a woman's hair can inflame a man's lust."

"That's ridiculous."

She shrugged, all too familiar with the oddities of men. "Jews and Christians do it too."

"No, they don't."

"Catholic women wear veils in church and orthodox Jewish women wear wigs. Maybe I should have a scarf with me just in case."

"Um, I don't think I can hold much more," I said, my left arm beginning to sag. Wendi had piled on six evening dresses. She led me to the back of the shop to the dressing rooms. Then she took the dresses off my arm and went in.

As she got dressed, she continued to talk to me. "So, why are you so interested in meeting David's father? I hate meeting a guy's parents. It always changes things and never in a good way."

She was right. Normally, I'd never have wanted to meet a guy's dad. In fact, I'd never met anyone's parents before. That didn't seem like a bad— "You know, I've never met a guy's parents before. Maybe I'll regret it. I don't know."

She came out of the dressing room wearing a shimmering lavender dress that gathered around her neck, exposed her shoulders like a halter and then plunged to the floor. It was about six inches too long but could easily be hemmed. Unfortunately, it made her look short.

"What do you think?"

"It's great," I said.

She looked in the mirror next to the dressing room and said, "I look like a shiny sack of potatoes."

"A *great* shiny sack of potatoes."

She hiked up the skirt and went back into the dressing room.

"The thing about meeting David's dad is that if he figures out who you are, he'll hate you. And if he doesn't figure it out, there's no reason to pay any attention to you."

I hated that I had to lie to her. I wanted to tell her everything. I wanted to know what she thought of sexy Agent Walker and whether, in her opinion, David could do anything truly wrong. Mostly I wanted her to tell me that what I was doing was right, that I was a good American, that I'd made the right choice.

Instead, I had to say, "Oh, that's pretty."

She'd come out of the dressing room wearing a black-and white dress. The top part was plaid with spaghetti straps and the white skirt was overlaid with black organza embroidered with stars.

Studying her image in the mirror, she said, "I don't know. It's a bit much."

"Gee, that's how I'd describe your style."

"Shut up. Let me try on another one." She slipped back into the dressing room.

"Are we even sure this party is formal?" I asked. "Maybe it's casual."

"Casual for you and casual for me are different things."

Which made me wonder what I was going to wear. The only suit jacket I had was from a prep school I didn't attend and was just slightly too small for me. Well, it *was* too small for me, but I looked good in it, especially if I pushed up the sleeves so no one could see how short they really were.

"Should we look for something you could wear?" Wendi called out.

"I don't have any money, remember?"

"You could go naked. Do you think the prince's father would like you then?"

"Ha-ha," I said. "I'll think of something."

Then she popped out of the dressing room in a new dress. It had a tightly fitted black bodice, a thick red ribbon at the waist and a knee-length skirt with vertical black and white stripes, and another red ribbon around the hem.

"This is the one," Wendi said, looking at herself in the mirror. The dress was eighty-five dollars. Used.

Even though it was a very-Wendi dress, I had to ask, "Are you crazy? Shouldn't we go to the Salvation Army and get something for, like, ten bucks?"

"I'm not going to a party given by a prince in a dress that smells like mothballs. Besides, I can't afford a ten-dollar dress."

"Then how can you—you're not going to steal this dress are you?"

She gave me a filthy look. "Of course not. This is a consignment store. I'm going to wear the dress once, have it dry cleaned, and bring it back and sell it on consignment for what I paid for it. Total cost, including their commission maybe six bucks. Unless you want to buy it for me?"

"No, no, I can't."

"Then I'm going to do this my way."

THE PRESIDENT'S DAILY BRIEF

September 27, 1980
Top Secret

Iraq-Iran War – *Full-scale war continues unabated. While neither Iraq nor Iran supply a great deal of oil to the U.S., their conflict could ensnare other nations in the Persian Gulf and threaten American supplies of oil. Conflict in the region involves complex historical and religious issues, including a 1,300-year-old battle that still causes bitter emotions on both sides.*

Iran – *Islamic Conference attempted to broker a peace agreement in the Iraq-Iran war. Iranian President Abolhassan Bani-Sadr rejected mediation. Prime Minister Mohammad Ali Rajai announced, "We will not accept any mission as a goodwill delegation and will never be ready to speak one word about negotiations."*

Hostages – *The majles debated resolution of the hostage-crisis and established a seven-man commission to outline conditions of release. Commission is prohibited from having direct contact with U.S. officials or rejecting any of the four conditions stipulated by Khomeini.*

Munich, Germany – *Terrorist attack at closing of Oktoberfest event kills 12, injures more than 100. A right-wing neo-Nazi group is suspected, though German officials downplay this possibility. The bomber died in the explosion.*

CHAPTER TEN

That night at work, Maxim was all a flutter.

"Pat*rick*, you have been especially requested. You will have only one party tonight. They want the Madison room all to themselves. This is a very important honor and you should be very proud."

"I *am* very proud. Thank you, Maxim," I said. One of the first things you learned about the headwaiter—aside from the fact that his accent was phony—was that you had to repeat whatever he said to appease him.

"There will be ten or twelve of them, perhaps. It should be no trouble for you, I'm sure."

"Ten or twelve? Absolutely no trouble."

"Good. I am very pleased." He turned on his heel and walked away.

It was going to be a relatively easy night. There might be a few tense moments when I had to get dinner for twelve out of the kitchen and onto the table all at once, but really it was going to be easier than the five or six smaller tables I usually served on a Tuesday night.

Since they wanted the room to themselves, it probably meant they were staying after dinner to talk. I doubted I'd have any parties afterward, so this would be my one table of the night. I just hoped they tipped like six tables.

They began to arrive around seven. Middle-aged men in gray suits. Big surprise. I took drink orders and ran to the bar. A lot of Cutty Sark and soda. They smoked cigarettes, sipped their drinks, and ignored me. I tried to figure out who might be in charge, but it seemed like whoever it was wasn't there yet. I stood calmly near the door.

Of course, I could hear everything they were saying.

"Carter is chasing Ronnie off the front page."

"Come on, man, there's a war in the Middle East and the Arabs are trying to expel Israel from the UN. Yeah, Carter gets his name mentioned, but people are associating his name with trouble. You'll see."

"We're sending planes to Saudi Arabia. If Carter gets us involved in a war over there people might just stick with him."

"The planes are to protect Saudi Arabia. They are radar planes, that's all. They're just going to let the Saudis know if anything's spilling over from Iraq."

"The Saudis don't have radar? What century is this?"

Then, the older guy with the round glasses walked in with a couple of other gray suits, Mr. Discretion. That explained why I'd been requested. Well, at least I knew I'd be getting a decent tip at the end of the night.

"Hello, Patrick. Glad you're here tonight," he said. It wasn't surprising that he knew my name. I usually introduced myself to each new party. What was surprising was that he'd remembered it.

"Hello," I said. He didn't introduce himself and I wasn't sure it was polite to ask. "How are you, sir?"

"Excellent." Then he and the men he'd come with ordered drinks. I ran to the bar and put in the order. There were eight men total at this point and I wondered if others were expected. When the drinks were ready I took them back to the Madison room.

"What if he gets them out? You know he'll win if that happens," said a man with a bad comb-over, obviously talking about the hostages. I set his drink down in front of him.

"I think the chances of Carter getting them out are pretty piss-poor," Mr. Discretion said. "They hate him over there. He'd have to give them something very big. And he can't risk that."

I set his drink, a Dewar's and water, on the cocktail napkin I'd already laid down.

"Can we get there first?" asked the grayest of the gray suits. "Make sure he can't get them out?"

"That would be a violation of the Logan Act. Private citizens are prohibited from negotiating with enemies. It might also be called treason," Mr. Discretion said.

"Only when the other side does it," Comb-Over said. The table erupted in self-satisfied laughter. When it died down, he added, "Seriously, when we win it won't matter."

"That's when it will matter more," said Mr. Discretion. "Was a special prosecutor put in place to investigate George McGovern?"

I put down the remaining drinks. The table was silent. You didn't even need to invoke Nixon's name to make these gentleman frown unhappily.

I leaned over and asked Mr. Discretion, "Would you like appetizers?"

"That's a wonderful idea. Why don't you choose for us, Patrick?" Then he turned back to the table. "Now, who has an idea that might be legal?"

I walked out of the room wondering what I should get them for appetizers. We only had a few on the menu: Coquilles St. Jacques—which was really meant for one person, so that was out—the brie & pâté plate, the champignons farcis, and the tarte à l'oignon were all better choices. Two orders of each should be enough for eight. I didn't want to ruin their appetites.

I put the order into the kitchen and went back to have a cigarette in the employee lounge. I wondered if some of the things I was hearing would be interesting to Agent Walker. Immediately though, I felt a pang of guilt. Mr. Discretion was paying me for my, well, my discretion. I really shouldn't say anything about it. He trusted me. But then, David trusted me, too. So why was I treating the two situations differently? *Were* they different? I had a little trouble seeing exactly how.

Putting out my cigarette, I went back to the Madison room. I emptied their ashtrays, carefully placing a saucer atop each one to prevent ashes from flying out. As I did, I tried to listen to see if they were calling one another by name. Bob, one was called Bob. Or was it Bill?

Going back to the bar, I ordered a couple of refills, then returned to the Madison room. I wanted to get the menus off the table—the menus at Le Marquis were over-sized and clumsy—before I brought out the appetizers. I walked down to Mr. Discretion and subtly spoke to him.

"Would it be all right if I took the order now? I won't rush it through. I'd just like to get the menus off the table."

"Of course, why don't you start with Judge Carlisle," he waved a hand at the man sitting next to him. I wrote Judge Carlisle on the very top of my pad then smiled at him, waiting for his order.

"Prime rib, pink, French fries—"

"I'm sorry, your honor, we only serve potatoes au gratin or baked. The au gratin is very good."

"All right, whatever."

I picked up the menu from in front of the judge and moved onto the gentleman next to him. Of the remaining gentleman, four ordered the prime rib exactly as Judge Carlisle had, one ordered the stuffed sole, two had the fruits de mer—a fish and pasta dish—and Mr. Discretion ordered the boeuf Bourguignon, which seemed to be his regular order.

After I dropped the menus off at the waiter's station—where a hostess would pick them up and bring them back out to the front —I went and checked on the appetizers. They were ready so I brought them out to the Madison Room.

"I for one was much happier in July. *Time* magazine has them deadlocked again. How did that happen? Our boy was up by twenty percent just a few weeks ago."

"The problem is the South, Bill. If it goes for Carter again, we're sunk. That's where Ronnie needs to be. This weekend he was at his ranch in California. Now I ask you, if he's already won California what's he doing there?"

I cleared my throat and told them what the appetizers were as I set them down. I went around the table and gave them each a small plate to set their choices on. Then I offered them another drink and got a couple of takers. Before I left the room, Mr. Discretion called me over.

"When you bring dinner, we'll have two bottles of the Pouilly-Fuissé."

"Of course," I said, then left the room. I ordered the drinks from the bar. Wendi came up behind me and asked, "How's your big party?"

"Gray suits. Drinking up a storm. Deciding the fate of the free world."

"Oh good, you'll make some money."

"I hope so. They just ordered two bottles of thirty-dollar wine."

"That helps. The dining room is dead. I've only got a couple of deuces."

My drinks came up and I went back to the Madison room. While setting down another Cutty Sark and water, I heard, "Carter has said we're neutral in the Iraq/Iran conflict. Can we make it seem like he's namby-pamby, that he's too weak to pick a side?"

"Obviously, we're on Iraq's side. Are we sending help to Hussein? He shouldn't have to go it alone."

"Don't you see, though, that's what we're not talking about. Now's the time to offer something to Iran. They weren't prepared for this. They need weapons."

"Do you think Carter will trade them weapons for the hostages?"

"He's not that bright," Judge Carlisle said.

"It could be a PR disaster if he did."

"That's what I mean," the judge said. "Carter's not bright enough to say one thing and do another."

I walked out of the room and went back to the lounge. I lit a cigarette and began to write out their check. Our system was to write orders on a scratchpad and then write out the check as neatly as possible. It wasn't a good system. Things got left off checks all the time, but it did leave the guest with a very neat check.

I stopped what I was doing and just smoked for a bit. Why was a judge at a meeting discussing such obviously partisan things? I'd always thought judges were meant to be impartial. Hadn't I learned that somewhere? And why would it matter to a judge who was president?

And why did it matter to me? It did kind of matter. I mean, it was my country too. Yeah, I knew being gay was sort of illegal in most places, but that didn't mean I wasn't an American. I could be an American and think that laws and customs were wrong—that seemed to be one of the basics of being an American. Along with the right to try to change things.

I supposed I would need to talk to Agent Walker about Judge Carlisle and what he'd been saying. It was entirely possible this group was trying to do the exact same things he thought David's father was up to, so he'd need to know about it. He'd need to stop them.

When was I going to see David again? I was getting off early. Maybe I should call him and have him come over. Was there a way

I could raise the issue of the hostages? Should I tell him what the men were saying in the Madison Room just to see the look on his face? Would he start to tell me what his father was doing if I brought it up?

Then I had a thought; a ridiculous and kind of scary thought: I'm Mata Hari. I'm seducing a man for his secrets.

CHAPTER ELEVEN

The telephone guy arrived at eleven o'clock in the morning, but still managed to wake me. I'd called David before I left work, but he said his father needed him and reminded me that he'd spent the night before. Bored and a little anxious, I was up half the night re-reading *The Persian Boy*. I liked it, though it seemed to be taking its time getting to Alexander. I fell asleep during chapter six. Not because it was incredibly late, but because I'd drunk most of a bottle of Lancer's. Mr. Discretion had tipped me a hundred dollars cash on top of his two hundred and ten-dollar bill and I'd bought the wine on my way home.

I stumbled over to the phone jack from the last tenant and pointed it out to the installer. He got onto his knees and started opening it up.

"I asked for the really long cord," I said. It was the only way either of us would get any privacy. "They said you'd bring it."

"It costs extra."

"I know. I don't care."

Bleary-eyed, Wendi came out of her bedroom on her way to the bathroom. She'd had the rest of my bottle of Lancer's plus some leftover Lambrusco. She glanced into the living room and said, "Uh."

The telephone guy looked up at me and said, "Wife?"

"Friend."

"Smart. Don't let 'em tie you down. Next thing you know

you'll be an old man and none of them will look at you. Get 'em now, while you can. Get 'em all."

"Thanks for the advice."

I went into the kitchen and made a shitty pot of coffee. It was almost brewed when the telephone guy stuck his head into the kitchen and said, "Done."

"Okay, thanks."

"It's a black desk-style phone. Is that what you wanted? I've got a beige princess phone in my van."

"The desk phone is fine, thanks."

I came out of the kitchen, since I wasn't sure he'd leave unless I showed him out. I followed him to the front door.

"Did you want to try it before I go?"

"You tried it, didn't you?"

"I did."

"Then I'm sure it's fine," I said, shutting the door behind him. As soon as I did, I ran to the phone, which he'd left on the floor rather than setting it on top of the wire telephone stand that Wendi had picked up at a little shop we stopped at after the consignment store. I snatched up the receiver and listened for the dial tone. It was, thankfully, there.

Wendi came out of the bathroom and stopped at the entrance to the living room. "So, it works?"

"Yes."

"Great. Let's not give anyone the number."

"Um, that kind of defeats the point."

She shrugged and walked back out. When I heard her bedroom door slam, I picked up the phone and hurried back down to my room. The cord allowed the phone a whole foot into my room. I shut the door, then went over and picked up *The Persian Boy* and took out Walker's business card.

Sitting down next to the phone, I called the number at The Publius Society and left a message for Agent Walker. "This is Liberty. Got the phone installed," I whispered. Then I gave the receptionist my new phone number.

"Have a nice day," she told me before I hung up.

After that, I thought about who else I might call. I should probably call David, but I wasn't awake enough to talk to him, or more accurately, spy on him. I could call my mother, but I *certainly* wasn't awake enough to talk to her. I hadn't spoken to her in almost a year. Whenever I imagined how the conversation might go, I decided not to call her.

I was thinking about crawling back into bed and taking a nap, when I heard the mail being dropped into the slot. I got up, brought the phone back out to the living room, and picked up the mail off the floor. There was a catalog for Brown University and one for Amherst. My mother was thinking about me, at least.

After the stupid thing with Andrew she could barely forgive me for screwing up my education. Well, not barely; she *couldn't* forgive me. The catalogs were a reminder not to forget what a screw up I was. I took them directly to the trash and threw them out.

Wendi came out of her room again.

"Does the phone work?"

"Uh-huh," I said.

"Did you call your mother?"

"No."

"I'm going to call mine. If she finds out we have a phone and I didn't give her the number she'll never speak to me again. And that means I won't be able to borrow money from her, so I'd better call. It'll probably be a very long phone call. Is there anyone you want to call first?"

"No, I'm fine."

I went back to bed and spent the next few hours fantasizing about Agent Walker. Eventually, I'd find out everything they needed to send David's father to prison or deport him or something. And David might go wherever with him. Then things could change between Walker and me. I wouldn't be an asset anymore. There wouldn't be any water to muddy. He could see me. He could be my boyfriend. Or, you know, whatever.

It sounded glamorous to be in love with a spy. But then I thought, he's not going to be able to tell me anything. He'll be sneaking off to secret meetings all the time and leaving me in the dark. But then I wondered if he'd break the rules for me. Would he tell me about everything he did? Would he talk to me about what happened in his secret meetings? Maybe he could get me a job with the CIA and I could be a spy too.

I mean, I already was a spy, I knew that. But maybe I could spy on someone I wasn't having sex with. Or maybe I could have an asset of my own. Wendi would make a good asset. She could get anyone talking. For a while I thought about what great spies Wendi and I would be together. And then it was time to get up.

I told Wendi I was going out for cigarettes and went to meet Agent Walker at our spot in Dupont Circle. He was supposed to be there by one o'clock but he didn't come. I didn't have a watch, but it seemed like I was waiting forever. I was starting to worry about what to tell Wendi. It didn't usually take a whole hour to get cigarettes.

I was just about to give up and go home when Agent Walker showed up.

"Where've you been?" I asked. "You're really late."

"I came out of the Metro and I was sure someone was following me."

"Were they?"

"No, I think I was wrong. I walked around a couple of blocks, just to be sure."

I couldn't help looking around. What if he was being followed? What if someone followed him right to me? Was I being followed? None of this had seemed particularly dangerous, but maybe I was wrong.

"Who would follow you?"

"You don't need to know that. Let me have a cigarette."

I gave him one and lit it for him. He touched my hand as I did, gently. Looking up at me, his dark blue-black eyes locked with mine for just a moment. There was a flash of something I couldn't quite read. Desire?

"Is this all more dangerous than I thought?" I asked.

"Don't worry, I won't let anything happen to you," he said, back to business. "What did you want to see me about?"

"I got invited to the party on Friday."

"Excellent," he said, exhaling. "That's wonderful, Patrick. You're doing a great job."

In his excitement, he rested his hand on my knee for a second, but only a second. I was far too aware of it. We both were, I think.

"David said they were having the party because of the war. But that doesn't really make sense. What good is a party going to do?"

"There will be a gentleman there named Faroukh Jafar. He's a family friend of the Qajar's. He's an arms dealer. The Iranians need arms. Jafar is attempting to broker a deal with an American manufacturer."

"I knew some of that. I mean, not the part about arms—David has been upset about the war," I said, although I didn't know much more than that. "Do you know who's winning?"

"The Iranians are doing better than expected, but they desperately need arms. That's why the party is important."

"Oh, that reminds me," I said, causing his eyes to open a bit wide. That really shouldn't have reminded me of anything. "I waited on this table last night. I should tell you about them."

"I'm sure that's not important. What we're trying to prevent is sale of arms to Iran by Jafar. You need to stay focused."

"Uh-huh, but the men I waited on last night were talking about the same thing. They were talking about getting arms to Iran. They want to help Reagan beat Carter, just like the Qajars."

He stopped and starred at me a long time. Then he finished his cigarette in two deep inhalations. He threw the butt on the path in front of us and ground it out with his foot.

"What men?"

"One was a judge named Carlisle, another guy was named Bill, I think. The main guy, the one who pays the bill, wears these round tortoise shell glasses. I don't know his name. He pays in cash."

He was thoughtful for a moment. "All right, I'll look into it."

"You will?"

"I doubt there's anything there."

"Isn't it weird that a judge was there? I mean, the whole conversation was about making sure Reagan wins. Shouldn't judges be impartial?"

"You know a lot for a waiter."

"I had a government class in high school. Everybody does," I said. It was a very weak answer.

"I doubt the judge was doing anything inappropriate."

But I had the feeling he was. Judges aren't supposed to be at strategy meetings for presidential candidates. Right? Don't they take an oath about things like that?

"So, David's father is trying to do the same thing, isn't he?" I asked. "He wants to give arms to the Iranians so they'll keep the hostages?"

And then when Reagan's elected they'll give Iran back to him, I added in my mind. But the monarchy wasn't exactly America's to give, was it?

"You don't need to think about things like that. We have lots of people thinking about it all. You just need to get the information I asked for."

My feelings were hurt by that. He seemed angry at me. "Does it bother you that I'm having sex with David?"

He gave me a long look. I couldn't tell what he was thinking.

"What you're doing is important. We'd be in bad shape without you." He put his hand on my thigh again, half of it on my shorts the other half on my bare leg. The heat from his hand made me dizzy. "I hope it's not too unpleasant."

It wasn't, but I didn't want to tell him that. Instead I said, "I— I'll get through."

"We've gotten off topic," he said. Thankfully he took his hand away. I could think again.

"At the party, I need you to try to keep track of everyone who's there. Particularly anyone who talks to Nasim el-din Qajar or Faroukh Jafar. Those are the two most important people to watch."

"Is David involved in any of this?"

"At the very least, he knows what his father is doing. He's definitely complicit."

THE PRESIDENT'S PERSONAL DIARY

October 1, 1980

The Iranian parliament has set up a commission to look at the hostage situation. It appears the commission will have little power. As has been the case since the beginning, it is a challenge to determine who exactly we should be negotiating with. Clearly, it is up to the ayatollah, but exactly who has his ear is sometimes a moving target.

Negotiations with Tabatabai, the Iranian Minister of State, have been underway for weeks now, there is no clear sense of how this commission will affect those negotiations. Given the split in the parliament it's not clear whether we will be allowed to even speak to the commission.

There seems little to do but to prepare for those of the ayatollah's conditions we're willing to meet and continue to negotiate on those we are not.

The hostages have been held three-hundred and thirty-two days. Each day I pray for their safe release and a resolution to this crisis.

CHAPTER TWELVE

The house was brick and stone, had a round turret on one end and a square tower on the other. The brick had been painted dove gray recently so it all looked clean and fresh. It was four stories tall, with an English basement like the one I lived in. Theirs, however, was devoted to its original purpose: laundry, storage and servants' quarters. There was a modest set of steps leading to the entrance.

Wendi and I arrived around seven-thirty, just as the sun was setting. It had rained most of the day and there was a distinct chill in the air, letting us know autumn had begun in earnest. A valet stood guard in front of the house. Since we'd come in a cab, we didn't need his services. We smiled as we breezed by, bouncing up the steps to the front door.

I was wearing a horrible light blue corduroy suit my mother had bought me in my last year of high school. It had three pieces, but I refused to wear the vest. To avoid the issue of a tie, I wore a dark blue turtleneck. It was a humiliating outfit, I looked like something out of the Sears catalog, but at least it was humiliating in solid colors. Wendi had suggested I wear a plaid leisure suit she found at the Salvation Army. She was joking, but I didn't find it very funny.

"Are you sure this is a good idea?" Wendi asked, in the cab. "What if David's father realizes who you are?"

"Then we'll get thrown out. Don't worry. I have the cab fare to get home."

"Don't act so calm, Patrick. You've got to be freaking out."

And I was freaking out, although not because I thought David's father would throw us out. I was freaking out because I was a spy on a mission and I had no idea if I'd be able to accomplish it. I had to keep track of people's names and what they said, and I couldn't write anything down since that would be suspicious. And I wasn't too happy about the idea that maybe I was in danger. Logically, I'd known I was in danger, I just hadn't wanted to think about it.

An ancient, British butler in a tuxedo opened the door for us and we walked into the house. The foyer was large, had doors on either side and a staircase directly in front of us. On either side of the staircase, hallways led to the back of the house. Oriental rugs in deep reds and oranges covered most of the floors.

The butler took the shawl Wendi wore over her dress and put it into a closet. While he was doing that, David stepped out of the parlor and hurried over. He wore a crisp white pleated tuxedo shirt open at the neck, with four onyx studs and cufflinks to match. The shirt was paired with a well-tailored pair of clingy black slacks. He looked remarkably sexy, as though we'd just caught him in the midst of taking off a tuxedo and if we just waited patiently he'd continue getting undressed.

"There you are." He kissed each of us three times on the cheeks. "Thank you, Cedric," he said, then to us, "Come in, please. There aren't many guests yet, so you'll have a few moments with my father. But first, if you'd take your shoes off and leave them here—"

There was a row of shoes next to the foyer wall.

"I don't mind. And neither does father. But the servants get very particular about these things and there's nothing worse than unhappy servants."

Wendi looked miserable as she took her shoes off. She'd spent a half an hour choosing which pair looked best with her dress. Of course, I was even more miserable. I had on a pair of dingy athletic socks that had been completely covered by my boots but were now on display.

Reluctantly taking off my boots, I asked, "What do we call your father? If you're a prince, is he a king?"

"We're not formal," David said. "Father prefers that you use his first name, Nasim."

"We shouldn't call him, 'your majesty'?" Wendi asked.

"God no," David said. "He saw the Pahlavi usurper on *60*

Minutes with Dan Rather calling him 'your majesty' every time he asked a question, since then he's never let anyone use that phrase."

We walked into the parlor David had come from. It was a large room with six windows: two on the front, one on the side and three in the round turret at the corner of the room. A baby grand piano sat in the turret, while two sofas and several overstuffed chairs took up the rest of the room. Beneath all of that were two opulent Oriental rugs in blue and brown. Like the ones in the hall-way, the patterns were intricate and incredibly detailed. The room was painted the same color as my hideous suit and for a moment I fantasized I could stand next to the wall and disappear.

Somewhere a stereo played classical music. A man in his late fifties sat in the largest of the chairs with two other Middle Eastern gentlemen around the same age on the sofa next to him. Of course, the man was David's father; I could see the resemblance. Though his hair was graying, much of it was still the same color as David's; his nose was similar and the way he held himself was something David had either copied or inherited. There were differences though, his eyes were dark, his lips thin and his chin not nearly so square.

"Father, these are friends of mine, Patrick Burke and Wendi Feinstein."

Nasim el-din Qajar looked at me and knew exactly who I was and what I meant to his son. I could see it in his eyes. It wasn't hatred exactly, but it was far from an offer of friendship.

"Thank you for having us, sir," Wendi said, filling the awkward gap I'd left.

"Nasim, David's friends call me Nasim," he said. It was such a casual request, and yet he managed to make it seem somehow formal. And then he stood and kissed Wendi three times on her cheeks.

"It's a pleasure to meet you, Nasim," I managed to choke out.

"Yes, of course," he said, as though agreeing with me. He sat back down and did not kiss me on the cheeks as he had Wendi.

I wondered if that was an insult. No one else seemed to notice, so maybe it wasn't a big deal. I glanced at the two men on the sofa waiting for someone to introduce us. Finally, Wendi jumped in and said, "Hi, I'm Wendi. And this is my friend Patrick."

They made no move to extend their hands or to kiss us on the cheek, so we stood their awkwardly. One of them said, "Gus," and the other said, "Fred." I doubted they were the names they were born with. The moment was uncomfortable, even more uncomfortable than meeting Nasim.

Luckily, the front door opened and David said, "Come with me" and the three of us went back to the foyer. On the way, I noticed that the dining room on the other side of the entrance hall had a table filled with food. My stomach growled.

Entering the house were three girls and a guy around our age. The girls wore trendy outfits, a peach-colored jumpsuit with Candies, a disco dress with spaghetti straps, and a black turtleneck over a brown skirt. The girl in the brown skirt was the only one wearing a hijab. The other two let their glistening black hair hang free. They easily kicked off their shoes and added them to the growing assortment.

With them was a tall, elegant young man wearing a white dinner jacket and a black bow tie. One glance told me he was desperately in love with David. It was that obvious. In those first few moments, David was all he saw. The girls he came with might as well have been invisible even as they kissed David on the cheeks in what I'd begun to realize was a common greeting. Among friends, at least.

For the young man, Wendi and I barely existed. He certainly didn't pay us any attention. He just stood looking at David the way a puppy watches his master, waiting for a command.

David introduced everyone: Nima, Roxanna, Shadi and Ebrahim. Immediately, I realized this was the Ebrahim David had told me about, his former lover. He was attractive enough, but he reminded me somehow of guys I'd slept with. The ones I was happy didn't come back.

"This is Patrick," David said. "And his friend, Wendi."

I smiled at them all, including Ebrahim. The girls rushed me and kissed my cheeks, again and again, then did the same to Wendi. Ebrahim took a moment to glare at me and then looked back to David, as though looking for an explanation or an apology.

Nima, in the jumpsuit, came close and whispered into my ear, "I was at Exile. I was the one dancing with Davoud when he saw you. The way you looked at each other, it took my breath away. It was so out of character for him. He's normally so prim and proper."

"I've noticed," I said.

"I gave him half a Quaalude, that might have had something to do with it," Nima said, blushing. It was a surprising revelation. If not for half a Quaalude I might not be there spying on David and his father.

"Wow, that's flattering," I said, dryly.

"Oh, I'm sure he likes you. I just don't know if he would have done anything about it without a little help." She turned to the others, "Davoud? Are you offering us a cocktail?"

"What would you like?"

"Champagne."

We all moved into the dining room where the alcohol sat on a buffet under the window. Nima stayed close, resting her hands on my arm as we talked, taking them off only to toss her very long, very straight black hair over a shoulder. "Be careful around Ebrahim. Don't turn your back, you might find a knife in it."

I leaned away from her and said, "You'll like my friend, Wendi. Her tongue is nearly as sharp as yours."

Nima burst into laughter. "You make me sound like a serpent."

Wendi tried to join us, but Ebrahim came over and asked, "What were you whispering in our new friend's ear, Nima?"

"Just how nice it is to meet him," she said. "And I was about to say—"

"Is it nice to meet him? Why?"

"Oh, stop it, Ebrahim. Don't be a bitch."

That's when David popped the cork on the champagne that had been chilling in a silver bucket. He immediately began pouring it into glass flutes that had been arranged on the buffet table. Roxanna and Shadi began to chatter in Persian, but from their gestures I suspected they were talking about me. Then Nima stopped them and made them speak English so Wendi could join in.

"Don't you have someone to do that?" Ebrahim asked, as David offered him a glass of champagne. "Surely you can afford servants."

"You know my father, he's loyal even to our servants. The staff has been with us for decades and they're now so old we wait on them as often as they wait on us."

"That's ridiculous. Give them a small pension and send them home."

I took two glasses of champagne, one for me and one for Wendi. She took her glass from me and went back to talking with the girls.

"Where is home, Ebrahim? Iran?" David asked. "Why do you think their fate would be any better than our own?"

"You cannot think the revolutionary guard so cowardly as to be afraid of a few ancient servants."

"Please, no politics tonight," Nima interrupted. "Ebrahim, talk about all the frivolous things you've been doing instead."

His eyes flashed. Briefly, I thought he might reach out and slap her. Instead, he said something in Persian.

Nima blanched.

David stepped in and said a few words, also Persian, I think.

Ebrahim nodded, then spit out an answer to Nima's question. "I've been doing what we've all been doing, I've been following the news and calling friends to talk about the fate of our country. And to bemoan the fact that I am not there to fight with them. If you want we will call that frivolous."

"But you're not a fanatic, Ebrahim," David said. "You know they'd never let you fight with them."

"I have beliefs. Why shouldn't I stand up for them?"

"Your beliefs have to do with fine wine, elegant clothes and expensive cars." David's voice carried more kindness than I thought Ebrahim deserved. "You're everything the ayatollah condemns. They're not going to let you fight with them. You're what they're fighting against."

"I am not. They fight against the evil of America."

"And you love everything American."

With a meaningful glance at me, Ebrahim said, "I do not love everything American." And then he walked away; two of the girls went with him.

Nima stayed with Wendi. She tried to smile.

"What did he say to her?" I whispered to David.

"He said 'A woman's heaven is beneath her husband's feet.' It's an old saying. I reminded him that a good Muslim respects women and treats them well."

"Sounds as confusing as Christianity."

David smiled and said, "Quite."

"I just bought the new George Benson album," Nima said, as though nothing had just happened. "I find jazz so relaxing. Don't you?"

Neither of us answered as other people, newly arrived, came into the dining room. David went over to greet them. Nima asked

Wendi about her dress, so I took two steps over to the buffet and began to make myself a small plate of food. There were several platters of exotic looking cookies and another of dates; some kind of red fruit in a bowl that looked kind of like corn kernels; a large bowl of hummus with thin slices of flatbread surrounding it; several bowls of mushy looking vegetables I couldn't identify and was certainly not going to taste; and, finally, a tray of bacon-wrapped chestnuts and chicken livers. I started with those and put at least one of each item on my plate.

Wendi slipped in next to me, saying softly under her breath. "I don't think Ebrahim likes you."

"I'd have to agree with you." Lowering my voice, I asked, "What is this?" I pointed at the red corn kernels.

"Pomegranate seeds," she said, before continuing with her thought, "Of course, I don't think David cares one bit whether Ebrahim likes you or not."

I caught David's eye and smiled at him. He returned my smile in a private kind of way that made my heart bounce. I tried to remember that he and his father were doing terrible things. Things I needed to help stop.

"No, I don't think David cares at all."

Just then, an old woman of about eighty came out of the kitchen. She wore a bright, flowered hijab and a full-body cloak in another flower pattern. On her feet, a pair of Nikes. What little bit of hair I could see had been dyed flat black but not recently as there was a one-inch stripe of white on either side of her center part.

I thought she might be straightening up the table, that she was a servant or with the caterer, but then, surprisingly, she reached under the tablecloth and slid a trash can out from under the table. She dumped the tray of chestnuts and chicken livers into it, set the empty silver tray back on the table and walked away.

"Did you see that," I asked Wendi.

"I did. She murdered the chestnuts wrapped in bacon."

"What have they ever done to her, I wonder?"

"It's a shame, I was looking forward to having a plateful."

"Wait, you're Jewish."

"Thank you for noticing."

"You're not supposed to have pork either."

She rolled her eyes. "My mother's father thanked God every

day he wasn't born a woman. I don't think my mother's been in a temple since before I was born. We glory in all things pork."

"Okay. You want me to pick some out of the garbage?"

"Gross."

With a shrug, I finished filling my plate, fearful that the woman might return and throw more food away. We found a corner where we could nibble and sip champagne.

People were arriving all the time. I assumed David had gone back into the entry hall. Wendi and I continued to haunt the food table for a while. Gus and Fred had come in for cocktails and stood behind us.

"There is new panel to deal with hostages. Some with the Islamic Republican Party."

I'd totally confused their names, so I had no idea which one of them said that. I really was a terrible spy.

"That will not end well."

"No, it will end badly."

"Do you know any of them?"

"One. He is a friend to Nasim."

"So, there's hope."

"Some. It is a small hope."

Wendi was eating a cheese cube. "Stop eavesdropping," she whispered. "It's not even an interesting conversation."

"I wasn't. I was just thinking about...things."

"What things?"

"Boy things," I said, though that was far from the truth.

"Seriously? Sex at a time like this. You're disgusting."

"What can I say? Hormones."

The party was filling up and I needed to find a way to move around more. I had to find this Farouk person Agent Walker wanted me to watch. I was also supposed to be watching Nasim, something I hadn't been doing a very good job of since he was nowhere near the food table.

"Let's go back into the other room," I said to Wendi.

"Why? All the young people are in here." She'd been chatting with Nima a little here and there, and I suspected wanted to chat with her some more. "David will come back."

"But I want see what's happening in there."

"People are talking, that's what's happening in there."

"Fine. I'll go by myself," I said and padded out of the dining room and across the entry hall to the parlor. I was right, David was at the front door greeting people as they came in.

In the parlor, there were a lot of people now. Many of them were obviously Americans. Nasim was speaking with a middle-aged, blond woman with hair that had been sprayed into a small hive. She wore a filmy purple gown with a knot of fabric on one shoulder. I stood close enough to hear her saying, "Such a charming custom, being barefoot I mean. I have to tell you the shoes I wore this evening were already beginning to pinch and all I'd done was ride in a taxicab."

"I'm so happy you're comfortable," Nasim said.

"Now, I wanted to ask you. Is it true what I'm reading, that the Iranian Revolutionary Guard are going into battle wearing burial shrouds they're so happy to die for the cause? What kind of people do things like that?"

"Christians, Jews, Muslims. At one time or another they've all done exactly that," Nasim pointed out.

"Oh, but I don't think—I'm Presbyterian and we would never..."

"It is hard to imagine, isn't it?"

"It is."

"Be on guard. Don't let your country be taken over by fanatics."

"Oh, that's simply impossible. Our national character is too reserved to be fanatical."

"One hopes."

The doubt in his voice clearly disturbed her. She smiled, and then said, "Vivian, Vivian is that you? Excuse me, Nasim, I must say hello." She walked across the room to a tall woman in a red satin dress.

The woman instantly launched into a much safer topic. "Did you hear? Steve McQueen is dying of lung cancer."

"Nooooo, really?" Vivian said, though something told me she already knew. Even I had seen it in the papers.

"Yes! I love his movies. I was sure he was invincible."

"An American icon, yes."

"Such a tragedy."

Nasim turned and left the room. That wasn't good. I was supposed to keep an eye on him, but I could hardly chase him from room to room. I walked casually around the living room. Two men were talking about the big fight between Muhammed Ali and Larry

Holmes. I wasn't sure whether it had already happened or not and if it did, who won. Their conversation didn't tell me much other than they were sort of racist.

Crossing the foyer, I went back to the dining room. It was packed. I squeezed my way to the buffet, careful not to step on anyone's toes, and poured more champagne from the open bottle sitting in the silver bucket. Then I hovered again near the food.

"If he can just be convinced to offer them help in fighting the war against Iraq, then there will be no question about the hostages."

"You mean a trade?"

"Of course I mean a trade. That's what diplomacy is. Horse trading."

These were two men behind me in gray suits, politicians, American politicians, I was sure. They were no use to me. I needed to find Faroukh. The fact that Agent Walker wanted me to find him suggested that if there was going to be horse trading, he would be at the center of it. So, where was he?

Suddenly, David was behind me whispering, "Come with me." I followed him through the crowd into the kitchen. It was large with a wooden table seating eight in the middle of the room with plenty of space to walk around it. There were caterers scurrying around and, of course, the colorfully dressed elderly woman I'd seen earlier busy glaring at their every move.

David led me through the kitchen out to a utility room where there was a washer and dryer. He closed the door behind us, shifted a full hamper in front of it, and then pressed me up against the wall. He kissed me, hard and fast.

I pushed him away. "David? What are you doing?"

"I couldn't spend all night with you and not kiss you."

He kissed me again, I leaned into him and kissed him back but then pulled away again.

"David, you have responsibilities."

"Just another minute or two. Please?"

This time, as he kissed me, he ran his hands up under my turtleneck. That had to stop. "Cut it out. We can't go back out there with hard cocks."

"Too late," he said with a smile. "Do you have any idea what you mean to me? I don't know what I'd do if I thought I could never kiss you again."

I didn't know what to say to that. It was too much. It was too soon. It was too late. Someday the kissing would stop. I didn't know if he'd ever find out that I'd been spying on him and his father, maybe he wouldn't, but still, I was using him terribly. The end would be sudden and unexpected. And it would come soon.

I kissed him again and then whispered into his ear, "Go back to your father's party. I'll be out in a minute."

"All right. But we may have to leave early to finish what we've just started." He moved the hamper and then adjusted himself in his pants so that his erection was less obvious. Then he walked out of the utility room.

I took a deep breath, reached into my jacket for a cigarette and lit it. The first drag was wonderful, they often were, but the others were not as good. Sometimes they were downright work. I should quit, I knew, but I was only twenty. There was time to quit later.

For a terrible moment, I admitted to myself that I wished things were different. I wished David was not a prince, that his father was not involved in international intrigue, that there had never been a reason for Agent Walker to talk to me. I wished David was just a boy I'd met, like all the others except that he came back. And that I could be happy he'd come back.

The door to the utility room opened and the ancient butler—Cedrick? Crispin? I'd forgotten his name already—was standing there.

"Patrick?"

Damn, he'd remembered mine.

"Yes."

"Come with me, please."

There wasn't anything to do but follow him into the kitchen. I stopped at the sink, ran water on my half-smoked cigarette and tossed it into a garbage can. The butler led me out of the kitchen to a room at the back of the house, behind the stairs on the other side. He tapped on the door. Someone inside said, "Yes."

Opening the door, the butler ushered me inside then closed the door behind me. I was alone with Nasim el-din Qajar and I had no idea why. Did he know I'd been kissing his son just moments before? Was I about to be thrown out of the house? Or did he know what I was really doing there? Had he somehow found out I was there to spy on him?

He sat behind a large walnut desk with a telephone that had

clear plastic buttons on the bottom to handle multiple lines. There was a large desk blotter, a short stack of papers and a daily calendar on a plastic stand. There was a page on each side, one marked with the hours of the day for appointments and the other blank so you could make comments about the day's events. I was trying to read upside down, something I'm not bad at, when he looked up at me.

My mouth may have dropped open. It was as close as I'd been to him all night and I could see where David had gotten his looks. Nasim was a solid man, much more handsome up close, and when he looked at me, he smiled; a charming smile, a sympathetic smile, a *kind* smile.

"You are the reason Davoud insisted he invite so many friends, aren't you?"

"I'm sorry? I don't understand." Although, I did.

"You wanted to come to the party and Davoud was afraid of what I might think so he hid you in a crowd."

"I don't think that's true."

"Let's not lie to each other, you and I." Like David, his accent was British though Nasim's had something more exotic underneath.

He waved a hand toward a chair inviting me to sit. I didn't have any choice but to do exactly that. "I had an older brother, Amir. He was like Davoud. Very close to his school chums. Better at friendship than romance."

"David is quite good at romance," I said, without thinking.

He smiled, almost sadly.

"My son will do his duty one day. Just as his uncle did. I hope you understand that."

"Yes, he's talked about that."

"Good, then we understand each other and can be friends."

In the spirit of friendship, I asked, "Is your brother here?"

"Alas, no." Offering no further explanation he said, "We should return to the party."

He stood and came out from behind the desk. When he was next to me, he tucked a hand under my arm, just the way my mother would when we crossed the street together. It was an odd gesture. Fragile and unexpected from a man who projected such strength.

"How do you find Davoud's friends?"

"They're very nice."

"No, I'm afraid they're not."

"Well, Ebrahim did give me a dirty look."

"Poor Ebrahim. I understand they kill the ones like him now. It is a shame. The imams have such power. I do not think it right."

I almost didn't understand what he was saying to me, but after I turned it around in my head, I did. Ebrahim was obviously gay, most people could figure that out. They were killing obvious gays in Iran. And they would not be if Nasim were shah.

He wanted my vote.

When I entered the parlor with David's father, I saw that a couple of new guests had arrived. One of them was Mr. Discretion, my gentleman with the round glasses and big tips. He came over to me, adjusting his glasses on his nose.

"Well, well, they say Washington is a small world and it certainly is."

"You know each other?" Nasim asked.

"Patrick is my favorite waiter at Le Marquis."

"I'm sorry, I don't know your name," I said.

"Barrett. Barrett Copeland."

The way he said it made me wonder if it was supposed to mean something. In Washington, there were so many people well known to their particular group, which was fine, but they always expected that you'd know them too.

"Barrett has been a good friend," Nasim said.

"It's easy to be kind to those who are kind, Nasim."

"Have you heard anything? Has Muskie made any progress?"

"They're playing their cards close to the vest—but let's not talk politics in front of our young friend," Copeland said. "Tell us, Patrick, what is your favorite dessert at Le Marquis?"

I didn't have to think about it. "Probably the tarte aux fraise."

"Nothing with chocolate? How interesting," Copeland said. "The coconut cream pie is my favorite. Nasim, you must have it. The bakers fold whipped cream into the filling so that the pie graduates from coconut filling to whipped cream without so much as a line. It's a secret exactly how they do it."

Nasim glanced at me for confirmation. "It is a secret. I have no idea how they do it. They make the pies in the middle of the night so no one can watch."

I worried I might get stuck with them discussing desserts for the rest of the party, so I said, "I think I need another drink, excuse me."

Giving them a last smile, I walked into the dining room to find it somehow even more crowded. Wendi was still in there, laughing as Nima, pressed up against her, whispering into her ear. David saw me and winked, then squeezed between several gray suits to get to me.

"Where have you been? I thought you were right behind me."

Quickly, I decided not to mention my conversation with his father. Instead, I said, "One of my customers from Le Marquis is here, I was talking to him."

"Are you having fun? Is this what you were expecting?"

"I guess. I don't know what I was expecting. But I'm glad I came. Could I have more champagne?"

"Yes, of course." He reached over a small woman who was laughing raucously and snagged a bottle from the bar, then poured the tiny bit that was left into my glass.

"Sorry, it'll be a nightmare getting more. So, how are we doing?"

"What do you mean?"

"Our party. You're sort of in the party business. How do we stand up?"

"I think the crowd speaks for itself. You've done a wonderful job."

"I think you're lying to me. Our servants are old and not well-behaved. And the food is, perhaps, too Persian. Everything American keeps disappearing almost as soon as we put it out."

I didn't have the heart to tell him that it probably wasn't disappearing because it was being eaten.

"The champagne, however, is well chosen. Don't you think?"

Other than a few rehearsed lines about the list at Le Marquis, I knew nothing about wine. I didn't know what to say, but was saved when middle-aged woman wearing a sedate hijab rushed up to David.

"There he is, my fine, beautiful young man," she said, practically pinching his cheeks. "We must find you a wife. She must be obedient, demure, attractive and a good Muslim girl, of course. My daughter, Banu, is just seventeen. A very malleable age. You can mold her into the woman of your dreams."

Without bothering to excuse myself, I stepped backward and fought my way out of the dining room. I walked down the hallway on one side of the stairway. The door on my left was Nasim's study,

I remembered. The door on my right might have been a bathroom. That gave me an excuse if there was someone—

I ducked into the study. The light was still on, though the room was empty. I knew exactly where I wanted to go. I hurried over to Nasim's desk and stood where I could read his calendar upside down. On the right side, my right, the day was broken down by hour. Next to the hour, you could write an appointment or other event. Nasim had not had any appointments that day, rather he had written PARTY over the entire day. Clearly, he'd left the day open to get ready. The facing page was blank, a place to write notes.

Flipping back a few pages, I saw that earlier in the week, Wednesday at three, he'd had an appointment with an F. Jafar. That had to be the Faroukh Walker wanted me to find. Since they'd seen each other two days before, maybe Faroukh wasn't there at all.

I flipped back another page, then another. On the previous Monday, Nasim had written the note, 'need TOWs.' I looked at that for a long moment, it didn't make sense to me. Had his car broken down somewhere? All the letters were capped which suggested an acronym of some sort. An acronym for what, though?

"What are you doing in here?"

Adrenaline shot through me like a spike. I turned around and there was Ebrahim glaring at me.

"I was looking for the bathroom."

"Well, it's not in here, is it?"

"No, it's not."

"What are you really doing?"

"It's a great party. But I still, uh, I kind of needed a break. You know?"

He stared at me, grinding me with his eyes. Then said, "He'll never be yours. Not the way you want. He's going to marry Nima. Very soon."

"Is he? He didn't mention it."

My jaw set, either Ebrahim or David was not being entirely truthful with me. I tried to remind myself it didn't matter, but I didn't do a very good job of it, and I could feel anger coloring my face.

"Yes, though why he's willing to settle for such an ill-behaved woman is beyond me. I will marry Shadi. A much better choice."

"Which one is Shadi?" I asked, voice terse.

"The modest girl with the hijab. I think it wise to marry a religious girl. They know how to be obedient."

This was beginning to sound more like fantasy than reality.

"Does Shadi know you're going to marry her?"

"She will be told when the time is right."

"That's so kind of you."

"This is what I don't like about Americans. You think you have the right to judge everyone else."

"The way you're talking about Shadi, it's like she has no rights."

"She has the right to be taken care of. By her father and one day by me. What other rights does she need?"

I smiled at him and said the meanest thing I could think of, "I'm sure the two of you will be very happy together."

WEST WING

Early October

"Let's move on, shall we? The next item to be discussed are the shah's assets in the United States."

"The Iranians continue to request all of the shah's assets held in the United States be turned over to them. They seem to be under the impression the shah held vast sums of money here."

"That's not true though?"

"No, it's not. Treasury believes the amount of the shah's assets held in the U.S. to be much less than the Iranians believe."

"At some point they'll want an accounting. We should be prepared for that."

"An accounting of assets currently in the country or of the assets held in the U.S. when the hostages were taken?"

"I imagine they'll want both, don't you?"

"There was quite a bit of time for the shah and his family to move assets out of the U.S. after the hostages were taken and before the funds were frozen."

"Yes, there was."

"Do you think they'll want to know where the funds went?"

"Probably. But they'll need to go through the courts to get that information. I don't know that we can tell them legally."

"Can we even give them the accountings legally?"

"Possibly not. That's one of the issues I'm attempting to clarify with the White House counsel."

"Do we know how much the Iranians think there should be?"

"Fifty billion is the only number I've heard, but I don't think even they believe that."

"Do we have a better number?"

"Fifty million is more likely."

"They're not likely to believe that, are they?"

"No. And it may be a challenge convincing them that our hands are tied and we can't simply seize the shah's assets. They will need to go through the courts. They're going to have to sue."

"We can promise them assistance with that?"

"I don't see why not."

"What if they request we simply pay them from the Treasury?"

"Well, that would be a ransom, wouldn't it?"

"A fifty billion-dollar ransom."

"We can't do that, can we?"

"Can you imagine what Reagan would make of our paying a fifty billion-dollar ransom?"

CHAPTER THIRTEEN

The phone was ringing and I was hideously hungover. Even before I managed to open my eyes, I regretted I'd had the damn thing installed. What kind of madness was it that people could reach you at any time of day? What was wrong with the mail, which had the decency to arrive only once a day? Who would have the gall to call at—I reached for the alarm clock I kept on the floor near the bed, found it and peeked—eleven o'clock in the morning? An ungodly hour.

I heard Wendi pick up the phone in the other room and say, "Hello?"

She waited. I wondered if she felt as bad as I did.

"No. I'm sorry. There's no one named Sylvia here."

Dammit. Walker wanted a report on the party. But I didn't want to talk to him. I wanted to go back to sleep. I closed my eyes and pulled the sheet over my head. But then Wendi was in my doorway saying, "You don't go by Sylvia, do you?"

"She must have had this number before we did."

"Her boyfriend sounds sexy." She got down and climbed into bed with me. "Scoot over."

"I can't scoot," I said, moving over gingerly. "I might puke if I scoot."

She slipped in beside me anyway. "Well, that was some party."

"Did you have fun?"

"More than I expected."

As she said that, I remembered something from the night

before. It was very late; the party was almost over and I was sitting in a chair near David. He and his father were talking.

"Do you think the ayatollah will come to terms?" David asked.

"It is challenging for the unreasonable to see reason."

"What about Bani-Sadr, what does he say?"

"He's irrelevant. He's but a president. He can't override the ayatollah. That's why our country needs a shah. It's the only way to stop Khomeini."

"Someday, Father. Someday."

There it was. Walker was right, David *was* complicit. I couldn't believe they'd been so open about what they were doing. Or had they just forgotten I was there? Was I that insignificant?

Wendi was saying something.

"What?" I asked.

"I said, 'Do I look like a lesbian?'"

"Huh? Why are you—What does a lesbian look like?"

"I think Nima was flirting with me."

"Maybe Persian girls are different."

"She kept accidentally touching my boobs."

"How do you accidentally touch someone's boobs? I mean, more than once?"

"Exactly."

"Ebrahim told me David is supposed to marry Nima. So if I were David's lover and you were Nima's, we'd be related in a way."

"A very awkward way."

"But it would be kind of cool."

"I'm not going to start sleeping with women just because you think it would be cool to be fuck cousins."

"Well, that settles it. You're a horrible friend."

"And speaking of flirting, what was with you and that British Attaché?"

"Huh?" I had no memory of that. Unless she meant the short little man at the end of the night who wouldn't go away. "Isn't an attaché a briefcase?"

"Not that kind of attaché."

I was a horrible spy. I didn't know what an attaché was and I was pretty sure I hadn't completed my mission.

"Do you remember anyone named Faroukh?"

"No. Why are you asking that?" she asked, making a face.

"A couple of people mentioned someone named Faroukh, but I

couldn't figure out who he was." I was surprised by how well I'd taken to lying. Well, maybe not that surprised. "I think he might be an ex of David's."

"No, I don't think so. We met all the young people who were there. Unless you think David was involved with one of the fossils. Besides, Nima said David used to be involved with Ebrahim."

"I knew about Ebrahim," I said. "David told me."

"Nima made it sound like it never meant much to David. It was always just friends fooling around for him."

"But not for Ebrahim," I agreed.

"No. Not for Ebrahim."

"Stop hogging the covers," I told her. "My feet are cold. When does the heat come on?"

"October fifteenth. Eleven days."

"Oh, God. Eleven very cold days."

She gasped. "You just reminded me. You remember those two old guys, Gus and Fred? They had this very strange conversation about toes. At first I thought they were into feet, but then it seemed like someone they knew wanted more toes. So, whomever they were talking about is the person who's into feet. Well, not feet, toes."

"I really don't understand that fetish. Do you?"

"Not really. I see how feet can be ugly, but I'm not sure how they can be sexy."

Forcing myself to sit up, I said, "I need a cigarette. And coffee."

"Coffee! The nectar of the Gods!"

———

I had almost nothing for Walker, so I didn't call him back. I wasn't even sure Faroukh Jafar had been at the party. I didn't learn anything about an arms deal. I didn't really learn anything. I found a note talking about TOWs and Wendi heard a couple of old guys talking about toes. Yeah, TOW and toe, so they were probably the same thing, but I had no idea what thing. And, yeah, I had confirmation that David was involved or at least knew about everything. But that wouldn't matter to Walker. He already knew that.

As a spy, I was an absolute failure.

Wendi and I crawled out to a deli on Connecticut Avenue, ate pastrami sandwiches with thick French fries for breakfast, and then crawled back to the apartment. When I walked in the door, I grabbed the phone and dragged it back to my room so I could call David.

"If you're not hungover I'm going to kill you," I threatened when he picked up. The telephone cord just made it into my room and I sat with my back against the closed door.

"I didn't drink anywhere near as much as you did," David said.

"I'm not a lush, honest."

"You're a very silly drunk."

"Oh thanks."

"Ebrahim told me you were snooping around my father's office?"

Okay, that was not good. Despite the fog in my head, I knew I needed to change the direction of our conversation quickly.

"Yeah, I was looking for the bathroom and took a wrong turn. It was stupid, too, since I'd just been in there half an hour before."

"What do you mean? You got lost in my father's office twice?"

"No, the first time I was invited. Your father and I had a little talk."

"Oh. I'm sorry."

"He said you're like your uncle. Did you know your uncle was gay?"

"My uncle died when I was small."

"Oh. Sorry. I guess he lived long enough to do his duty though. It seems like your father doesn't care much about me, not as long as you do your duty too."

"Well, that's interesting."

"He didn't say anything to you about this?"

"No, he wouldn't talk to me about this kind of thing. I'm surprised he talked to you."

"Well, he didn't speak bluntly, or even directly, but I did understand what he meant."

David was silent.

"I didn't know he knew," he finally said, softly.

"Isn't it better that he knows?" He didn't answer that, so I asked, "What else did Ebrahim say?"

"Oh, he thinks I should marry Nima."

"Does Nima get a say? Ebrahim told me it was all set."

"It's not. But she might not mind. We're good friends. She wouldn't expect me to love her."

"That sounds awful."

"I imagine it does to your ear."

"My American ear, you mean," I sniped.

"Yes, that's what I mean."

"Tell me how marrying Nima makes either one of you happy?"

"It would be a good match. Our families would be pleased; our future secure. We would make lovely children. And we would allow each other to find happiness elsewhere."

"Well, I guess you've got it all figured out," I said. The anger in my voice surprised me. I tried to get it through my thick skull that it didn't make any difference what David did. As soon as I got the information Agent Walker needed, we would be over. He wasn't my boyfriend.

"Please don't be angry," he said. "Nothing is decided."

"I have to go now," I said. I was getting confused so I thought it best to end the conversation.

"You're angry. I shouldn't have talked about this. Ebrahim is trying to cause trouble. I know that and yet I let him."

"Everything's fine. I'm just a little hungover and a lot grumpy."

"All right."

"And I have to go, I need a nap."

It was damp and drizzling when I finally went to meet Agent Walker in Dupont Circle. I didn't have a raincoat, so I tried to sit under a tree to keep the anemic rain from falling on me. This was it. I was really a spy. I was about to give my first real report. Not that there was much to tell. To tell the truth, I wasn't sure Walker wouldn't be furious with me.

When he sat down next to me, Walker wore a heavy trench coat and carried an umbrella. We looked like we had nothing to do with each other—him in business attire and an all-weather coat; me shivering in a jean jacket, T-shirt and 501s.

"Couldn't we have met at your office?" I asked. "Don't we look suspicious sitting here in the rain?"

"This won't take long," he said. "How was the party?"

"Great. Everyone had cake and ice cream."

"Tell me what happened," he said, ignoring my nervous flippancy.

Cupping my hands, I lit a soggy cigarette to give myself a moment to collect my thoughts. Walker reached out for one, without asking.

"David invited some friends our age so there was a whole group of us. It was hard to break away and listen to the grown-ups."

"Are you telling me you didn't find out anything? Nothing at all?"

"Well, Barrett Copeland was there. Does that mean anything?"

"Copeland is an influential Republican operative. One of the money guys. He can pull a million dollars out of a hat like it's a rabbit. Were you introduced?"

"Yes and no. I already knew him. I've waited on him at Le Marquis, but I didn't know his name. We introduced ourselves. He's the guy I told you about. I mean, he gave the party I told you about. You remember, they talked about—"

"Yes, yes. I remember. I passed your concerns along and they're being looked into."

"Oh, um, thank you."

"So, who did Copeland talk to?"

"Everyone, I think."

"Did you hear any of what was said?"

"No. I mean, he talked about desserts with me and Nasim."

"Nasim? You're on a first-name basis with the crown prince?"

I shrugged and wiped the rain off my face. "He tells everyone to call him Nasim."

"That's rather informal."

"Especially for someone so formal. I think it has to do with Americans' awkwardness with royalty." Suddenly, I remembered something. "Wait a minute. Copeland mentioned someone named Muskie. Does that mean anything?"

"Edmund Muskie is the secretary of state," he said patiently.

"Oh."

"Patrick, you should read a newspaper once in a while. What did they say about Muskie?"

"I have been reading the new—" I stopped. It was pointless trying to explain myself. "They just wondered how he was doing, negotiating to get the hostages back, I guess."

"Well, it makes sense they'd want to know, doesn't it?"

I didn't say anything and he changed directions. "What about Faroukh Jafar? Did you see who Jafar spoke to?"

"Um, I didn't actually see anyone named Faroukh. I don't think he was there."

"He was there. We saw him go into the house before you arrived. He was the whole point of your going to the party. And you couldn't figure out who he was?"

They were watching David's house? That shouldn't have surprised me, but somehow it did. I thought I was doing this alone, but there must be other people involved, other agents, perhaps a lot of them. I just didn't know who they were.

"I couldn't exactly go around asking if anyone had seen him. That would have been suspicious. I mean, it would have helped if you'd had a picture or something," I said more stridently than I'd intended. They always had pictures in the movies.

"Okay. Calm down. I know you did your best," he didn't give that a very convincing line reading. "Did you find out anything at all?"

"What are TOWs. T-O-W?"

"Anti-Tank Missiles."

"Okay, Nasim had a note on this desk that said, 'NEED TOWs.' And then, my friend Wendi told me about a conversation she overheard where two guys were talking about TOWs. She thought they meant toes, like on your feet."

"Wendi? You brought your roommate with you?"

"Yes. It was how I got David to bring me. People assumed she was my girlfriend. Well, they didn't, but—"

"Have you told her anything about me?"

"No, of course not."

"She has no idea what you're doing?"

"No."

I didn't tell him that I hated that she didn't know. I didn't tell him how much I wanted to blab it all to her.

"So, who was it she heard talking about the TOWs?" he asked.

"These two old Iranian guys. They called themselves Gus and Fred."

"Fred is Faroukh."

"Really? Why not Frank? That would make more sense."

"I don't know why not Frank. He likes Fred. So tell me everything you can remember about Fred."

"Well, he was there with Nasim when we arrived. Just sitting on the sofa with Gus. He wasn't friendly. Later I heard him talking about some panel negotiating to return the hostages. He said Nasim had a friend on it."

"Things are moving along quickly. There's no time to waste. Can you get back into the house? You need to find out more about the TOWs. How many are they shipping? When are they shipping them? How will they be getting the weapons to the Iranians?"

I gave him a nasty look and said, "Sure, I'll just ask Nasim."

"There has to be more information at his desk. Notes, at least."

"What about gadgets?" I asked, abruptly.

"What do you mean?"

"I mean, why can't you just give me a bug and I'll put it in Nasim's office, and you can listen to everything he says yourself. I could have put one in there during—"

"Don't you think we've tried that? They keep finding them."

I didn't know what to say to that. I mean, I thought I was being really smart—and utilizing everything I'd learned from James Bond movies—but I guess I was wrong.

"I had an interesting conversation with Nasim," I admitted.

"What are you talking about?"

"It seems he accepts my relationship with David, as long as I'm willing to disappear when it's time for David to marry."

"Are you saying he wouldn't mind if you stayed over?"

"I don't know. Maybe."

"You need to be staying there. You need to spend as much time as you can there."

CHAPTER FOURTEEN

When all was said and done, I'd found out more at the party than I'd realized. And, more importantly, I wasn't the disaster of a spy I'd thought I was. Walker went away happy. I returned to my apartment to crawl back into bed. It wasn't just the hangover knocking it out of me. No, spying was much more nerve-racking than I'd expected.

I lay there for a while, very still, imagining that the information I'd given Agent Walker would lead to the hostages being freed within the week. I thought of the headlines and the satisfaction I'd feel from having helped. And then, I couldn't help myself, I imagined what it would be like if people knew. I imagined my face on *Time* magazine, imagined being interviewed on *60 Minutes*. Who would interview me? Mike Wallace or Dan Rather? And which was which again?

I'd have to be careful what I said about David. I could say we were just friends. I didn't have to tell the entire country that David and I were doing *it*. And I think I'd want to say that I hadn't actually seen David do anything wrong. And he hadn't, exactly. His father was the one doing bad things. He's the one everyone should hate, not David. I'd have to tell that to Mike or Dan and then cross my fingers that it got on the air. It didn't matter. The fantasy was silly. There was no way it would ever come true. Not even close.

I spent the rest of Saturday reading and sleeping; sleeping and reading; and doing both at once a couple of times. I woke up pages from the last thing I remembered and had to go back to find my place. Armies were marching around Persia and Alexander was still offstage. I was sure I remembered a lot more sex scenes.

Of course, for a lot of the day I worried about how I was going to get to spend more time at David's house. It seemed completely impossible. I was sure Walker was overestimating how nice Nasim wanted to be to me, while underestimating how much David wanted to please his father. I was sure I wouldn't be able to get David to ask me.

Short of burning down my apartment and telling David I was homeless, I couldn't really think of any way to get him to invite me there. I could think of reasons I couldn't stay in my own apartment—fighting with my roommate, bedbugs, a gas leak—but not David saying, "Why don't you spend the night with me then?"

It was nearly eight when he called me.

"Have you recovered?" he asked after we'd said hello.

"Almost."

"What are you doing?"

"I'm just reading *The Persian Boy*."

"Would you like some company?"

"Oh, not tonight."

"I'm disappointed."

"I'm kind of embarrassed," I said, improvising.

"Embarrassed? Why are you embarrassed?"

"Your house is so beautiful. I don't know why you'd want to come here and sleep on the floor with me."

"Patrick, you don't sleep on the floor. You have a mattress."

"A mattress on the floor. And you're a prince. You shouldn't have to sleep like that."

We were silent for a long moment.

"It really bothers you?" he asked.

"It does."

"Let me think about it."

Well, that was easy. He was going to think about it a little and then maybe, probably, possibly, he'd ask me to stay with him at his place. I wouldn't have to tell lies about leaky pipes or fighting with Wendi. It was all going to work out just the way I needed it to.

Sunday morning, I walked over to the deli where we'd had breakfast the day before and bought onion bagels. I picked up a Sunday paper and went back to the apartment. I made a pot of weak coffee, toasted a bagel, spread a thick layer of cream cheese all over it, and sat down with the paper.

I scanned the front page for stories about Iran. I found one midway down. Two of Iran's major ports were on fire and there was no sign of a truce with Iraq. After I read most of that article, I skimmed an article about Supreme Court judges and what they were planning to rule on this term. There was a case about statutory rape and whether it applies to just girls, a case about presidential immunity, another case was about whether women should be drafted, and one about affirmative action for women. A lot this year about what women did and did not get to do.

I was only part way through the article on the Supreme Court when Wendi walked into the tiny kitchen.

"What the hell are you doing?"

"Having coffee. Reading the newspaper."

"I've never seen you read a newspaper. I thought you hated the news."

"It's okay," I said.

"It's okay? That's what you have to say about the state of the world?"

"Well, no, I mean things could be better."

"Give me the front page when you're done," she said, pouring herself the rest of my coffee. "What are you going to do today?"

I was done with the front section so I gave it to her, then said, "I think David and I are going to a movie."

"What are you going to see?"

"David wants to see *Somewhere in Time*."

"Oh, romantic."

I cringed.

"What do you want to see?"

"I'd kind of like to see *La Cage Aux Folles*."

"Again?"

I shrugged.

That afternoon, I got my way. At four o'clock, we went to see *La Cage Aux Folles*. It had been running forever and this was my third time, so I spent most of the movie watching David watch the movie. He spoke French, which meant that he laughed before the rest of the audience since the subtitle track was late.

Afterward, despite the fact that I was starving, David insisted on driving us to a mysterious destination. A half an hour later we were in an area of Georgetown, almost in Virginia really, that I was completely unfamiliar with. He pulled the Lincoln up to the curb in front of a furniture store called Modern Home.

"What are we doing here?"

"I'm going to buy you a proper bed," David said, jumping out of the car. A proper bed? Something with a headboard and a box spring, and maybe even a mattress that didn't come from the Salvation Army?

For a moment I was thrilled, but then I thought about it. It was the opposite of what I was trying to do. Sure, I wanted the bed, but at the same time I was supposed to start spending my nights at David's house. If he bought me a bed we'd be spending all our nights at my apartment and I wouldn't be learning anything about what Nasim was doing. My half-assed plan had backfired.

I hesitated when I got to the sidewalk.

"What?" he asked. "What is it?"

"Nothing," I said because I had no other answer.

He led me into the furniture store. Inside, it was all very modern, Norwegian or Swedish, I think. A lot of medium-toned woods with rounded legs and arched backs. The bedroom furniture was in the back, sleek and elegant. I loved it.

A salesman walked over and before David could get a word out, I cut him off, saying, "You know, we're just looking."

"Take your time. I'm Buddy. Just ask for me when you're ready." And then he walked away.

I bit my lip and looked at David, and told yet another lie. "This isn't really me."

"No? I thought you'd like it."

"That's so sweet of you."

"Let's go, then. There are a couple other stores nearby," he said.

"How did you even find this place? I mean, you're not from Washington." Neither was I, I'd have never—

"Yellow Pages."

We walked out of the store and he said, "So there's another place that's all antiques and a place that's more traditional. Are you an iron frame kind of guy or are you more of a four-poster fellow?"

I didn't know what to say to that. I couldn't go to either place. This was a disaster. I looked longingly at the Lincoln.

"Something's wrong, I can tell," he said.

"No, it's all right."

"Well, no, it's obviously not. This isn't working for you, is it?" I could hear the fear in his voice as he asked that, so he had to be talking about us and not the shopping trip. It made me feel bad. It was all such a sham.

"No, it's working just fine. It's just— David, I want to sleep with you in *your* bed."

"In my bed? At my house? With my father in the room across the hall?"

"Well, your father doesn't have to be there...it's just, I want to be a part of your life. If we spend all our time together at my apartment, even if it's in a brand-new bed, then it's like you're in my life but I'm not in yours."

"You don't know what you're asking," he said, flinging open the car door.

I walked around to the other side and got in. He didn't start the engine right away. We just sat there.

"I don't think your father will mind," I said.

"Why? Because he spoke to you at a party? I think he'll mind. I think he'll mind quite a lot."

"But, basically, he told me it was okay for me to see you. So why—"

"That's not what he was telling you. Patrick, he was putting you in your place. He told you that you didn't matter."

"Oh, I see." I hadn't thought about it that way. I suppose I'd just been happy he wasn't yelling at me. "And now you're going to tell me he was right. I don't matter, do I?"

"Patrick."

I felt terrible. I was being manipulative and knew it. But that's what I was there for; to manipulate him.

"Well, do I matter?"

He remained silent for a long moment then said, "I wish it was easier to say no to you. You can stay tonight. Father goes to his room around nine; we'll slip in after that. Then we'll sneak you out in the morning."

"Sneak. So, he won't even know I'm there?"

"Oh, he'll know. He knows everything."

And so, I slept with David for the first time in his bed. It was a lovely bed too. The headboard was tufted blue velvet surrounded by an ornately carved mahogany border. The sheets were amazing. I didn't know sheets could feel like that, so soft and cool to the touch. The pillows were thick and full of goose feathers. Climbing into it was like being embraced.

David slipped me in around nine-thirty and we made love in the wonderful bed. We were slow, deliberate and quiet, so very quiet. Neither of us moaned or spoke or called out. Instead, we gasped and panted and hummed softly. We were even careful with the bed. It did squeak a bit. To avoid that, I stood, bent over the bed, David behind me, both us biting our lips so as not to make a sound.

Afterward, I put on David's robe and slipped out to go to the bathroom. The hallway was wide, and like the other rooms it had a lovely, long intricately patterned carpet. Across from David's bedroom was his father's. On the floor in front of Nasim's door was a tray with dark tea in a glass cup and a plate of cookies. The cookies were shaped like small beige apples with a slice of pistachio used as the stem.

Getting back into bed with David a few minutes later, I said, "Someone left tea and cookies outside your father's door."

"Samira. You saw her at the party. The old woman in the flow-ered hijab. She was my father's nanny."

"Well, he doesn't need a nanny anymore, does he?"

"No. Her duties are self-assigned. We ask nothing of her."

"So, what does she do?"

"She brings him cookies and tea each night before bed. They're always gone in the morning. He wouldn't dare not eat them. She brushes his suits some days. Some days she yells at the cook."

"At the party, I saw her throw away a tray of hors d'oeuvres."

"Was it the chestnuts wrapped in bacon? She made a fuss about them in the kitchen. Father wasn't pleased. He'd wanted something especially American for the guests."

"That was thoughtful of him," I said, resting my head on David's chest.

"I think she throws away the whiskey too."

"You're not supposed to drink?" I asked, a little surprised. Alcohol had flowed freely at the party.

"It is haram. Samira wishes we were more observant. It's quaint."

I didn't ask what haram meant; my guess was abomination. Christianity was full of abominations, why wouldn't Islam be the same? It *was* a funny thing to say, though. He found it quaint that a servant threw away food and liquor. I'd grown up without servants, but I'd never have thought their misbehaving was quaint.

David turned onto his side and pulled my arm around him. I pressed myself against his back and kissed the nape of his neck. In a few moments he was asleep. He seemed so real, so vulnerable. Part of me wanted to protect him. I reminded myself that he was bad. He was helping his father do terrible things. I shouldn't want to protect him. I should want to destroy him.

But I didn't.

And what about Walker? What did I really feel about him? He was sexy, in a dark, distant kind of way. And it was certainly fun to think about what it might be like, after this was over. But—

Sex. The problem was sex. I was having sex with David and I wasn't having sex with Walker. That's why I was confused. Sex messed up everything. It made you feel like you knew someone when really you didn't. Having sex with David made it seem impossible that he could be a bad person. And yet he was. I'd heard it myself. He was involved in everything his father was doing.

And then, between the wonderful bed, David's warm, sweet smell, and the fuzzy hum I felt after making love, I was asleep a minute or so later.

When I woke the next morning, David had already gotten up. It was after nine o'clock, which confused me since I'd thought the plan was to sneak me out of the house before Nasim got up. I put on my clothes and snuck out of the room to go to the bathroom. The tray in front of Nasim's door was gone. The house was quiet.

In the bathroom, I used some Scope and then tried to pat my hair down. I wondered if it might be a good time to snoop around Nasim's office. Of course, he might be in there already. Did he keep regular hours? What exactly was involved in getting a kingdom back? Probably a lot of phone calls and promises and meetings and, I guessed, arranging for weapons to be delivered.

If I weren't a spy, I'd be trying to get out of there as quickly as I could, so I needed to at least pretend to do that. After going back to the bedroom, I looked around to make sure I'd gotten all my things. When I was sure, I left the room and slowly descended the staircase into the large entrance way. Nasim's office was behind me when I reached the bottom. The house felt completely empty. Did I dare go back and check the office?

Suddenly, there were voices in the parlor in front of me. Persian, they were speaking Persian, or at least I assumed that's what it was. It wasn't English, that's for sure.

I decided I should walk quickly to the front door and leave. As I passed by the living room, the double doors were open. I glanced in and there was Nasim sitting in his grand chair. In front of him sat a man and woman on their knees, holding Nasim's hand and kissing it.

I hurried out of the house, hoping he hadn't seen me. There was something regal about the tableau but also something intimate. Almost religious. It felt like something I shouldn't have seen. I felt like an intruder. Well, I *was* an intruder so it was a natural way to feel.

Hurrying down the front steps, I turned toward my apartment and began to walk. It wasn't far, just on the other side DuPont Circle. I was almost all the way to the Circle, when I saw David jogging toward me. He looked amazing in nothing but his tiny nylon shorts and a tank top. When he saw me, he came to a panting stop.

"Good morning," he said.

"I thought you were going to sneak me out before your father woke up?" I asked, my voice a bit agitated.

"I changed my mind. If I want him not to meddle in my life, I have to stop accommodating him."

"Yeah, I guess that's smart."

"Did he see you?"

"I'm not sure. I walked by the living room and he was in there with this couple who were…bowing to him, I guess. You know, treating him like a king."

"He is a king. Those people are expats. They support the return of our dynasty."

"Does he give them money?"

David smiled and gave me a puzzled look. "No. They give us money. I know it looks like we have a great deal, but the truth is we don't. That's not our house for example. It is simply being rented from a friend, a good friend who's letting us pay a scandalously low rent."

"But yesterday you were going to buy me a bed."

"We're not destitute. You know, there is a place between great wealth and poverty."

I knew that, logically, it's just that my mother and I had never been able to find it. For a moment, I imagined what it might be like to have friends who could loan me a mansion.

"Was the shah, the other shah, really that bad?"

David shrugged. "He did some good things, that is true. But then he allowed Khomeini to rise to power. It doesn't matter what good you do if you allow it to be ruined."

Then he smiled at me and it was like the sun coming out.

"I'm sorry I didn't get back sooner. I would have liked to kiss you goodbye. I wish I could do it right here."

"I wish you could, too."

David invited me to come back for lunch, but I suggested dinner. It would be easier to spend another night if I came in the evening. Besides, it was laundry day. If I didn't do my laundry on Monday, it meant that I'd spend the week sponging off my waiter pants and rinsing my white shirts out in the sink or dousing them with cologne.

I hated Wendi on Monday afternoons because her mother came into town, took her out to lunch, and then left with her laundry—returning it the following week neatly folded. Meanwhile, I packed my dirty clothes into a shabby duffle bag and rode a bus to the nearest laundromat.

The highlight of my afternoon was reading all about a congressman from Maryland who was being investigated by the FBI for being gay. It was the top story in *The Blade*. The FBI was worried the married congressman might be blackmailed by communists, though when it came down to it, he was only blackmailed by a bartender at the Naples Café.

The congressman claimed his real problem was alcohol and now that he'd stopped drinking everything was fine. He did admit that he suffered from homosexual tendencies. That almost made me laugh. People suffered from acne or constipation or halitosis.

Things you could find a cure for at the corner drugstore. Saying you *suffered* from homosexual tendencies was just weird. It was like saying I suffered from a tendency to be twenty-years-old.

I mean, I know not everyone felt that way, but people were just who they were, right? You could try to be nicer or you could try to be smarter, but you couldn't really be less gay no matter how hard you tried. I mean, did straight people really think they could just be gay if they woke up one morning and wanted to?

And I think the congressman sort of proved that since it seemed like he was trying really hard not to suffer from his homosexual tendencies. And not managing very well.

David and I met for dinner at a little pizza parlor on the west side of Connecticut Avenue. It was one of those places with red-and-white checked plastic tablecloths and pizza that came by the slice on a paper plate.

He had mushrooms on his pizza, while I had extra pepperoni. I'd decided I needed to be more assertive with David and ask more questions. If I couldn't get into Nasim's office again, then I had to work with what I had. And I had David.

"So at the party, which one was Ebrahim's father?"

"Fred."

"What does Fred do?" I asked, hoping I sounded casual.

After a shrug he said, "He's an importer. Mostly Persian carpets. Although we shouldn't talk about that."

That wasn't exactly true. I was fairly certain he was more arms dealer than rug dealer. Still, I played along.

"Why shouldn't we talk about rugs?"

"There's an embargo. Fred has to ship them out of Iran to Turkey. And then they're shipped here. As Turkish rugs. The customs inspectors can't tell the difference."

"How is a Turkish rug different from a Persian carpet?"

"Don't ask that in front of Fred. You'll upset him terribly."

"Is that the only thing he trades in?"

David shrugged. "He dabbles in this and that."

That was annoying. I couldn't exactly ask him to be more specific. I tried another way. "Ebrahim makes it seem like they have money. It can't all be from rugs?"

David reached over, picked a piece of pepperoni off my pizza and popped it into his mouth. "A Persian carpet can cost more than an American car. And the embargo has only increased the prices.

Not to mention demand. Why are you so interested in how Fred makes a living?"

I shrugged. "I've always been poor. There's nothing wrong with asking how people get rich, is there?"

"You know, in many parts of the world what you call poverty is considered wealth."

"I don't need a prince to tell me that," I said. That was the wrong answer. I was being petulant and obnoxious. Not the best way to get information from someone. I tried to backtrack. "I'm sorry."

"No, don't be sorry. You're right. Who am I to tell you what you should be satisfied with? So you want to be a rich man one day? How should you go about it?"

And then the conversation went awry. We spent the rest of the meal imagining ways I might become wealthy. None of which were realistic. None of which would ever happen.

CHAPTER FIFTEEN

Later that night, after a couple of drinks at the Fraternity House, a romantic walk around Dupont Circle, and another round of muffled lovemaking, I waited impatiently for David to fall asleep. I hadn't been able to turn the conversation toward anything useful. Though in all honesty I shouldn't have expected to get much out of him. He was hardly going to jump into a conversation about anti-tank missiles no matter how cleverly I asked the question.

I knew what I was going to have to do, and just the idea of it was making it nearly impossible to hold still while I waited for David to fall into a deeper sleep. I rolled over onto my side facing away from him, so I could stare into the darkness and worry. The only thing I could think of was to go downstairs in the middle of the night and look through Nasim's desk.

Sometimes when I'm nervous I make a list of all the books I've ever read. (I tried this once with all the guys I've slept with, but that's only twenty-four including the prince, so it usually doesn't take long enough.) I work backwards because I can't remember the first book I ever read. I'm sure it was some picture book, some Dr. Seuss or Mother Goose. No, I start with now and try to find my way back to the beginning. *The Persian Boy*, *The Boys in the Band* (Act One), *A Confederacy of Dunces*, *The Dead Zone*, the three books about Merlin: *The Crystal Cave*, *The Hollow Hills*, *The Last Enchantment*. Wait, those should have been backwards. Oh well. *Sophie's Choice*, *The Rubyfruit Jungle*, *Fear of Flying*—not as dirty as advertised. *Looking for Mr. Goodbar*, *Ragtime*, *Watership Down*, *The*

Once and Future King. I'm skipping some and getting them out of order. All of Jacqueline Susann. *The Great Gatsby* for a college class (also high school). *The Front Runner*—hidden under my mattress while I still lived at home. *Maurice,* after I moved to D.C. Yes, things are completely out of order now. *Maurice* was one of the first books I bought at Lambda Rising, along with *The Lure. Gravity's Rainbow*—also in college; only for three chapters, then I dropped the class. *The Summer of 42,* but that was in high school, as was *The Captain and the Kings,* which had a gay character. *Carrie, Salem's Lot, The Stand, Interview With the Vampire.*

There were more. I was missing books, but one thing was clear. I should have been reading other books. Spy novels: Ian Fleming. John le Carré, Ken Follett. I picked their books up in the grocery store, read the blurbs, studied the covers, and then read something else.

My mother tried to get me to read Gore Vidal, though she always mentioned that he was queer: "Even though he's a queer, he writes about American history with such novelty."

Finally, the clock next to David's bed read 2:37. It was time. He was snoring softly and didn't stir as I slipped out of bed. Moving carefully, I opened his door and stepped into the hallway.

As I headed to the stairway, I didn't make a sound. I hadn't thought about it much before, but the house was full of Persian carpets, expensive carpets, carpets that I now knew cost as much as automobiles. They made it easy to walk around quietly. Even though the house was old, the floorboards didn't creak under the thick rugs. I made it downstairs without making a single sound.

I couldn't remember if the moon was full, but there was a lot of light in the front of the house. *Wait, there's a streetlight. That's why it's so light.* I turned and looked down the hallway to Nasim's study and it became much darker. I crept down the short hallway and carefully opened the study door. It was barely more than a click, but to me it sounded insanely loud. I stood there and listened. Nothing. No one came running.

Inside, the room was much darker than the rest of the house. I didn't think I could risk turning on the overhead light so I felt my way over to the desk. I remembered there was a desk lamp with a green shade in one corner. I found it and turned it on, illuminating only the desk.

The desktop was very clean, there'd been papers before but now there were none. In fact, there was nothing but the calendar, the telephone and the blotter. Sitting down behind the desk, I tried the drawers. The ones on the side were open, but they didn't have anything that looked interesting: phone books in one of the bottom drawers, boxes of stationary in another. The papers which I'd seen sitting on the desk were probably in the locked center drawer.

I could try to break the lock, but then Nasim would know someone had been in his office and, since I was the only person new to the house, I would be the likely suspect. I looked through the other open drawers. In one I found a legal pad. There was nothing written on it, but I could see indentations from the sheet above. I decided to try a trick I'd seen in some old movies on the Late, Late Show.

Finding a pencil, I lay the pad on the desk and began to carefully brush the lead point over the impressions. Soon words began to form. They were hard to read since there were impressions coming from the sheet before and even the sheet before that. Nasim seemed to press down hard when he took notes.

TharsBente Aeroo RioBlahense
   TeF Amv-Tahnan

I was getting gibberish. Below the top two lines I found:

1000 missib.
   50E Oze
   Pans

Staring at the sheet, I tried to make sense of it. I didn't think the list had anything to do with pans. Then I saw it: 1000 missiles. The L and the E had gotten crushed together. There was no S. 50E was 500. Ghost impressions from the sheet before turned Uzi into Oze. And Pans was Parts. This was a list of things needed by the Iranians. This was what Walker wanted.

Looking closely at the two phrases at the top of the page I tried to work them out, but then I heard movement outside the door in the hallway. Quickly, I turned off the desk light, slipped the pad back into the drawer, and, not knowing what else to do, hid under the desk. Seconds later I realized how stupid that was.

What would I do if someone found me there? I couldn't exactly say I was looking for the bathroom underneath Nasim's desk. I could pretend to be sleepwalking or, I guess, sleep-crawling, but no one would believe that.

I didn't believe it.

Barely breathing, I folded the sheet of pencil-brushed paper and slid it into my underwear, which was really all I was wearing.

The door to the study opened. *Oh God.* I hoped it wasn't Nasim coming down to do some work in the middle of the night. If he tried to sit behind his desk his knees were going to bump me in the chin. The overhead light came on.

Silence.

Someone stood at the door looking into the room. They must have heard something that made them suspicious. Perhaps I hadn't been as quiet as I thought. Maybe when you lived in a house full of carpets you heard things normal people couldn't. God, I hoped I was being quiet now. I was barely breathing. Sitting perfectly still under the desk. I imagined myself a statue: solid and motionless.

After what seemed like ages—but wasn't—the light went off and the door closed. I stayed under the desk for quite a while, not daring to breathe. I was afraid whoever opened the door might have just stepped inside and was waiting there for me to come out.

I had to pee. I didn't know whether I had to pee because my bladder was full or if I'd just had the piss scared out of me, so to speak. While I waited, I wondered who'd opened the door. I didn't think it was David. If he'd woken up he would know that I wasn't in bed. I had the feeling he'd have said my name. That meant it had to be Nasim or one of the servants.

After waiting for what was probably twenty minutes—a very long twenty minutes—I crawled out from under the desk. Then I hurried over to the door, cracking it a little and peeking out. There didn't seem to be anyone out there so I stepped into the hallway. I hurried up the stairs and was back in David's room a moment later.

I found my jeans on a chair, took the page from my underwear, and put it into one of the back pockets of my jeans. Then, I went over to the bed and carefully crawled in.

"You were gone a long time. Did you go downstairs?"

"I did. I was hungry."

"What did you find?"

I had to think quickly. What did everyone in the world have in their refrigerator? What could I say that they were sure to have?

"I had a piece of bread with butter."

"Bread and butter? There's a jar with cookies on the counter. Samira makes them. They're a lot better than bread and butter."

"Thanks. I'll remember that."

I rolled over and slipped an arm around David.

I lolled in bed until nearly lunchtime, exhausted after not sleeping well. David kept getting back into bed with me, trying to ease me awake. Around eleven thirty he went for a run and I went downstairs to see if I could find something for breakfast.

On the way, I peeked out the windows and saw that it was cloudy but not raining. The kitchen was large with the kind of things you didn't normally see in a kitchen, or at least that I didn't normally see: a six-burner stove and double-doored refrigerator. There was a large wooden table in the center of the room where Samira sat polishing a piece of silver.

"Um, hi. David said I should help myself to some breakfast."

Samira simply shrugged and continued what she was doing. Coffee percolated on the counter. I would have liked a cup, but I didn't want to ask where the cups were.

I peeked into the refrigerator and found some orange juice. I set the bottle on the counter and continued my search. There were eggs in the refrigerator, but I didn't want to cook them. I could, but my desire to run out of the kitchen as quickly as possible made scrambling eggs impractical. I noticed a breadbox and opened it. There was a loaf of bread in there so I decided on orange juice and toast. I searched the counters for the toaster and found it on the other side of the room. That was odd; I would have put it near the breadbox.

Crossing the room, feeling Samira's eyes on my every step, I wondered if she was the one who'd stood in the doorway of Nasim's study? Nervously, I went over and put two slices of bread into the toaster and pressed the lever down. Now I needed a plate and a glass for my orange juice. As I was searching the cupboards, Nasim came into the kitchen with a newspaper tucked under his arm.

"Patrick, I see you're up."

"Oh, yes, um, David said I should help myself to breakfast."

"And where is my son?"

"He's gone for a run."

Samira said something in Persian. Nasim replied and then, switching back to English, said to me, "I hope she hasn't been rude to you. She's very set in her opinions."

"No. I mean, she hasn't said anything to me."

I found the dishes I was looking for and put them on the counter. Then the toast popped up. I picked up the dish and went back toward the toaster.

Nasim said something in Persian and Samira got up and snatched the plate out of my hand. Then she took the toast out of the toaster, put it on the plate then walked over to the refrigerator.

"Would you like coffee, Patrick?"

"Oh, yes, please."

He gave some instructions to Samira. To me he said, "She will make some fresh. Come sit with me in the dining room. Samira will bring you some scrambled eggs with your toast. Come."

We went out to the dining room and sat at the large mahogany table, Nasim setting his newspaper to one side. I'd only been in the dining room during the party the week before, and then the table was covered with a white tablecloth and pushed up against the wall. Now, it sat regally in the center of the room.

"It's important to have patience with servants, though at times it can be a challenge," Nasim said, obviously meaning Samira.

"David mentioned that she's been with you a long time."

"Yes. Long enough that lines begin to blur. She is family but not family."

Samira came out with two cups of coffee, clearly not having made fresh, and set them down. Nasim asked me, "Do you take cream and sugar?"

I did but decided to say I didn't since I didn't want to see him argue with Samira. Twenty seconds later she set a creamer and sugar down in front of us.

"Samira, when you make Patrick's eggs please make him some fresh toast so that it's warm."

She raised her chin and left the room.

"She's really not meant to cook. She was my nanny and then Davoud's. She's itching for Davoud to get married and have children she can take care of."

Since I was standing in the way of that, I could see why she might not like me. I really wanted cream and sugar for my coffee even though I'd turned it down.

"Are you sure you won't have cream or sugar?" Nasim asked, seeming to sense my dilemma.

"Well, maybe a little." I made my coffee light and sweet. Then tipping my head at his newspaper I asked, rather boldly, "Do you think the hostages will be released before the election?"

"I know Mr. Carter is working very hard on that. I wish him well."

I studied Nasim. It wasn't exactly an answer; it was also an obvious lie. I knew he didn't want the hostages released. He was good at lying. I must have made him uncomfortable since he said, "I know that we Persians are difficult for a young American like yourself to understand. We are a very old people, a great civilization that once ruled half the world. We have fought off the Greeks, the Romans, the Arabs, the Mongols, the Russians, the Turks and the British. And now it is clear that our greatest enemy has always been ourselves. You will never have to face a truth like that. Your country is too young. You are lucky."

Samira came out of the kitchen with a plate of scrambled eggs and two slices of buttered toast. She set them down in front of me and then left. I stared down at my breakfast. The eggs were a fluorescent yellow with white chunks.

Nasim noticed me, "She's added turmeric, a spice used often in Persian cooking. It's mild; you won't burn your mouth."

"And the white things?"

"Feta cheese. Also, very mild."

I took a tentative bite. It wasn't terrible. Maybe it was even good. I nodded at Nasim.

Smiling, he stood and said, "I'll leave you to your breakfast. I'm glad that you've made yourself comfortable. I want you to be comfortable while you are with us."

Taking his coffee and his paper, he walked out of the dining room, leaving me to wonder what he'd meant by that. "…while you are with us." He didn't expect me to be around long. Had he been the one who'd nearly caught me the night before? Did he know I was a spy? Did he know that the CIA was on to him? Did he expect to be expelled from the country? Or did he think Reagan would win and make his first order of business invading Iran and installing Nasim onto the throne?

Either way, he didn't expect me to be in David's life much longer. For that matter, neither did I.

When David returned from his run, I told him I needed to go home and get ready for work. I needed to call Walker and meet with him before I went to work. It was almost twelve-thirty, I was cutting it close. He didn't want to let me go, but what could he do?

Instead of going home though, I went directly to the pay phone at the drugstore and called Publius. Instead of taking a message, they gave me one.

"Liberty, I have a message for you. You're to go to 1344 E Street NW. Suite 9423."

"When?"

"Any time today."

The Munsey Trust Building sat at one point of the Federal Triangle, across from the Old Post Office. The Old Post Office was draped in scaffolding and from the signs they'd put in front it looked like they were turning it into a shopping center, or at least part of it.

A woman in front of Munsey Trust held a sign that said not to tear it down, though no one seemed to be paying her any attention. That it was coming down soon explained the empty storefronts on the building's first floor. I found the lobby and took an old, creaking elevator to the ninth floor.

When I got out I was in a marble hallway with high ceilings. I walked the halls until I found a glass door marked 9400. Pushing it open, I walked into a room full of neatly arranged desks. Around the edge of the large space were offices.

At most of the desks there was nothing but a black desk phone. About half of the desks were occupied with various sorts of people, each with a few short stacks of paper in front of them, and all were talking on their phones.

Nobody bothered with me. I walked down a sort of aisle and stood in front of an office numbered 9419 occupied by Robert

Winthrop. To my left was 9420 James Kettle, 9421 Andrew Bauhaus, 9422 Clement Hastings, and then 9423 no name. I stood in the doorway looking at Agent Walker as he sat behind a desk. His desk was stacked with computer printouts.

I stepped inside and said, "I thought your office was on K Street? That's what your business card says."

"Close the door."

I did and the sounds of the busy office became muffled. Without being asked, I sat down in the green vinyl guest chair.

"I'm undercover. You're not my only assignment, you know."

Well, that made sense. A ten-minute meeting with me every few days was hardly a full-time job.

"What kind of place is this?" It looked like telemarketing, but why would a CIA agent—

"You don't need to know that," he said, quickly moving on. "Tell me what you've done."

"I've been staying at David's, like you told me." I started to reach for the piece of paper in my pocket.

"Ah, you're in," he said. "Good. Have you seen the crown prince?"

"Not much. He goes to bed early. Well, he goes into his room, I'm not sure he's asleep. One of the servants leaves tea and cookies outside his door. It's usually still there when I arrive about ten, but it's gone—"

"Who else is in the house?"

I was itching to show him the list, but he wasn't letting me. I mean, for some reason I wanted to be casual about it. I wanted to simply set it in front of him and watch his eyes light up. He was going to be happy with me, I was sure.

"There are the servants, of course. A woman and a man. They're old."

"Who's come to the house?"

"I thought you knew that kind of thing. Aren't you watching?"

"Of course, we're watching the house. But I'm not here to talk about what I know. I'm here to talk about what you know."

"Yesterday when I left there was a middle-aged couple kneeling to Nasim like he's royalty. I mean, I know he *is* royalty he's just royalty without a country so—it seemed odd."

"The ex-pats come from different parts of Iran, different tribes.

Nasim settles their disputes. Takes their money. Promises them they'll go home one day."

"They hope to put Nasim back on the throne."

"More than hope. They've got the British in their pockets. They've come to do the same with America. They never stop plotting and scheming."

"Isn't that what we're doing, though? Plotting and scheming?"

He smiled. "Yes, but we're the good guys, remember?"

"Speaking of which," I said, finally taking the sheet of paper out of my pocket and putting it in the middle of his desk.

"What's that?"

"I searched Nasim's desk in the middle of the night. I found a pad in his desk. I don't know what you call it exactly, but I rubbed a pencil across the sheet. You can see what he was writing."

Walker unfolded the sheet of paper and read. "Why are these words all jumbled?"

"It looks like Nasim presses really hard on his pen. Some of the marks are from whatever he wrote on the pad before."

"Tel Aviv," he read. "I think this is the name of an airline. Spanish or Argentinian. They're flying in weapons from Tel Aviv to Tehran." He looked up at me, his night eyes jolting me. "When?"

I licked my lips. "I don't know. This is all I found. I did good, didn't I?"

"Yes, of course you did. Very good. We need to know when."

"I almost got caught. It was kind of terrifying."

"But you didn't get caught. That's what matters."

I took my cigarettes out of my pocket and lit one. Walker bummed one and as I gave it to him said, "If you're really quitting I should started telling you no."

"I *am* quitting. This actually helps."

"Smoking is helping you quit smoking?"

"I didn't say it was logical."

I asked something I'd been curious about. "How did you get into this kind of work?"

His eyes flashed, annoyed that I'd asked. "What kind of work?"

"Being a CIA agent."

"I was recruited in college."

"Because?"

"I was a political science major. I wrote an interesting paper. And, no, I'm not telling you what it was about." He gave me a very intense look and said, "You have to find out when this deal is happening."

I didn't relish the idea of sneaking round the house again. I didn't have an excuse to be places I shouldn't be. 'I'm looking for a bathroom' only works so many times, even in a large house like theirs. But I also couldn't find a way to say no to Walker.

He got up and came out from behind the desk. When he was standing next to my chair, he tilted my chin up and bent down to kiss me. As he did, he slipped his hand into my lap and squeezed. I gasped.

"This will all be worth it, Patrick. I promise you."

WASHINGTON STANDARD

October 7, 1980 – Evening Edition

Iraq attacks oil industry

By Winslow Crain
Middle East correspondent

TEHRAN, Iran—Recent attacks by Iraqi forces against the Iranian oil industry, primarily in the embattled city of Khorramshahr, have begun to show results in the capital city. The use of private cars has been restricted by the government and the number of air raids into Iraq has declined.

A few days ago, Iranian jets were bombarding Iraqi targets up to a dozen times a day. Yesterday, Iran attempted to do similar damage to Iraqi supplies by bombing the northern oil city of Kirkuk, one of only three raids attempted.

Iraq claims to have devastated Iran's oil industry, crippling their military capacity. If true, Iran is at a serious disadvantage and may not be able to mount a defense much longer.

Meanwhile, Iraq again attacked Tehran's Mehrabad International Airport on Monday, as well as nearby oil refineries. Reports from Iran's national radio stated that four persons were killed and dozens injured in the bombing.

Continued on page 8, col. 2

CHAPTER SIXTEEN

That night I went to work. My station was four tables in the main dining room for a change. Wendi worked the station next to mine. When I arrived, she said, "Long time no see."

"I stayed at David's."

"Yeah, I figured. Nasim must be enjoying that."

"We sat up all night playing gin rummy."

"Sounds cozy."

My first party was a priest and his elderly mother. I'd waited on the priest before, so I knew to stand next to his mother and out of his reach. During their last visit, he'd gotten hold of my wrist and worked his way up my arm while trying to convince me to sign up for his private Bible study. I'd wiggled out of the situation by telling him I was Methodist. My mother was Methodist, so close enough, right?

The priest and his mother ordered Jameson Manhattans straight up and the champignons farcis to share. I put the appetizer order into the kitchen and then went to the bar. An anchorman on the television hung above the bar was telling the nearly empty room that Mohammad Ali was retiring from the ring due to health issues. Barrett Copeland sat alone about midway down, nursing what looked like his usual Cutty Sark and water. He saw me and slid over.

Pete came over, glanced at my ticket, and started to make the Manhattans.

"You keep interesting company, Mr. Burke," Barrett said.

"Did you enjoy the party?"

"Very much so. I don't agree with Nasim al-din Qajar's politics but no matter. He's civil and an excellent host."

"What don't you like about his politics?" I asked. I'd kind of thought they were on the same side.

"It's no secret he'd like to be the new shah. I'm not sure that's the best thing for America."

"But Khomeini's terrible. For everyone."

"Religious regimes don't last. The Iranian people will rebel soon enough. Sometimes it's best to simply let nature take its course."

Even though my understanding of history was sketchy at best, I was pretty sure there were a lot of religious regimes in the Middle Ages. Regimes that lasted for centuries.

"How did you meet the Qajars?"

"I met David at a party," I told him. A disco is *like* a party.

"The young are so fluid. I can't tell you the last time I met anyone new at a party. I only seem to meet the people I already know. There's nothing quite so depressing as an evening with people you already know."

"Are you staying for dinner?" I asked, to be polite.

"No, I'll just have some onion soup here at the bar."

We were kind of famous for our onion soup, which was ninety-percent French bread, a well-chosen Gruyere and sherry. Onion being the least relevant ingredient.

Pete had put the Manhattans on a small round tray for me. Smiling at Copeland, I picked it up and left the bar. When I got back out to the dining room, I noticed that I had a new table and came to a complete stop when I saw that the party was made up of Ebrahim, Nima and Shadi.

"Behind you," Maxim said, coming through with a tray over his shoulder. Once he was by me, he stopped and glared. "Don't just stand there Pa*trick*. Serve those drinks."

Taking a deep breath, I went over to the priest and his mother, and gave them their Manhattans. "Your mushrooms will be ready in just a few minutes."

Unfortunately, since I'd had to set his Manhattan in front of him, the priest had an opening to grab my arm.

"Patrick, my parish is starting a study group on Monday nights at my residence."

"I'm sorry, sir, you must have forgotten I'm not Catholic."

"Don't be ridiculous, with a name like Patrick you have to be Catholic."

His mother chuckled. I tugged my arm away from him, saying, "I have another party. Please excuse me."

I stepped away from the table, took a deep breath and turned to face Ebrahim and his friends. I pasted a smile on my face and said, "Welcome to Le Marquis. I'm Patrick and I'll be waiting on you this evening."

"Hello, Patrick," Nima said, winking at me. The other two remained silent.

"Our specials tonight are confit de canard and a delicately poached salmon. The side vegetable is ratatouille. And the soup of the day is vichyssoise, in addition to our famous onion soup which we have every day. Can I start you off with a cocktail?"

Nima ordered first, "Beefeater martini, straight up, very dry, olives."

"I'll have a ginger ale," Shadi said.

Ebrahim simply sat there. Finally, he ordered, "Old-fashioned. Maker's Mark."

Old-fashioneds were annoying to make since you muddled the fruit, which I'm sure was what took Ebrahim so long to order. He must have assumed I made the cocktails myself.

"I'll bring those right out for you."

As I walked toward the bar, Wendi came up alongside me. "What are they doing here?"

"I think Ebrahim wants to humiliate me."

"You want me to take them? I'll trade you the four top I just got."

"No, that's okay. Go over and say hello, though. I'm sure Nima would like to see you."

I winked at her. She rolled her eyes at me and went into the kitchen. I slipped into the bar and put in their drink order. Pete picked it up and began building the drinks.

"You come here a lot," I said to Copeland.

"Proximity. K Street is nearby. There are several popular hotels where the people I need to see stay. And, yes, I do eat at other hotels. Often."

"Do you only eat at hotels?"

That made him laugh. "It does seem that way at times." He shrugged. "The life of the political animal."

I watched as Pete muddled fruit for the old-fashioned.

"Do you think Iran will ever have another shah?" I asked Copeland.

He gave me a surprised look, then answered, "It depends on the shah. The ayatollah might decide to take the title himself."

"And people would just let him?"

"The country has isolated themselves. An impoverished, starving population will always choose the most fanatical leader they can find. Yes, many in Iran long for the old days, but too many simply long for bread they'll never get."

"But wouldn't they rather be free? Even if they are hungry?"

He shrugged, "Spoken like a young man who's never been truly hungry." Then he added, almost unbidden, "Freedom's Achilles' heel is that it allows the freedom to destroy it. By its nature, freedom is fragile."

"But it's still worth dying for, isn't it?" I said, unconsciously paraphrasing my distant relative.

"I think it is. Do you think so, Patrick?"

"Um, I guess. Yes, I do."

Pete had finished my drinks and put them on a tray for me. I raised an eyebrow at Copeland and scurried back to the dining room. What an odd conversation to have in the middle of waiting tables. Freedom is fragile, would you like an appetizer? And yes, I would die for freedom. I felt all jumbled up as I set the drinks in front of Shadi, Nima and Ebrahim.

I pulled myself together and asked, "Do you know what you'd like?"

"Are any of these dishes halal?" Ebrahim asked as he studied the menu intently.

At first, I wasn't sure what he was asking me. Fortunately, Nima stepped in. "Don't pay any attention to him. His family doesn't keep halal. He barely knows what it is."

"Don't attack my faith, Nima. I won't have it."

"I liked you better when the only thing you believed in was Bette Midler."

He replied with something in Persian, which was clearly rude given the look Nima gave him.

"He was asking for me," Shadi said. "My family, we try to keep to the old ways. But it is hard in this country."

"I'm sorry," I said to Shadi. "I doubt we have anything like that."

"It's all right. I didn't think you would."

Wendi came over to say hello, so I slipped away and ran out to the kitchen to get the priest's mushrooms. What did Ebrahim think he was doing? Well, obviously he thought he'd be able to humble me by coming in, but why? Why was I that important? How did my humiliation benefit him?

I brought the mushrooms out to the priest and hovered near his mother as I set them down in the center of the table.

"How are the Manhattans?" I asked.

"Lovely."

"Did you want to order quickly? Or should I come back?"

"No, our order is simple," the priest said. "We'll each have the cote de beouf. Medium rare."

"Yes, sir."

"That comes with the potatoes au gratin and the ratatouille?"

"It can, yes."

"Wonderful."

Even though Wendi was still talking with the table, I went over to Ebrahim and friends to get their order. Before I could do anything, Nima pinched the sleeve of my waiter's jacket and pulled me close.

"I didn't know you worked here. It was a surprise when Ebrahim requested you. I'm sorry if you're embarrassed. He shouldn't have brought us here."

"It's fine. I'm not ashamed of being a waiter. I don't happen to have a wealthy family to live off."

She giggled. "Don't say that to Ebrahim. We all live off our families."

"Sorry, it's just...he's not better than I am just because his family has money."

"No, he's not."

"But, why did *you* come? He's so rude to you."

She shrugged. "Shadi needed a chaperone. I was the best she could do."

I imagined she was safer with Ebrahim than she wanted to be, but I didn't say anything. Instead, I stood up and said to the table, "Would you like to order?"

Wendi took that as her cue and went back to her own tables.

"You go ahead, I'm still deciding," Ebrahim said. I wondered about that. Normally, I took women's orders first. Why did he assume he'd be going first? Was that a Persian thing? Or an Ebrahim thing?

Shadi ordered a salade nicoise. I suspected that was as close as she could come to being halal. Nima ordered the Marseille shrimp with an onion soup to start. Then I stared at Ebrahim waiting for him to order.

"The food here is so bloated and spoiled, just like American society."

"I'll let the management know," I said politely. "Can I get you a simple salad like the one Shadi is having?"

"No, of course, not. I'll have the cote de beouf. Rare."

"Excellent choice. Not at all bloated or spoiled."

I smiled and walked away. Ebrahim jumped out of his chair and hurried after me. He caught up to me as I was about to go into the kitchen.

"Did you change your mind?" I asked.

"I know what you're doing."

Adrenaline rushed through me like wildfire. He knew. How did he know? Did he know? He could mean something else. But what?

"I'm taking your order to the kitchen," I said as evenly as I could. "Is that what you know?"

"I see right through you. David will too. Just wait and see."

"Go back to your seat Ebrahim."

He gave me a filthy look and did exactly that. Instead of going into the kitchen and putting in my two orders, I stepped into the bar. It was quiet and dark, and I thought I could gather my thoughts for a moment, but didn't have the chance.

Copeland stood next to the stool he'd been sitting on. He took money out of his pocket and laid it on the bar. When he saw me, he said, "I was hoping I'd see you again."

"Leaving so soon?"

"I thought I'd go home early for a change."

"Well, have a pleasant evening."

He stepped in close to me and said, "Be careful, Patrick. Your friends are on the wrong side of history. People on the wrong side of history get hurt."

Then he walked away. Holy shit. Why was everyone playing 'warn the waiter?'

I didn't stay at David's that night. Whether it was because I almost got caught in Nasim's office the night before or the run-in with Ebrahim I wasn't sure, but I knew I had to stay away. For at least a night. Besides, it was hard to find anything out if I was only there late at night. It might be better to stay over on Friday or Saturday. Then I could try to linger and spend most of the weekend there. I'd find out more.

Naturally, that isn't what I told David.

"I don't want you to get sick of me," I said when I called him after work.

"I'm not sick of you. I'm sick without you."

"I just want to spend a little time with my book and my roommate."

"I'm jealous of them both."

"You'll see me plenty. Don't worry."

I did get to spend time with my book. I was in chapter eight and still Alexander was only being talked about. Still no sex scenes, even though the eunuch was practically a prostitute. On the other hand, I did *not* get to spend time with my roommate. She'd been cut early at the restaurant and wasn't home when I got there. And she still wasn't home when I fell asleep around one.

The next morning, I went to the kitchen to pour a bowl of cereal and found a naked man standing in front of our refrigerator. He saw me and asked, "Do you have any eggs?"

For a moment, my tongue was thick and difficult to move. "Um, well, if you don't see them, they're not there."

"Bagels it is, then."

We usually didn't have much more than bagels and milk in our fridge, so it wasn't a big surprise to me. Certainly not the surprise his naked presence was.

"Who are you?"

"Lefty. I'm...you know, with Wendi."

"I didn't think you'd wandered in off the street. Lefty, huh?"

"It's a nickname. It's really Leonard, but who wants to be called Leonard?"

"Leonard Nimoy?"

"Yeah, but I'm not that cool."

I wasn't sure I agreed. He seemed pretty cool at the moment.

He looked to be in his late twenties, had red hair, very pale skin and a whole lot of freckles. He was in good shape, his waist trim, his biceps thick. I tried not to look below his belly button. Tried, but failed. Repeatedly. Like when he turned his back to me to slice a bagel.

Starring at his very nicely rounded ass, I asked, "So, have you known Wendi long?"

"We met last night at the Lafayette Pavilion."

Wendi had an affection for the basement bar at the Hay-Adams, mainly because it was a block from The Hotel Continental and was a comfortable place for a woman to go alone. And apparently a good place to pick up straight men.

"I should go put some clothes on, shouldn't I? I'm making you uncomfortable."

"I'm cool," I said, though I really wasn't.

We were saved from the awkwardness of agreeing on whether he should dress or remain naked by the telephone ringing.

"Excuse me," I said and went out to the living room to answer it.

It was David.

"Nima called and told me about last night. Why didn't you say anything? Is that why you wouldn't come over? I'll call Ebrahim and talk to him."

"No. Don't. That's why I didn't say anything to you about it. I don't want you to call Ebrahim, it will just make things worse. He's really upset about us and I think if you call him it will only make him more upset."

"Did he at least tip you well?"

He hadn't.

"Let's not talk about it," I said. Ebrahim hadn't tipped at all. I'd wondered if it was a religious thing. "How did he even know I worked there?"

"I don't know. Why? Do you think I told him?"

"I don't know what I think. All I know is I didn't tell him."

"I haven't discussed you with Ebrahim. I wouldn't."

"All right. It was just a question."

"Did you ask Wendi? Maybe he spoke to her at the party."

"I will ask, I guess. Later. She's a little busy now." I'd just heard Lefty walk back into the bedroom with his toasted bagel.

"I have news," David said, a little more upbeat. "Father is

having a dinner party Friday night. He specifically asked that I invite you."

"Um, sure, that sounds fun." It sounded kind of horrible, but maybe I could pick up some information.

"I don't know that it will be particularly fun. I've seen the guest list."

"I don't have anything to wear."

"Don't worry about that. It's not that fancy. But if you want, you could wear something of mine."

"You're taller than I am."

"Not pants. I could loan you a nice shirt and maybe even a jacket." He paused a moment, seemingly a bit nervous. "Patrick, I missed you last night. I know I was reluctant to have you stay at first, but now I love it. I love having you in my bed. It's terrible when you're not here. You've ruined me."

"Ruined you? I'm sure there's not a thing wrong with you."

"I love you. I was a fool to think I could ever set you aside. This is it for me. This is it for always."

"You mean, you're not going to do your duty one day?"

"I couldn't dream of it."

That took my breath away. Softly, I said, "I love you, too. I don't want you to do your duty."

I said it because I was supposed to. It was the only way to keep spying on him. But did I mean it?

I had no idea.

TABATABAI TELEX

0515 EST
WHITE HOUSE WPB
V
VIA WUI*
WHITE HOUSE WPB

STRAUSSE GBP25844

TO: WHITE HOUSE
FM: SADEQ TABATABAI, DUSSELDORF

ATTN: EDMUND MUSKIE
NEGOTIATIONS ON TRACK. IGNORE NEWS REPORTS.
HOSTAGES RELEASED BEFORE NOVEMBER 4, 1980. DO
NOT WORRY.

REGARDS,

SADEQ TABATABAI

WHITE HOUSE WPB
STRAUSSE GBP25844

CHAPTER SEVENTEEN

As soon as I got off the phone with David I called The Publius Society and left a message for Agent Walker to call Liberty. David loved me. Should I report that? No. Walker didn't need to know. I didn't want to know. I needed to harden my heart against him. But how did you do that? How did you build a wall around your heart? I felt really sad. A part of me wished none of this was happening, wished I could love David back, and that loving him would be right and true.

But I knew how this was meant to turn out. Walker would get the information he needed. The good guys would win. And David would hate me. And I hated that he'd hate me.

I sat down on the couch and tried not to listen to the noises coming out of Wendi's bedroom. They must have made short work of the bagels and had moved on to more interesting things. The phone rang and I snatched it up.

"Yeah?"

"Is Sylvia there?"

"Speaking."

"That's not funny. You can talk?"

"Pretty much," I said. Wendi and her date were unlikely to stop what they were doing any time soon.

"Why did you call?"

"Nasim is having a dinner party Friday. He asked David to invite me."

"Who else is going to be there?"

"I don't know."

"Did you ask?"

I hadn't but I hated his tone. "David wasn't sure," I lied. "Hey, I was thinking…shouldn't we be using some kind of code, you know, other than Sylvia."

"Why?"

"Shouldn't I say *the target* instead of Nasim? And maybe, like, *the target junior* if I'm talking about David? You know, in case someone's listening?"

And I might be falling in love with David, but I was definitely not falling in love with *the target junior*.

"No one's listening."

"How can you be sure?"

"Because you're a waiter. No one spies on waiters."

It was a humiliating thing to say to me and I was sure he meant it to be. Then he said, "Try and find out who's going to be at that dinner and call me back."

———

That afternoon it was cloudy and suddenly warm again, so Wendi and I took the Metro the one stop to work. It meant we walked five blocks instead of ten, but since it was also kind of humid it was worth it.

"So, who's the guy?" I asked, while we waited on the platform.

"His name is Lefty."

"Yeah, he told me that."

"He works at a not-for-profit trying to solve hunger. He's very deep into the Uganda famine," she said.

I, of course, had no idea there was a famine in Uganda. I also couldn't tell you exactly where Uganda was on a map. "Well, that's very noble of him."

"It is."

"It's funny too. David went out with a guy who did stuff in Africa."

"Africa is like three times as big as the United States. There's a lot to do there."

I shrugged, sure she was exaggerating how big Africa really was. "I didn't mean anything by it. Lefty's cute."

"Oh my God, he told me about this morning. I can't believe he stood there talking to you while he was naked."

"He looked like he was enjoying himself. Do you think he's an exhibitionist?"

"No, no, I don't think so. He said the look on your face was hysterical." She got a kick out of imagining the look on my face. "And that you were trying really hard not to look at his cock."

"Did he want me to look at it?"

"I just said he's not an exhibitionist. Did you want to look at it?" She asked, getting a little defensive.

"You do realize that when a naked man stands in front of you it's challenging not to look at his cock."

"Is it? I'll have to try it more often and get back to you."

It seemed like a good time to change the subject. "Where does he live?"

"At the Watergate, if you can believe that."

The train arrived and we got on. Our stop was the end of the line so it always seemed to wait there an extra-long time.

"Why didn't you go to his place?"

"He's got two roommates."

"You've got a roommate."

"Two roommates in a one bedroom. No privacy."

"Maybe that explains why he's so comfy walking around naked. Did you look at his wallet?"

"He didn't take a shower so there wasn't time."

"So, he might be lying. He might have a wife and kids in Maryland."

"No, he'd definitely take a shower if he did."

"What? Why do you think that?"

"You can't go home to wifey smelling like sex. Amazing sex, by the way."

"Be careful, Wendi."

"No. Absolutely not. For once, I'm not going to be careful. I don't want to be so careful I end up not having a life."

"Okay. Don't be careful."

"Thank you, that's wonderful advice."

Then the train pulled out and we were on our way.

———

"Are you staying over with David, tonight?" Wendi asked me, as we picked up our last orders of the evening.

"Yeah, he missed me last night," I said. Then I yelled out to the cook, "Ramon, this fish is burned."

"No, it's not!"

"Do you want me to get Maxim and let him decide?"

A surly Ramon came over and snatched the fish off the pick-up line.

"Good, I'm glad you're staying with David," she said. "Lefty is coming over and I kind of want the place to myself." She blushed a bit. Of course, it was no surprise. I'd caught her talking to him on the employee pay phone twice during our shift.

"Why is he called Lefty? Is he left-handed?"

"No. He comes from this very conservative family. It's their idea of a joke."

"He must think it's funny. I mean, he's having people call him that."

"He's very proud of his politics. And he should be. He's doing great work. Isn't it terrific that we have boyfriends at the same time?"

"Um, wait a minute, isn't tonight your second date?"

"Uh-huh," she said, shrugging. "Don't look at me like that. He's coming back so he's obviously not a one-night stand. And... he's coming back the next night. I think that means something."

"Yeah, but I wouldn't pick out a china pattern quite yet."

"Why can't you be on my side, Patrick? I'm rooting for you and the prince."

She was rooting for us? I wasn't always sure. Well, maybe she was now that she might have her own boyfriend.

Her order was completely assembled, so she lifted her tray over her shoulder and went back out to the dining room. I stayed there waiting for my fish. After it was ready and not burned this time, I delivered the orders to my table and checked my one other remaining party who wanted to dawdle over coffee and after-dinner drinks.

I went into the bar and found that it was empty. Pete leaned against a cooler looking up at the television. *Nightline* was already playing. Tom Brokaw was saying it was day 339 of the hostage crisis. Then he continued, "Tonight a Chinese freighter has been trapped in the middle of an ongoing battle in the Persian Gulf. Forty-nine sailors are without water, while Iraqi officials claim to have taken control of the Iranian port Khorramshahr. Meanwhile, there is little to report on negotiations to release the American hostages held in Tehran."

Pete was shaking his head.

"Three VSOPs," I said.

"Reagan will get the hostages out, you wait and see," Pete said, unbidden.

"So, they'll be stuck there until February or March?"

"Carter's a bungler. And I think the Iranians are smart enough to know that Reagan will bomb the shit out of them."

That was an uncomfortable thought. I didn't think bombing the shit out of them was good foreign policy. Pete, however, seemed to disagree. When he'd finished pouring the cognac, I picked up the snifters and was about to bring them out to my party when I stopped and asked, "You worked for the State Department, didn't you?"

He nodded. "Fifty-four through fifty-seven under John Foster Dulles. A great man. So was Eisenhower."

"But they threw you out, right?"

"Doesn't mean they weren't great men."

Confused by that, I went back out to the dining room and delivered the drinks Pete had made. Afterward, I went back to the employee lounge for a smoke. I was almost finished when Wendi came up and asked, "Do you think he's cute? I think he's amazingly cute."

"Lefty? Yes, he's cute," I said. Fortunately, he *was* cute even though I would have had to say so even if he weren't. I hoped this phase didn't last long. She was either on the phone talking to Lefty or off the phone talking about him. I wondered for a moment if she was talking to her tables about him.

"He told me all about the work he's doing in Africa. Bringing water to villages, distributing food, I mean, it's amazing."

"When does he go back?"

"Go back where?"

"To Africa."

"Oh, no, he's a stateside facilitator."

"A what?"

"He works with American companies to provide food and other materials to Uganda. And other countries. He's never even been to Africa."

"So, he sends them Cheerios?"

"Yes. Basically."

I thought Cheerios were about as close as you could come to eating cardboard without actually eating cardboard, so if it was a choice between Cheerios or starvation, I'd have to mull it over.

"Pat*rick*!" I heard Maxim screaming as he walked into the kitchen. I stubbed out my cigarette. I was sure I was going to get into trouble for taking too many breaks. But I only had two tables left and they didn't want me staring—

"Pat*rick*," Maxim said when he reached me. I was standing awkwardly next to the tiny café table "I have noticed that Mr. Barrett Copeland asks for you quite often. You know who I mean?"

"Yes, I know who you mean. He's been very kind to me."

"An unusual thing to say about a politician. Anyway, he has a reservation on Saturday. Do you think you can work on Saturday?"

That meant a lot of money; probably as much as I'd make all week. "Can I work on Saturday? Yes, of course," I said quickly before Maxim changed his mind. "Thank you."

"Good. I must warn you, though. In order to avoid a mutiny, I'll have to cut you first."

"You'll cut me first. I understand."

"Excellent."

And then Maxim walked away. Wendi looked at me and raised her eyebrows. In the little world of Le Marquis, I was rising.

The next morning I woke late. David was already up and gone. I didn't have much there, so I put my waiter clothes back on, grabbed my bow tie and cummerbund, and left the room. I went down the front stairs, unsure whether David was even in the house. Then I heard Nasim's voice coming from the dining room. I wasn't quite sure what he said, but the tone of his voice seemed serious. David answered him in a similar tone.

They were having breakfast. I was close enough now that I could hear their silverware clinking on their plates. Then I heard Nasim say, "I don't trust him."

My heart flipped over. Was he talking about me? Of course, he was, there was no one else—

"I don't trust him either," David replied. "I should tell him not to come here anymore."

I stood quietly outside of the dining room.

"No. You can't do that," Nasim said. "We need to try to figure out if he's up to something. And if so, what."

"He's not up to anything, Father. He's just a silly boy."

They *were* talking about me. I *was* a silly boy. They didn't know anything really, but they suspected. I decided I'd better step in and say good-bye so that I could leave. I needed to call Walker and ask him what to do about this.

I stood in the archway to the dining room. "Good morning. Sorry to interrupt, I just wanted to say good-bye."

"Oh, don't leave," David said. "I've been waiting to take you to breakfast."

I glanced down at the table and saw that there was nothing but a cup of coffee in front of him. It was his father who'd been clinking cutlery.

"That's okay. I have things—"

"No. I'm putting my foot down," David said with a big smile on his face. He got up and came around the table. "It'll take an hour. You'll still have time to do whatever you need to."

"I don't know."

"It'll take an hour."

My face was turning red even though it felt like my blood was running cold. "All right. An hour."

David said good-bye to his father and we left the house. Out on the sidewalk, I suggested the deli Wendi and I liked on Connecticut. "They have really good bagels."

"That sounds lovely," David said, and we turned toward Connecticut Avenue. "Father and I were just talking about tomorrow night's dinner. He wants it to be memorable. What do you think we should serve?"

"I don't know."

"Come on, Patrick, you work at a restaurant. You must know something about food."

"Something with a sauce. People like sauce. Or something wrapped in pastry. Saying something is en croute also makes people excited."

"I had a salmon wrapped in pastry with hollandaise once. I could suggest that."

"Uh-huh." I wasn't paying that much attention to what he was saying. I was wondering how long it might take me to eat a bagel with cream cheese. Ten minutes? Could I be on my way home in half an hour?

When we got situated in a booth with our toasted bagels, I asked, "The dinner is in two days. How are you going to find a caterer? I mean, there will be a lot of people, right?"

"We'll use the same company we used for the party. They always find room for us."

That didn't tell me anything about how many people would be there. I wondered if I should press it. Even if he knew I was spying on them, I didn't want to be obvious.

"Will there be people I know?"

He considered. "I think you'll know everyone."

That meant everyone there would have been at the first party. That was good. That was something I could tell Walker. I was about to start asking about specific names when David asked me, "You never talk about your family. Tell me about them."

I was a little taken aback. Why did he want to know about my family? He didn't trust me. He was on the verge of telling me to go away.

"Um, well, there's just me and my mom really."

"Are you close to your mom?"

"Not anymore."

"You had a falling out?"

"She wants me to go to college. Keeps sending me catalogs to places I couldn't get into and couldn't afford if I could."

"That's not a terrible thing for a parent to want."

"I had some trouble at school," I admitted. "I might not be able to get back in. Even a lousy school might not take me."

"Is there anything Father could do? He knows people."

I couldn't imagine why he was asking that. Was it just a way to get rid of me, packing me off to school?

I chewed my bagel for a minute and then, reluctantly, told him what had happened at school. The whole sordid story of giving my paper to a boy named Andrew and getting myself tossed out of school.

"But that wasn't your fault."

"It kind of was."

Suddenly, I realized something. I'd done something stupid chasing after a guy. And now I was doing stupid things chasing after another guy. If I didn't have a sort of crush on Agent Walker, would I be doing any of this? Maybe not. I mean, I told myself it was about patriotism, but, if I was being really honest, it was more about the way Walker kissed me. Right? Or was it about the way David kissed me? Had I just been using Walker as an excuse to get closer—

"Are you okay?" David asked. "Is this really upsetting you?"

"I'm fine. The bagel is giving me a stomach ache," I lied, pushing the half-eaten bagel away even though I really wanted the rest of it.

"I wish we could spend the whole day together."

"Tomorrow," I said, not meaning it.

"I don't want to wait that long."

"I have to go to work. I'm not a prince, remember?"

"Being a prince isn't as easy as you think."

"No. I guess it's not," I said. Walker was right. No one spied on a waiter. Which I guess is one of the nice things about being a waiter.

David finished his bagel, took another sip of his coffee, and we left the deli. We walked a half a block down Connecticut Avenue. He was quiet, seeming to be working up to something, but I didn't care. We were three blocks from my apartment. I would be home soon and on the phone to Publius. Walker would put an end to this. I was in too much danger.

"Come in here," David said, abruptly pulling me into a trendy men's shop.

"David, I don't have time. We could say good-bye here and then you can go shopping."

"I'm not shopping for me though. I'm shopping for you."

Since it was fall, there were thermal T-shirts in the window in a rainbow of colors, as well as a selection of matching jockstraps. David quickly picked out a pair of designer jeans and a boxy, aqua-colored rayon shirt. "Try these on."

"David."

"Please."

The dressing room was in the back of the store. I went back there, opened the door, and went in. Quickly, I slipped out of my waiter clothes, realizing as I did that they smelled of cigarette smoke and Caesar dressing. God, how could David stand being around me?

I pulled on the jeans. David had done a good job of picking out my size, the jeans fit really well. This shirt was big and loose, but I was pretty sure that was the look. Once I had everything on, I stepped out of the dressing room.

Glancing around the store, I found David at the checkout counter handing the telephone receiver back to the sales guy. He saw me and came over.

"That looks pretty good. Well, the jeans. I'm not as sure about the shirt."

"Who were you calling?"

He got a devilish look on his face. "I called Le Marquis. I told them you're too sick to come in to work today."

"They're never going to believe that. I'll lose my job."

David shrugged. "It's a job in a restaurant. You'll get another one." He squinted at me. "The shirt's wrong. Why don't we try one of the thermal ones? What's your favorite color?"

"David, I won't be able to get another job. Not if Le Marquis tells them I'm unreliable."

He was still moving toward the thermal shirts. "If you lose your job I'll have Father get you another. You'll probably end up better off."

"Le Marquis is one of the best restaurants in the city."

"There are others." Pointing to a rack he said, "I want to get you one of these jackets too. I think you'll look good in one."

The jackets were Members Only and, yes, I really wanted one. But I was still worried about my job. I wasn't so sure Nasim helping me get a job might not land me at a Persian restaurant in Maryland or someplace.

I ended up with the jeans, three thermal shirts—turquoise, navy and red—a gray Members Only jacket, and a pair of red high-tops. While I was happy about the clothes, I wasn't happy about being stuck all day with David like this. Unfortunately, I couldn't think of an excuse to go home since David had made me put on my new clothes before we left the store. Now, I didn't exactly have a reason to go home. I was trapped.

"So, what exactly are we going to do all day?" I asked when we got out to Connecticut Avenue again. "I mean, we just ate. We can't go to lunch."

"It doesn't matter what we do. We just need to do it together."

CHAPTER EIGHTEEN

Having just made love, David and I lay in his bed, naked, sweaty, sticky, legs wrapped together. We'd spent the day at the movies— we finally saw *Dressed to Kill* (which didn't do much to bring down my level of paranoia) and *Divine Madness*. Then when we got back to David's around dinnertime, Nasim wasn't there so we made sandwiches and ate in David's room.

"What are these?" he asked, pointing at the brownish marks on my hips.

"Waiter bruises. I bump into tables."

He kissed them.

"Are you going to let me go home tomorrow?"

"I don't know. Maybe, maybe not."

I tried to think of a way to contact Walker, but I didn't know how to get to a phone. The one in Nasim's office was out of the question. There was one in the kitchen, but there was usually someone in the kitchen, Samira or Cedric. There was a phone on the third floor, but I couldn't think of a reason to go up there without David.

"Wendi has a boyfriend," I told David.

"She does? That's great."

"His name is Lefty."

"Is that a common American name?"

"No. It's not at all common."

"Well, I hope she's very happy."

I bit my lip.

"You don't like him?" David asked.

"I don't know him. But I'm not sure I trust him." I wasn't exactly the person to be talking about trust, but...

"Why don't you trust him?"

"Well, for one thing I think he's too good-looking for her."

"That's a silly reason to be suspicious of someone."

"Not really. I don't know why he's with her."

"Did she sleep with him on the first date?"

"Yes."

"Perhaps that's why he is with her. She might be good in bed." David paused, then added, "Besides, I'm too good looking for you. I'm not holding that against you."

"You are *not* too good-looking for me," I said. "You're exactly the right amount of good-looking." Like so much of what I said, it was a lie. He probably *was* too good-looking for me, but I wasn't about to admit it.

"Do you miss not having a mother?" I asked.

"Do you miss not having a father?"

"Sorry, stupid question."

"It's hard to miss what you don't know," David admitted. "I don't remember having a mother. I mean, sometimes I think about what it might have been like, but I doubt it would have been as wonderful as I imagine."

"What kind of a woman was she?"

"She came from an excellent family. Expatriates, of course; but then, after she died my grandparents went back to Iran. I'm not sure if they're still alive. They were more religious than we are."

"And your mother? Was she religious?"

"More than my father, yes. I suspect if she'd lived I might be more like Ebrahim."

I groaned a little. "That's a terrible thing to say about your mother."

"Perhaps it is."

"Your father wants to be shah, doesn't he?"

"Yes, of course."

"Isn't that, I don't know, kind of selfish?"

"Not as selfish as it sounds. He *is* the rightful heir, after all. But my father favors a constitutional monarchy. He believes in democracy and he believes in a secular government. The fanatics who've taken control are no better than the usurper. In fact, they may be worse. The country was becoming Western in nature before the revolution. Now…well, now it has turned in a terrible direction."

I didn't have a response since I knew nothing about Iran and almost as little about kinds of governments. I mean, I believed in democracy, I just never bothered to vote. It never seemed to make a difference before. But now I think, well, maybe it does make a difference.

"Ebrahim will be at dinner. But don't worry, I'll make sure he's not seated near us."

"Can he eat in the kitchen?"

David chuckled. "If it were up to me, yes."

"I'm going to have to leave sometime, you know."

"Of course. I'm sorry if I've been selfish. I'm just not happy when you're not here."

I was sure it was a lie, of course, but it was a very nice one.

I woke early the next morning. The sky outside was gray and a sense of doom had settled over the house. Or perhaps just over me.

David was already up and gone. I climbed into the clothes he'd bought me, grabbed my crumpled up waiter's uniform and left the room. When I got downstairs things seemed quiet. I turned back toward Nasim's study. It was the perfect time to use the phone. If Nasim was in there, I could ask him to tell David I'd gone home for a little bit. And if he wasn't, but came back while I was on his phone, I could simply say I was calling my roommate.

I rapped on the door and then opened it. The study was empty. I hurried over to the phone and quickly dialed the number at Publius.

"This is Liberty." Okay, so maybe a code name wasn't a great idea. It wouldn't have been good to get caught saying something like that into the phone.

"Tell Walker to meet me at the circle at ten o'clock." The clock on Nasim's desk said it was almost nine thirty. I had plenty of time to get there.

I hung up.

Quietly, I left the study and walked toward the front of the house. The front door was right in front of me. I was about to walk out of it, when I heard Nasim's voice.

"Patrick, come sit with me. I'll have Samira make you some breakfast."

"Oh, I, um, actually need to run home."

"You can run home after breakfast."

"My roommate's expecting me."

Just then, the front door opened and David walked in, dressed in a matching jogging suit. A thin layer of sweat on his forehead.

"Davoud, tell your friend he should stay for breakfast."

"Oh yes, of course, and afterwards there are a few errands I need to run for the party."

"I promised Wendi I'd be home soon."

"She won't mind," David said. "Isn't she busy with her boyfriend?"

"I think they're having trouble already," I lied. "I think that's why she wants to see me."

"I'll go with you."

"Davoud, perhaps we are wrong to monopolize Patrick. Let him go be a friend to his roommate. If she needs him we should not stand in the way."

David looked from his father to me and then said, "Of course. I'm sorry."

"It's okay."

"We'll see you tonight, won't we Patrick?"

"Yes, sir. I mean, Nasim. You'll see me tonight."

I walked into Dupont Circle a little before ten and found our regular bench. The morning was cold and foggy. A jogger ran by me attached to one of those new Walkman things. I wanted one but knew they were about two hundred bucks, more than I made in a week, so I doubted I'd be getting one any time soon.

Of course, I also needed a watch. I was pretty sure it was after ten and Walker wasn't there, but I couldn't be sure. About ten minutes later, when Walker finally showed up, I was absolutely certain.

"You're late. Were you followed?"

"No. I had to run an errand."

I took my pack of Salem's out of my pocket, shook one out for Walker and one for me. I lit them.

"I think you only like me for my nicotine," I joked.

"Who said I like you?"

I could tell he was teasing, but I still didn't like his joke. I said, "Ouch."

"It's not a good idea to like your assets too much. They come and go."

"Except I'm not just an asset."

He looked me in the eye and admitted, "No. You're not."

"What kind of errand?" I asked.

"What?"

"You said you had to run an errand. Did your kids miss the bus so you had to drive them to school?"

"What makes you think I have children? I've never told you that."

Now it was my turn to tease him. "You're the kind of closet case who does everything that's expected. It's expected that you'd have a wife and two-point-three children living in the suburbs. So I bet you do."

"Tease me all you want. I don't mind." The tone in his voice said the opposite. Then he asked, "Why did you want to see me?"

"I overheard Nasim and David talking. They don't trust me. They're only keeping me around so they can figure out who I'm working for. I don't think I should go back."

"We're almost done, Patrick. I just need you to go back tonight, and then you're done."

"Why? Why do I have to go back?"

"The crown prince is going to Paris on Monday. He has an important meeting on Tuesday. After that, he won't be coming back to America. That's why he's having the dinner. It's a good-bye party."

"Oh. David didn't say. But why do *I* have to be there?"

"The crown prince cannot get to Paris. You have to stop him."

"Me? I can't—"

He took something from his jacket pocket and put it on the bench between us. It was a white powder in a glassine envelope.

"What is that?"

"I want you to put this into the crown prince's tea when it's left at his door tonight. Be careful not to touch the powder or inhale it."

"It's poison?"

"Yes. I'm not sure what kind it is. We have people who understand these things," he said. "I picked it up on my way here. That's why I was late. The death will look like a heart attack. No one will suspect you."

"No, I can't do that," I said. "You didn't tell me I'd have to kill someone. You said I'd just have to give you information. I won't. I can't."

"Patrick, it's been three hundred and forty days. Nearly a year. Fifty-two Americans trapped, God knows what's being done to them. You can help bring this to an end. You can stop his interference. You can bring them home."

"No," I said again, but my voice was weaker. What would happen if I didn't do this? Would people be hurt? Would they die?

"Pick it up, Patrick. It looks like we're making a drug deal with it just sitting there. We don't want some overzealous police officer to see it."

Numbly, I picked up the poison and slipped it into my shirt pocket with my cigarettes. I watched Walker, waiting for him to tell me what to do next.

"Do it tonight. Nasim el-din Qatar cannot go to France. We have to stop him."

"Tonight? He's not going until Monday."

"We don't want to take any chances."

I didn't say anything. He put a hand high up on my thigh and rubbed. "When he's dead this will be over. And we can be together."

I looked deep into his eyes; he held them very still. He was offering me sex if I killed a man. More than sex maybe. A life together? Was that a bargain I wanted to make? Or was it a bargain I'd already made?

"Couldn't I just give him enough to make him sick? Sick enough that he couldn't go?"

"Meetings can be rescheduled. You know that."

"I'm not sure I'm invited to stay over tonight." That was a lie. I knew I was. David expected me to—

"Find a way to get invited. You're good at that."

"All right," I said, barely audible. I felt deflated, as though I'd never be fully whole again.

"Can you do this, Patrick? Can you do it for your country? Can you do it for me?"

CHAPTER NINETEEN

Kill a man. I was going to kill a man. I had the means to do it in my pocket. If I killed him, the hostages would get released. *When I killed him*. When I killed him, I'd be stopping people working against my government. That was good, right?

But, why me? Why not someone else? Nasim didn't even seem that bad. Yes, he was going to Paris to do something terrible. Couldn't they just stop him? Throw him in jail for a while? Why did he have to die? And David. I liked David. Or maybe loved him. I don't know. It was all getting so confusing.

Later that afternoon, I returned to the house just as the caterers arrived: Three men in their thirties wearing white shirts, black slacks and red bolero-style jackets. They parked a van nearby and carried all the food, much of it already prepared, into the house. They must have all been gay because when I walked by one of them made chicken noises and winked at me. I blushed. Chicken was slang for a cute, young, gay guy. I hurried inside.

Samira seemed particularly aggrieved by the caterers' presence. She went into a loud tirade and would not be silenced until Nasim came out of his office to say a few harsh words to her. That was the only time I saw him, though. He and David spent much of the afternoon in the office.

At loose ends, I went up to the third floor. Most of the floor was a large room that had once been a nursery, back in the days when people kept their children at home to be educated—and had a lot of them. Now, it had a long, comfortable sofa and a large console television with a Betamax sitting on top. I spent part of that afternoon curled up on a lumpy sofa watching *Moonraker*. The irony of watching a spy movie on my very last day of being a spy was not lost on me.

I must have fallen asleep, because David woke me up saying, "It's time to get ready."

We went downstairs, took showers, and then, in our underwear, stood in front of his closet as he flipped through his wardrobe choosing our outfits for dinner.

"We'll start with something basic for you," he said, pulling a crisp, laundered white shirt off a hanger. Handing me the shirt he added, "Put this on." I did as I was told. Meanwhile, he flipped through some more hangers. "Your Calvin's will be fine. Do they need to be pressed?"

"I think they're okay."

"Yousef can press them." I couldn't remember which one was Yousef, certainly not the British butler whose name I'd finally settled on, Cedric. I hoped David wouldn't make me ask this mysterious servant for help.

"Ah, yes, this," he said, and then pulled out a dark gray sweater vest out of his closet. He frowned. "This shouldn't be on a hanger."

He took it off the hanger and held it up to me. I hadn't buttoned the shirt so I could feel the incredibly soft sweater teasing my chest.

"Is that formal enough?"

"Father will be wearing a dinner jacket, but he doesn't expect anyone else to."

I took the sweater from him and he went back to nosing around his closet. I glanced at the sweater's label. "This is cashmere."

"Of course it is," he said, seeming to think it odd that I noticed.

"I've never...I've never worn a cashmere sweater."

"Really? Oh, well, keep it then."

"No, it's yours."

"You'll let me borrow it, won't you?"

"Of course," I mumbled, knowing the end was close. Lying was more and more tedious. "What are you wearing?"

"I have a black tuxedo shirt I like. It sounds more formal than it is. And a pair of tuxedo pants with the satin stripe down the side."

"Okay." If we weren't dressed appropriately, at least we'd look like we belonged together. Kind of.

David took the sweater away from me and threw it on the bed. Then he slipped his hand into my shirt and caressed my chest. "You're so beautiful," he whispered.

"Stop it. You're better looking than I am."

"No, I think you are the beautiful one. But it's good that we think that way, isn't it? We each feel like we're getting a prize."

My stomach tied itself in a knot. Why did he have to say things like that? I mean, it really seemed he was in love with me. But he couldn't be. He was just keeping me around to find out who I was working for, but—he barely seemed to be trying. He wasn't asking me anything. How did he expect to find anything out when all he did was say lovely, poetic things to me.

There wasn't a thing I could say, so I pressed myself up against him and kissed him. I whispered, "I love you, David," into his ear and he squeezed me so tight I could barely breathe.

"Stop. You'll wrinkle the shirt." Though as soon as I said that I remembered it would be underneath a sweater.

"Take it off then," he said, but he didn't wait for me to take it off, he slipped it over my shoulders and threw it onto the bed on top of the sweater. Then he kissed me again.

We hadn't been together long, but I was beginning to recognize the meaning of each kiss. He kissed me hello and goodbye, I knew those kisses. They were easy. There was a 'we have to hurry' kiss, which was a kiss that wanted more when there was no time. And an 'I want you' kiss, a kiss that was a beginning. That was how he kissed me then, with an 'I want you.' Pliable, warm lips pressing against mine, promising so much more.

Pushing me back onto the bed, he swept away the sweater and shirt I was going to wear in just over an hour. It didn't matter. Someone would come and press them, make them nice. For now, all we needed was each other.

We wriggled out of our underwear and then he was on top of me, like he always was, kissing me, letting his hands roam over my body. I wrapped my legs around him, pulling him in closer. Feeling him on me, waiting, and then he flipped us over and I was above him.

"What are you doing?"

He shook his head. "No. I want this."

"You—really?"

"I trust you, Patrick," he said.

I pushed away the foolishness of his saying he trusted me. He shouldn't trust me. I wasn't worth trusting. And, he didn't trust me. I knew that. But still, I took him. The way he wanted, the way he trusted me to. I took him.

Afterward, sweaty and tired, I said, "David, your father said something this morning."

"What did he say?"

"He said he was glad I was coming to dinner because there might not be another chance. He said things may change quickly."

"He's going back to London."

"Oh. And you would go with him?"

"I might. Or I might stay here. It depends."

"It depends on what?"

"It depends on whether you want to go to England."

"Me? I don't even have a passport."

"That's easy enough to arrange. We'll call the embassy."

"Um, I think normal people go to the post office."

"Well, we can do that if you insist. It would take much longer."

"I don't know what I'd do in England."

"We'll get you a work permit."

"So I can work in a restaurant?"

"We can find you something better than that. You like to read. Maybe a job with a publisher?"

"What will you do?"

"Believe it or not, prince is actually a job. More is expected of me in Europe simply because there is more royalty there. Which means there are more invitations."

"Your job will be going to parties?"

"Your job will be reading books?"

I rolled over. It was a lovely fantasy, running off to England and working for a publisher and, presumably, joining David at parties and dinners. Living happily ever after in a way that wasn't going to happen for us. Whether he was going to London or not, I was leaving him.

And I was doing it soon.

CHAPTER TWENTY

Guests began arriving around seven. David and I had been down-stairs for only a few minutes. Our clothes were pressed, our hair blown dry and styled, and we smelled, probably not too subtly, of the same lemony-cologne. Smiles were stuck onto our faces like masks at a costume party. Just as David had predicted, Nasim wore a white dinner jacket and looked like a cross between Cary Grant and a Middle Eastern sovereign—which I guess he was.

Fred, Ebrahim and Shadi were the first to arrive. Fred wore a three-piece gray suit, while Ebrahim and Shadi were both dressed in what I assumed was traditional clothing. She wore a brown hijab and a heavy black dress that covered her to the floor, while Ebrahim wore what looked like a white nightshirt with an embroidered collar.

One of the cater waiters appeared almost immediately, offering us each a flute of champagne—which I was beginning to think was the national beverage of Persia. After serving the drinks, the waiter was back almost immediately with a tray of mushroom-filled pastries. They were delicious and conversation revolved around them even though Ebrahim and Shadi had both declined the champagne and the appetizers.

A tall woman named Vivian, who'd been at the previous party, arrived alone. She had dusty brown hair and kind blue eyes. Her hair had been shellacked into the shape of a Roman helmet, very round with a curl along her jaw. The only thing I remembered about her was that she'd talked with another woman about Steve McQueen having cancer. I didn't understand why she was there again. And when David introduced us it didn't get any clearer.

"Vivian Townsend, this is my friend Patrick," he said.

"It's a pleasure to meet you," she said. "I remember seeing you at the last party, but we didn't actually meet."

"Vivian, would you like a glass of champagne?" David asked.

"Oh yes, that would be lovely."

"I'll be back in a moment," he said and then walked away.

"Did you enjoy the party?" I asked.

"Oh, very much," she said.

I didn't know what to say after that. I felt like I should say something, my relationship with David made me a sub-host of sorts. After an awkward pause, I asked, "Have you lived in Washington long?"

"Yes, I'm afraid I have. It's turned me into something of a political creature."

"Is that how you know Nasim? Through politics?"

"Sort of. We met at a fund-raising dinner."

"For?"

"Oh my, I'm not sure I remember. It may have had to do with women's rights in the Middle East or perhaps it was for Senator Packwood. I don't know."

"And you became friends," I asked.

"Yes, of course, who wouldn't become friends with Nasim? He's so charming. Just as charming as his son," she added with a wink.

And then David was back with her champagne and a fresh glass for himself. They briefly talked about some people they knew in common. Gus arrived a bit later with a tall, elegant woman of about forty. She had straight black hair and was dressed in an elegant Western-style, and yet it was somehow obvious she was from the Middle East. She was introduced as Miriam.

Conversations swirled around us. They all seemed to center on current events. Something that was true everywhere I went in Washington. Everything was about politics all the time. In Boston, people talked about music and movies and television. Or at least that was my impression. It might have been that the general age of the people I talked to in Boston was thirty years younger.

Miriam said, "I suppose you saw in the papers that Khadafy has thrown his support behind Khomeini."

"Yes. Of course, completely expected. People like Khadafy think war is a kind of party and they hate not being invited."

Then behind me, I thought I heard something that sounded like "…Publius maybe…old tricks…"

I turned and scanned the room. It had been a man's voice, but whose? The room was getting loud. It could have been Fred or Gus or even Ebrahim. I drifted closer to their group to better hear what they were talking about.

"They're sending rockets now. Hundreds are dead. Hundreds more injured," Fred was saying. "There must be a ceasefire, if only to give us time to regroup."

"But Father, we need allies," Ebrahim said. "The Soviets are sending arms to Iraq."

"Not true," said Gus. "The Soviets are arming both sides."

"Of course, the Americans would be too if they could only get their hostages back."

"It's the Khomeini's doing," Gus said. "He has too much power. He'll bring the country down."

"You shouldn't say things like that about the Imam Khomeini. It's a blasphemy," Ebrahim said.

David came along, carrying more champagne, and pulled me away, whispering into my ear as he did. "Try to stay on the other side of the room, away from Ebrahim. Nima is worried about him. He's getting more and more fanatical. I don't want him saying anything to you."

He led me across the room to another small group made up of Nasim, Vivian and Miriam. Had Nasim made the remark about Publius? Wouldn't I have recognized his voice? And if he had, who had he been talking to? David?

Something began to distract me. It was the way Vivian and Nasim were standing next to each other, slightly too close, making me realize something I'd missed at the previous party. They were together. I wasn't the only one in the room who'd been regularly kissing royalty.

"We saw that Gertrude Stein play at the Kreeger," Vivian was saying to Miriam.

"Who's in that?"

"Pat Carroll. You've seen her on television."

"How was it?"

"Oh, it was wonderful. It's remarkable that one lone woman

can talk for that long and remain interesting," Vivian said. "Oh, that reminds me. Nasim, I have opening night tickets for *Sweeney Todd* on the twenty-fourth. You're coming with me."

"We'll talk about it later, Vivian."

Clearly, she didn't know that Nasim was returning to London. The look on her face changed slightly. She'd realized something was happening that she didn't know about.

"David, be careful of the champagne, you're going to have quite the head in the morning."

And she was right. He'd been drinking more than usual. Was he nervous? Was there more going on than I understood?

One of the cater waiters came in and subtly said a few words to Nasim. Then he turned to face the room and said, "Ladies and gentlemen, it's time to go in to dinner."

We trickled into the dining room in dribs and drabs. Nasim sat at the head of the table with Vivian on his left and David on his right. I sat next to David. Miriam was next to Vivian with Gus on her left. Fred was at the foot of the table, opposite Nasim. That left two seats next to me for Ebrahim and Shadi. Even though Shadi was directly next to me, I was still much closer to Ebrahim than I wanted to be.

Dinner was French. We had a chilled vichyssoise, and a salad with vinaigrette and brie cheese. The entrée was a delicious coq au vin over rice and dessert was a fruit tart. And, of course, several kinds of wine.

Ebrahim mumbled after each course was served. It was obvious he preferred the meal be Persian. It was a strange idea to me. I'd grown up loving Italian food, spaghetti and lasagna, my mother made one or the other every week. We were hardly Italian, but it never felt unpatriotic.

Vivian told a story about meeting Rosalynn Carter. "I thought that country bumpkin routine was just an act, but it's real. She has absolutely no guile. Neither does her husband, for that matter. It's surprising that they've gotten as far as they have."

"Have you met Mrs. Reagan?" Miriam asked.

"I have met Nancy. The opposite of Rosalind Carter in every way. It's like comparing one of the Borgias to Shirley Temple."

The conversation meandered along. Mostly about the recent weather—warmer than anyone liked—and the smog in Los

Angeles—which was apparently terrible, leaving us all relieved we didn't have any reason to go there.

During a lull, David abruptly—and perhaps a bit drunkenly—said, "Patrick is a direct descendent of Patrick Henry."

"Who is Patrick Henry?" Gus asked.

"An American patriot," David explained. I sat there silently. There was something mortifying about this. "He was the first governor of Virginia."

"Why is that important?" Fred asked. "I thought Virginia was a minor state."

"He was a great ora—ora—" David stopped, cleared his throat and tried again. "Orator and a founding father of this country. He helped get the Bill of Rights added to the Constitution."

"What is the thing you like most about America, Patrick?" Nasim asked.

I was tempted to give a silly answer like *American Bandstand* or Chevrolet. Instead, I sat back and thought. What was the most truthful thing I could say? Democracy? Representative government?

"Inalienable rights," I replied, recalling the term from a civics class.

Nasim glanced at me curiously for a moment and said, "How interesting."

"Isn't that the same thing as freedom?" Ebrahim asked.

"Kind of. Except it means freedom for everyone no matter what. Everyone has the right to be free. It's basic and can't be taken away," I explained.

"Be careful my friend," Nasim said. "Freedom always favors the rich and the powerful; as does tyranny. That is the problem with the world. Well, one of the *many* problems of the world,"

"You think your country is so very different from ours," Ebrahim said bitterly. "But it's not. At home, the right people must be paid and flattered. And here, the right people must be flattered and paid. You see, it is really the same. We just don't pretend to be better than we are."

"Ebrahim, if you can't be polite to our guest you'll have to leave," Nasim said. It was more Ebrahim's tone that was offensive than what he'd said. I really wasn't *that* innocent of the world I lived in. Or at least, didn't think I was.

Fred leaned over and said something into Ebrahim's ear.

Ebrahim flushed, pursed his lips and then raised his chin. To me, he said, "I'm sorry if my passion for our country offended you."

I doubted that was the kind of apology Nasim was looking for, but I figured I should accept it anyway.

"I understand," I said. "It's hard to live somewhere that doesn't feel like home."

"Especially when your home is a fantasy because you've never lived there," David added.

I could practically see Ebrahim biting his tongue. There was no way he'd insult David, even though he looked sorely tempted.

Nasim stood up and said, "Our dinner tonight was French, which was not simply a question of taste, though I'm sure you'll all agree that it was delicious. No, I wanted to let you know I'll be leaving for Paris on Sunday on business."

"How long will you be gone?" Vivian asked quickly.

"I'm not entirely sure. It depends on whether my business is successful."

Of course, I knew that the meetings had something to do with keeping the hostages where they were for a few more weeks. I wondered if it would be safe for him to come back to the U.S. if he was successful.

"In fact, I may not return right away. It may be time for us to return to London."

Vivian let out a little squeak. She'd clearly had no idea this was coming. I'm not sure, but I think her eyes began to water.

"I'm sorry if this comes as a surprise to any of you," Nasim said without looking directly at her.

Abruptly, Fred stood up too. "Excuse me, I must too make an announcement. I am sorry, Nasim, to steal your, what is the word—?"

"Thunder," Ebrahim said, eyes lowered.

"Ah, thunder, yes. You will forgive me, but my beloved son, Ebrahim, is engaged to his lovely Shadi." He raised his wine glass and said, "Salam ati."

Ebrahim was blushing, while Shadi could do nothing but stare at the table. I wondered if she understood what she was doing, marrying a man who had little real interest in her. I glanced at David and he didn't seem happy.

"If you'll excuse us, Fred and I must prepare for my meetings next week," he said. He and Fred stood up from the table, Gus followed them. The three of them walked out into the foyer going down to Nasim's study.

Vivian looked to be in shock. I had the feeling Nasim had just broken up with her. That the idea of her accompanying him to London was out of the question for one reason or another. I couldn't look at poor Shadi for fear the pity I felt for her would be too obvious.

"If everyone would go into the front parlor I'll ask for coffee to be served," David said.

"I'm sorry," Vivian said, seeming to rally. "I must dash. I promised a sick friend I'd stop and check on her as soon as we were finished."

"Yes, yes, of course," David said. "I'll tell Father. He'll be very sorry."

"Thank you." She came forward suddenly and kissed David on the cheek, saying under her breath, "Charming boy."

Miriam walked with Vivian to the door, while Ebrahim and Shadi had already headed to the parlor. David and I were suddenly alone.

In a low, sloppy voice he said, "When Faroukh announced Ebrahim's engagement, looking at poor Shadi, I knew that I could never do that to a woman. To take her whole life from her and offer so little in return. It is simply unkind."

He looked down, almost as though he'd been shamed and said, "You were right to break up with me, Patrick. I've learned a lot about myself this fall and it's all because of you. I don't know what I would do without you."

I didn't know what to say. Was this real? No, it couldn't be. It was an act for my benefit. He couldn't possibly mean it. Not after the things he and his father said.

"I think we can slip away now." There were still people to have coffee with and eventually walk to the door, but none of that seemed to matter to David. "I want to be alone with my lover."

He pulled me up the stairs to the second floor. As we entered his room, I noticed that the cookies and tea were already waiting for Nasim. That was my opportunity. The hairs on the back of my neck stood up. Would I really kill a man tonight?

David had pulled me into his room and was kissing me. He tasted sweet, overly sweet. The alcohol giving his breath an undertone of rot. I pulled away.

"You're drunk."

"I know."

"I'm going to get ready for bed," I said.

"I'm ready for bed," he said, guiding my hand to his crotch.

I kissed him quickly and said, "Not tonight. I'm feeling a little queasy."

I pushed away from him and began to pull my clothes off. The poison was still in the shirt I'd worn there. Right where it had been since Walker gave it to me. I'd hung the shirt in the closet earlier, not wanting a servant to come by and launder it.

Now, I went to the closet and got a hanger. I was going to hang up the sweater I'd worn and snag the poison while I was in there, but David said, "What are you doing?"

"I'm hanging up the sweater you gave me."

"We don't hang sweaters. We fold them and put them in a drawer."

I turned around and looked at David. He'd flopped on the bed and was trying to look sexy. Actually, he was succeeding. I leaned out of the closet against the door jamb and said, "You mean, even if I want to hang up the sweater I can't?"

Even as I said it, I was reaching behind me, my fingers slipping into the pocket of my shirt, reaching for the poison.

"The sweater is cashmere. It will stretch."

I got hold of the packet and casually brought my hand down and slipped it into the pocket of my Calvin's. I took the sweater off the bed and folded it. Then I put it on top of David's dresser.

"I have to use the bathroom," I said.

"Don't be too long."

"I won't be."

I smiled at him and then slipped out of the room. Closing the door behind me, I stood there looking at the tray of tea and cookies on the floor. I hadn't thought about it before, but his tea must be cold. I wondered if he liked it that way. I didn't think I would. I'd want nice hot tea with my cookies. I pushed the thought from my mind, reminding myself I had to act quickly. Slipping a hand into my pocket, I took out the glassine envelope, opened it and bent over—

And then I couldn't do it. Just couldn't. I couldn't kill another person even if other people's lives hung in the balance. I couldn't make that trade. I closed the glassine envelope, slipped it back into my pocket and went to brush my teeth. When I came back from the bathroom, David had fallen asleep and was already snoring. I curled around him and wondered what I was going to do.

Agent Walker was going to be angry, I knew that. But could he do something to me? No, I'd just tell him a lie. I'd tell him that the tea and cookies weren't there, that Nasim had already taken them into his room. That there was nothing for me to poison. Walker would have to let me off the hook. He'd have to find another way to stop Nasim from getting on the flight to Paris. One that didn't involve me.

THE WASHINGTON FINANCIAL JOURNAL

Friday, October 10, 1980
Economic Forecast

While the economy has recovered from the recession of early 1980, it is a weak recovery. Unease due to the presidential election and the situation in the Middle East continue to negatively affect markets, keeping gains in check.

Looking forward, if President Carter wins re-election expect the markets to remain ambivalent. Carter's challenging relationship with oil-producing countries, as well as the current Iraq-Iran War, will continue to provide uncertainty regarding energy supplies.

Should Ronald Reagan secure the White House, expectations on Wall Street suggest a possible boon. Should Reagan implement the tax proposals included in his platform, markets are expected to respond enthusiastically. However, should Reagan be unable to right the course of Middle East policy and establish a secure and reliable supply of energy, then periods of instability and uncertainty will continue.

Opportunities abound for investors willing to place bets on the ups and downs of world events.

CHAPTER TWENTY-ONE

"I shouldn't tell you this, but father is helping the Carter administration to get the hostages released. He's acting as a liaison to factions within Iran who have influence over the ayatollah. That's why he's going to Paris."

I stopped breathing. We were in the dining room having breakfast. David was terribly hungover, his voice deep and raspy.

"What? No, that's not— " I said before I could stop myself.

"That's not what?"

"I mean, that's great."

I was screaming inside. I'd very nearly killed Nasim. Nasim who was trying to get the hostages released. Agent Walker had lied to me. But that didn't make sense. Why would the CIA lie about this? Did they want Reagan to win? Was the CIA engineering some kind of coup? I had the vague feeling I'd read somewhere that George Bush, the guy running with Reagan, had been involved with the CIA somehow. Was that true? Was there a connection?

Or was it David who was lying to me? Was this simply a move in the game?

"What about the weapons?" I asked, impulsively.

David looked at me oddly. "How do you know about that?"

"I overheard Gus and Fred talking." Well, Wendi had.

"Technically, that's a separate thing. No one at the White House knows about it. But it's part of how father is applying influence."

Was that the truth? Was that what was really happening? I was so confused. It was entirely possible David was lying to me. That Nasim was doing just what Walker said he was doing. Things would look the same whether they were trying to keep the hostages in or get them out. I needed to get out of the Qajar's house. I needed to figure things out.

"You should go back to bed," I told David.

"I look that bad?"

"You kind of do."

Ten minutes later, we'd said our goodbyes and I was on the street heading for the Metro. As I waited for the train, I tried to put things together. Nasim and Fred were definitely trying to get arms for Iraq. That part was true. But who was lying to me? Was it David who was lying? Or was it Walker? I had to find out.

I got on the train and took it down to K Street. I had to see Walker and I didn't want him to know I was coming, didn't want to call him to meet me in the park. I wanted him unprepared. Off center.

The address of his office on K Street was easy enough to remember, 1313. And it was right around the corner from the Metro stop, right across the street from Farragut Square. Except it wasn't.

There wasn't any building on K Street with the address 1313. There was nothing there but a wide, hard-edged building from the 1950s: 1325. It took up most of the block. The buildings went 1307, 1325 and 1329. There was no 1313.

I turned on my heel and walked five blocks south. *What was going on?* The phone number for the Publius Society worked, so why didn't the address? Was this how the CIA normally operated?

When I got to the Munsey Trust Building I went directly to the ninth floor. Things in the 9400 suite looked pretty much the same. If anything the office was busier. I went directly to the office where I'd met with Walker. Empty. I turned around and spoke to the first person I saw, a dour looking man of about fifty.

"Do you know Gary Walker? He was working in this office the other day. Good-looking. Blond."

"Yeah."

"Do you know when he'll be in?"

"Well—" He shook his head. "He doesn't exactly work here. I think he was an auditor or something. I don't think he's coming back."

"What company is this?"

"Turnbull and Franks."

"And, what do you—"

"Polling. Most of this year we've been doing internal polling for the Carter/Mondale campaign."

"So—like Gallup?"

"Not exactly. Our polls are confidential and only used by the campaign. So, who are you?"

"Gary Walker—I had a meeting with him. We're—" I couldn't bring myself to say he was a friend of mine. "We're associates."

"So you're an auditor too? Why does the campaign keep sending—"

"Thanks. You've been really helpful."

I walked out of the office and then out of the building. Walker was there to steal the confidential polling for the Carter campaign. *So why had he had me meet him there?* He'd said he had other assignments. Had he wanted me to know that? Why would he—because it made him look more like a CIA agent. Which I was beginning to think he wasn't.

I went home, woke Wendl up, and I told her everything. When I was done, she said, "Yeah, there's no way he's a CIA agent. For one thing, they don't exactly tell you."

"Never?" I was beginning to feel really stupid.

"It kind of defeats the purpose."

"So if someone tells you they're a spy?"

"They're probably not."

"So, what is he?"

"He might be a spy, just not for the CIA. What did you say was on the business card?"

I jumped up off the sofa and ran into the bedroom. I came back a moment later holding my copy of *The Persian Boy*. Sitting back down, I opened it up and took out the card Agent Walker gave me. I'd been using it as a bookmark.

"When he gave this to me, he said it was his cover," I said, handing her the business card.

"The Publius Society?" she asked, as she read the card.

"He said it was a nonprofit and a lot of agents pretend to work there."

"I feel like I've heard of it somewhere."

She got up and grabbed the phone, then sat back down on the sofa with it on her lap. She dialed a number from memory.

"Who are you calling?"

"Someone who can help us figure this out."

———

The Old Ebbitt Omelet Room was an old-fashioned saloon about a block from the White House. A narrow storefront, it had a long bar, a collection of beer steins and wooden stools on one side, on the other rows of small tables crammed up against the wall and covered with gingham tablecloths. The ceilings were beamed and the walls covered with a menagerie of stuffed animal heads.

Even though it was a Saturday, the restaurant was packed when we got there just after one o'clock. We squeezed down the narrow aisle between the bar and the tables until we reached a table where an earnest looking man of about thirty was standing up to greet us. He wasn't especially tall, already balding and had skin so pale that it managed to look chapped though the weather was still in the mid-sixties.

Before we even said hello, he started, "Did you see? The teamsters endorsed Reagan. It's insane. What are they thinking?"

"It's not smart, that's for sure," Wendi said. "Glen, this is my roommate, Patrick."

"Nice to meet you," he put out his hand. I shook it. It was dry and a bit dusty. "Wendi says you're related to Patrick Henry."

"I am," I replied.

"That's *fucking* amazing."

"Not really. There are—"

Wendi kicked me and said, "We should all sit down." Then to me she said, "Glen is a researcher for the Carter campaign. I did some work with him looking into Reagan's time as governor of California."

"Do you remember that he actually sent the National Guard to occupy Berkley?" he asked. His intensity level was about twelve on a scale of ten.

I shrugged.

"Yeah, like, no one does. Even though they wounded hundreds of students. Seriously, he should be in prison, not running for president."

Wendi smiled at me. "Glen, we need to talk—"

A waiter of about fifty came over and asked if we wanted something from the bar. We all ordered draft beers. It was that kind of place. He didn't walk away, though. Instead, he asked, "So, what are you having?"

I was going to say that we hadn't even looked at the menu, but Glen went ahead and ordered a bowl of chili. Wendi said she'd have the Reuben. I hadn't asked, but I suspected she'd been there before. Possibly with Glen.

"Um, sure, I'll have the Reuben, too," I said. And then our waiter ran off to the kitchen.

Wendi started again. "Glen, can you tell us everything you know about The Publius Society?"

Glen sat back and stared at us for a minute. "Don't you know your American history, Mr. Henry?"

"Actually, it's Burke. Patrick Henry Burke. And yes, I know my American history. The Pilgrims came to America to establish religious freedom and make friends with the Indians."

"I hope you're joking. Neither of those things are true"

"Oh sure, I'm joking," I said, though I did remember being taught those things.

"Does this have something to do with Patrick Henry?" Wendi asked.

"Not directly. *The Federalist Papers*, written by John Jay, John Madison and Alexander Hamilton, were originally published under the pseudonym Publius. Patrick Henry was anti-federalist."

"But I thought he was a great patriot. My mother—"

"He *was* a great patriot. His opposition to the Constitution and the opposition of many others resulted in the Bill of Rights."

"What does that have to do with The Publius Society?" Wendi asked.

"Not very much, really. Publius is a shadowy bunch who've wrapped themselves in the language of patriotism. That's all."

"So what is it? What is it *exactly*?" Wendi wanted to know.

The waiter came by with the beers and set them down in front of us. We thanked him and waited for him to walk away. Glen took a moment to collect his thoughts, then began, "As far as anyone knows, The Publius Society is a group of lawyers. They call themselves conservatives, but they're not that exactly. They call themselves originalists and claim to believe in the original meaning of the Constitution but they don't actually believe in the Constitution at all. In reality, the only thing they believe in is taking away everyone's rights but their own. They believe in a strong ruling class."

"In other words, a bunch of old white men," Wendi said.

"Yes, which is what our government originally was so that part they've got right. Look, they're not like John Birchers; they don't come out and say what they're really doing. They're more behind-the-scenes, orchestrating things. Bad things."

"But, don't we have checks and balances to prevent—" I started.

"It's about the judiciary," he said. "They seek to control the White House so they can control the hundreds of judicial appointments the president gets to make. If they pack the courts with super right-wing judges, then the only real checks will be on liberal administrations."

"I see," I said. "So, they support Reagan?"

"Of course. But he's only the beginning. They intend to destroy the country by turning its own institutions against it."

"That seems extreme, Glen," Wendi said. "They can't really—"

"No, it's not extreme," I interjected. Too late, I realized she may have said that to downplay the whole thing. But I couldn't play that part.

"So, why do you want to know about The Publius Society?" Glen asked.

Wendi glanced at me and quickly I thought up a lie. "I got offered a job with them, filing, answering phones. It doesn't sound like the kind of place I'd like to work."

"If you don't want to tell me, just say so."

"It's the truth. It is," I lied. Poorly.

"First of all, they wouldn't hire liberals and they wouldn't hire gays. More importantly, they don't have an office for you to answer phones in."

I didn't worry too much about how he knew I was gay. Wendi might have told him—or she might not have needed to. It didn't matter; or at least it didn't matter much. I had bigger problems than whether people could tell I was gay.

And then our lunches arrived. Somehow, we ate. My head was full of everything that had been said. I barely tasted my sandwich. I knew that it was good, delicious in fact. But I was so distracted it was like chewing cotton.

Wendi and Glen had a depressing conversation about the campaign. The polls for Carter weren't great. He looked better in some states than others and there was the possibility he could catch up but not with the hostages still in Tehran. Honestly, I hadn't thought about it much, but now I really wanted him to win. Maybe he wasn't the greatest president we'd ever had, but he was so much better than the people trying to replace him.

We finished our lunches and our empty plates were whisked away.

"Iran is at war. Why doesn't Carter just trade them arms for the hostages?" Wendi suggested—of course I'd told her what Nasim was doing. "The Iraqi's will be pissed, but who cares."

"He can't give arms to our enemies. Not in the middle of an election, at least. Can you imagine what Reagan would make of that?"

"Glen, do you know Nasim el-din Qajar?" I asked.

"I know who he is, certainly. I know they've seen him in the West Wing. Several times."

"If he could influence the hostage situation, would he get them out or leave them where they are?" I had to ask, just to be sure, my stomach sinking even before he answered.

"He'd get them out. Why are you asking me—"

"I have to go," I said, standing up. I reached into my pocket and put a ten on the table. Then I rushed out. On the sidewalk, Wendi caught up with me.

"Patrick, wait. What are you going to do?"

"I don't know. I just need to go. I have to think."

"I have a date with Lefty later, do you want me to cancel?"

"No, no, go ahead. I'll be fine."

MISSION STATEMENT

The Publius Society

The Publius Society was founded by conservative legal professionals seeking to preserve the values and beliefs of our founding fathers. To that end, the Society works to encourage the selection and promotion of judges who interpret the law as it was written and in the context of the time it was written.

We believe deeply in the separation of powers and that laws should be written by Congress, not judges. We believe in small government, limited interference in individual lives and the fundamental principles of freedom. We will not lobby Congress or the president. We do not promote particular policies or outcomes. We do not endorse candidates.

Anyone may join the Society and be assured complete anonymity.

CHAPTER TWENTY-TWO

Except I didn't know where to go.

Escape. I wanted escape. Even if it was just into a fantasy. But as I walked along I couldn't do it. A prince was not going to save me, nor was a CIA agent. I was on my own. I had to save myself and I really had no idea how to do that.

And I was in danger. The Publius Society had tried to trick me into killing someone. That meant they were dangerous. That also had to mean—something hit me in a way I hadn't quite thought about before. Publius had its own clandestine operations; their own spy bureau, I guess you'd call it. Agent Walker wasn't a CIA agent, but he was an agent. A Publius agent. A dangerous Publius agent.

I should escape. For real.

I wouldn't get far, though. I didn't have any money and it was hard to hide without money. The only place I could run away *to* was back to Boston and Walker knew all about Boston. He'd find me in a matter of hours.

And even if I did manage to run away to some other place, Walker might go after my mother. He'd at least try to find out if she knew where I was. We weren't exactly on good terms—okay, we didn't speak, but that didn't mean I wanted her hassled or hurt. Or worse.

I could go to the police. I should go. But would they believe me? What was my evidence? A business card, a small bag of poison and a history of not exactly telling the truth. No, that wouldn't work.

What about the CIA? The real CIA? They might already even know about Walker. Although, that might be wishful thinking. And, in all honesty, going to the CIA might go as badly as going to the police. I had all the same credibility issues.

And then I was at the Metro Center Station. I found the escalator and let it float me down to the platform. The station was cavernous with a waffled concrete ceiling. I wondered if it was waffled like that to reduce noise. It wasn't very loud, at least not as loud as you'd think. But then the T back home wasn't loud either.

That's when I noticed him. At first, I thought he was cruising me. He was tall, a few years older than me and had that kind of blond hair that was dark underneath, sun-bleached I guess you'd call it. He wore a jean jacket, a pair of Calvin Kleins and a nice new pair of cowboy boots. I caught him looking at me as we waited for the train, but he quickly looked away.

I was flattered and, at that particular moment, I needed to be flattered. If I wanted to, I could go home with this stranger and hide out at his place for days, weeks maybe, and by the time I came back everything would be over. He could save me, at least temporarily.

All he needed to do was look at me again. But he didn't. He looked everywhere but at me. My fantasy of escape evaporated into thin air. Still, I kept watching him. I could tell he was aware of me, but he didn't want me to see him look at me, which wasn't how cruising usually went.

Usually, a guy glanced at you and then looked back. He might do that a couple of times depending on how intently you were looking at him. But this guy wasn't looking back at all, even though he'd already looked too much.

A chill ran across the back of my neck and the little hairs stood up. They were watching me. I knew they were watching me because I'd been told they were watching me. I wondered if this guy had been in Old Ebbitt's while we were having lunch. He could have been sitting at the bar and I wouldn't have noticed him. Or he could have been at another table. He could have been close enough to hear what we talked about.

The train pulled up. I got on. The guy in the jean jacket boarded the car behind me. A few minutes later, the doors closed and the train pulled out. Through the back windows I could see the car behind us. In it, I could see Mr. Jean Jacket. He was trying to get a good view of the car I was in. He was trying to look at me again now that he didn't think I could see him. I leaned back, very nearly behind a shallow partition.

There was another car in front of me, the first car. I got up and hurried into the front car. I picked out another seat where I could see through the window into the car behind us. As I'd suspected, Mr. Jean Jacket had seen me leave and moved up into the car behind me. He was following me. Definitely.

I looked straight ahead, hoping to make him think I had no idea what he was doing. An old woman sat across from me with her teenage granddaughter. The girl wore a Redskins sweatshirt and a Georgetown baseball cap. I had a feeling about them, so I went with it. Mr. Jean Jacket wouldn't bother me if I was talking to someone.

"Are you visiting from out of town?"

"We're here from Pittsburgh to visit my grandson. Marybeth's brother."

Marybeth gave me a look that suggested she didn't hold her brother, or me for that matter, in high esteem. But I didn't have to rely on Marybeth, her grandmother looked ready to talk, and talk, and talk.

"Your grandson lives here in Washington?"

"Oh, yes, he works for the president. He's very worried about his job, though. What with the election. That leaves me in a real pickle, you know. I really want to vote for Ronnie. I always liked him when he was in the movies. He's just the kind of man you can trust. But then, I feel like I *should* vote for Mr. Carter and then maybe Bobby can keep his job. But Mr. Carter is something of a bungler. I mean, I don't think he's as bad as they say, but he's not good."

We stopped at Farragut North and I watched to see if Mr. Jean Jacket got off. He didn't. I caught a glimpse of him sitting in the car behind us. The doors closed and we began moving.

"Does your grandson live in Dupont Circle?"

"Oh no, he lives in Foggy Bottom. Ridiculous name for a neighborhood, don't you think? I want to giggle every time I say it. No, we're going to the Smithsonian," Grandma said.

"Oh, well, I think you got on the wrong train. The next stop is Dupont Circle and it's the end of the line."

"Oh no, really? Marybeth, did you know we were going the wrong way?"

The girl shrugged.

"She's mad at me. I wouldn't let her call her boyfriend back home. But really, the money they charge for long distance. We can't come here and run up Bobby's phone bill. That would be rude."

"I was going to put five dollars under the phone," Marybeth said.

"Yes dear, I'm sure you were."

"At Dupont Circle just get on going the other way," I said. "You'll need to get off at Metro Station and get the blue line down to the Smithsonian stop. There are maps all over."

In fact, I could see one from where I was sitting. I think Marybeth may have been having one over on her grandmother. The Metro was so small that it took real effort to get lost. Marybeth must not be in the mood to look at dinosaur bones.

We were almost to my station, the last station, which meant Mr. Jean Jacket would be getting off with me. I had to figure out what to do. I could stick with Grandma and Marybeth until they got on their train going back downtown. Or I could very briskly walk out of the station and try to lose Mr. Jean Jacket on my way home. I knew my neighborhood; there had to be a way to shake him.

The train came to a stop at Dupont Circle. I stood up, saying goodbye to my human shields. The doors opened and I hurried out onto the platform. Walking briskly, trying not to look panicked, I headed toward the escalators. I wanted to look behind me and see if Mr. Jean Jacket was still there, but it wouldn't be smart.

When I got to the escalator, I didn't stand still for the leisurely ride to the top. No, I rushed up the steps, weaving in between people. And then I was on street level. All I had to do was cross over Connecticut Avenue, which dove under Dupont Circle, cross Mass Avenue, and then I'd be at P Street and just a couple of blocks from my apartment.

I still didn't know whether he was behind me. At some point, I'd need to stop and see if he was still there. I might be rushing around for nothing. I crossed Mass Avenue and then, a few steps later, turned onto P Street. It really was a lovely street, trees just beginning to turn, stately Greystone and brick townhouses pressed together in a way that felt more chummy than overcrowded.

Looking over my shoulder, I saw that Mr. Jean Jacket was still following me. He was about a half a block away. I needed to get farther away I needed it to be at least a full block. I picked up my speed but wasn't running. He must have known I was trying to get away at that point. He couldn't have been foolish enough to think I'd be walking around that frantically if I didn't know he was following.

I made it to 17th Street and turned north. Almost immediately, I broke into a run. I thought if I could get to the next corner Mr. Jean Jacket would be confused as to which direction I took.

I should work my way back over toward the park. There would be more directions to turn in and more things to hide behind. But I didn't turn that way. I got to 18th street and turned south to P Street again. I was running. Mr. Jean Jacket had to know I was running. I glanced over my shoulder and saw he was nearly half a block away, walking slowly but still coming toward me.

I dashed down 18th—heart pumping, breathing heavily—turning onto P street again, running, looking over my shoulder to see if he was anywhere to be seen, then hitting something hard and solid. I spun my head around and saw that I'd slammed into Lefty.

"What are you doing?" he asked.

"Let's get inside."

I rushed down the steps to my apartment, took out the key, opened the door, and hurried in. When Lefty was inside too, I shut the door and locked it. I peeked out the front window, moving aside the secondhand drapes Wendi's mother had given her. I waited, but Jean Jacket didn't walk by. It was over.

"What is going on?" Lefty asked again.

"I thought someone was following me."

"Why would anyone follow you?"

"I think he wanted to mug me," I lied.

"In broad daylight? In a good neighborhood like this?"

"Maybe I'm being paranoid." I wasn't. But I really didn't want to talk to Lefty about this.

"Where's Wendi?" he asked.

It wasn't a good idea to say she was still at lunch with another guy, so I said, "She's collecting signatures for Planned Parenthood. Or no, maybe she's gone to Carter campaign headquarters, I'm not sure."

He smiled, like she was an adorable misbehaving child off

doing silly childish things. "Good, it's just as well. I want to surprise her. Should I get tickets to the opera? They're doing *Barber of Seville* at the Kennedy Center or... there's this play called *The Shadow Box* at Ford's Theater. Which would she like better?"

"The opera is dressier. She likes dressing up." Probably more than she liked opera or theater. "Do you have a tuxedo?"

"I can rent one."

"She'd like that."

Two hours later, I went into work. I didn't know what I would do next, but I knew I would need money. The phone kept ringing, beginning before I could get rid of Lefty.

"Don't you want to get that?"

"No. I'm having a fight with my boyfriend. It's probably him." Mentioning your boyfriend was always a good way to get a straight guy to shut up and go away. The boyfriend didn't even have to be real.

Of course, the calls—which continued while I took a shower and put on my uniform—were probably from Agent Walker. By now, he had to have figured out that Nasim had not died in the night of an apparent heart attack. And I was sure he wanted to know why.

I could have simply answered the phone and made up some lie. But, now that I knew Walker wasn't a CIA agent, that he was actually a fraud, I didn't want to talk to him. Actually, I'd prefer not to talk to him ever again.

When I walked into Le Marquis, I was immediately waylaid by Maxim, "Pat*rick*, we are not an answering service. Your friends should not call here leaving messages for you."

"I'm sorry. Who—"

"Someone named Wal*ker*."

"I'm sorry. It won't happen again."

I did the pre-shift side work that had been assigned to me. I had the bread station. That meant lining baskets with napkins and stacking them so that when we got a new party we just sliced up some bread from the warming drawer and plunked it into the basket. Cleaning out the drawers. Then slicing up baguettes until the drawers were full and steaming. After that, I went and checked my station, making sure the silverware was sparkling and the napkins folded just right.

Being at the restaurant gave me a surreal sense of normalcy. It was almost like nothing had happened. I hadn't been tricked into spying on my boyfriend. I hadn't almost killed a man who was only trying to bring an international crisis to an end. I had to stop what I was doing and take a few deep breaths.

And then everything was done. The Madison room was ready, all I needed were the diners.

Barrett Copeland and his guests arrived on time. There were eight of them in total—including Judge Carlisle again. Politicians by the look of them. That shouldn't have been surprising. It was a company town after all. When I asked if they'd like anything from the bar, Barrett said they'd like two bottles of wine.

"The wine steward is here tonight. Let me send him over," I said, before I left the table and walked through the dining room. I found him in the bar talking to Pete. His name was A.J., and as soon as I told him he was wanted he grabbed a wine menu and hurried out to the Madison room.

"I guess you're moving up to the big time," Pete said to me. I knew what he meant but still couldn't deal with it, so I went back to the employee lounge and had a cigarette. When I was done, I figured it was time to go see if Barrett wanted a round of appetizers. I wondered if he'd want me to pick them out like I had before. I hurried out to the Madison room and when I walked in the first thing I realized was that I had another party.

A single man sitting alone at a four-top. Walker. It was Walker. He was a bit under-dressed for Le Marquis in a Georgetown sweatshirt and a pair of faded jeans. Had he come on a whim? No, wait, he knew I didn't normally work Saturday nights. So how had he known—

"What are you doing here?" I asked. I'd walked over to the table without deciding to, as though I'd had no choice.

"I've been trying to reach you. You didn't do what we'd agreed to."

"I wasn't able to. The cookies weren't there," I lied.

"That's fine. You should have let me know that. We need to make another plan."

I decided not to answer that. "Would you like something from the bar?"

"Don't be ridiculous. You know I'm not here—"

"You need to order something. Or you need to go." Honestly, I was hoping for the later.

"All right I'll have a ginger ale. But you need to meet me after work."

Ignoring the last, I turned and walked away. As I walked to the bar, I wondered how to get rid of Walker. I could call the police, but what would I say? I couldn't prove Walker wanted me to kill someone. And that made me think about the police walking through the restaurant to get to the Madison room, Maxim screaming at them, "Stop! Stop! You must stop!" And all for no reason, really. No one would arrest Walker.

I set the ginger ale down in front of him. "Did you want to order dinner?"

Softly he asked, "Do you still have the poison?"

I shook my head violently. Of course I still had it, but I didn't want him to know that.

"I'm going to wait for you."

"You can't do that."

"Don't worry, I'll order dinner. Eventually."

"I have plans after work, so there's isn't a point in your waiting."

"That's fine."

"I don't want you to wait for me."

"I have nothing better to do. I don't mind."

"I'm sorry. I really can't. Another time maybe." And with that I walked over to Barrett's party. I stood there for a moment, attempting to get my bearings.

"Reagan's in Detroit," one of the men said. "Do you think he'll have any luck there?"

"Sure, he's just got to tie the idea of crime and the inner city together and no respectable white person would ever vote for Carter."

"There are white people in Detroit?" another asked.

The table laughed.

I leaned over to Barrett and asked, "Did you want appetizers this evening?"

He shook his head. "No, I think we'll just go ahead and order."

I took their order. It was challenging to focus with Walker sitting right there. Plotting how he could get me alone so he could —what? Kill me? Force me to kill Nasim? Both?

"I'm sorry, did you say the stuffed sole?"

I needed to pay enough attention to get the order right. As soon as I served the entrée I could tell Maxim I felt sick and have someone take over. They never ordered desserts. Just coffee and after-dinner drinks. That was easy enough. Anyone could do it.

But how would I get out of the building? Walker might have a friend watching the employees' entrance. And another watching the front of the building. Who knows what they might do if they saw me trying to leave the building without Walker?

I finished taking the order, went back to the kitchen, gave the check to the expediter, and then busied myself with their salads. A few minutes later I had eight Caesar salads neatly arranged on a tray. I lifted it above my shoulder and went back to the Madison room. I set each down in front of a customer, then I picked up a chunk of parmesan cheese wrapped in a napkin and went over to Barrett. I started to grate cheese over his salad.

Walker watched my every move. I could feel his eyes on me like heat from a fire. It made me nervous. As I grated cheese onto Barrett's salad, my hands shook and I had to stop and steady myself. When I began again, he asked, "Is something wrong, Patrick?"

I had no reason to trust Barrett. In fact, I had every reason *not* to trust him. His political beliefs would put him in line with The Publius Society, or at least on that side of the aisle. Still, he'd been kind. And I had very little to lose.

"The guy in the corner. He wants me to kill Nasim. He works for The Publius Society. They tricked me into spying—"

"Enough. That's already more than I want to know."

For a moment, I thought that meant he was going to do nothing. That I was completely on my own with no one to help me.

Barrett picked up the napkin from his lap, set it on the table, and stood up.

"What are you doing?" I whispered.

"Gentleman, I'll be back in just a moment. Patrick, come with me."

Making sure to put himself between me and Walker, Barrett led me out of the Madison Room and through the restaurant. He had me by the arm and his grip was quite a bit stronger than I'd have suspected.

"I'm not sure if this is a good idea?" I asked. I felt sick to my stomach. I had no idea if I was being saved or sacrificed.

"Keep moving. I know what Publius is. I know what they're capable of."

I looked over my shoulder and Walker had just stepped into the dining room, looking lost and confused. Whatever Barrett and I were doing, he hadn't expected it. And neither had I.

We hurried across the lobby area outside the restaurant to the elevators. Barrett pressed the button and, luckily, a bell went off and the elevator furthest to our left opened. We hurried down there as two women in lacquered hair and mink stoles stepped out.

As soon as there was room, we jumped into the elevator. Walker was rushing toward us. Barrett hit the button to close the door. Walker got there in time to slip his foot into the closing doors, but Barrett stomped on Walker's foot. His foot disappeared and the doors closed.

We began to descend and I asked, "Why are you helping me? I thought you wanted Reagan to win the election? That's what Publius is doing, they're trying to make sure the hostages—"

"I know what they're trying to do. I want Reagan to win because the American people chose him fairly. Not because they've been tricked into it."

"You have integrity," I said.

"Don't tell anyone. It can be a liability in this town. I'm going to put you in a cab. After that you're on your own."

"Yes."

The elevator opened and we rushed out into the lobby. We were practically running. Barrett still had hold of my arm and I was sure I'd have a bruise in the morning.

We burst out of the hotel and dashed over to the cabstand. A taxi was idling and Barrett pushed me into it. As he did, he said, "You need to get out of Washington as quickly as you can."

LATE NIGHT TV MONOLOGUE

The host, in a thousand-dollar suit, pulls a piece of paper out of his inside jacket pocket. Smugly, he begins, "I have here a list of items President Carter is thinking of offering the Iranians in exchange for the hostages: a trip to Disneyland, an Atari 2600, Angie Dickinson, Chewbacca, the Osmonds, one hundred cases of TAB, New Jersey and…"

Drumroll.

"…the Chicago Cubs."

Laughter.

The host raises his eyebrows and holds out his hands. When the laughter dies down, he starts again, "The Iranians don't refer to the Americans they've detained as hostages. They call them guests. Guests at Komiteh Prison. So, here's my question: when you're given a two-inch straw mattress, do you still get turn-down service?"

Laughs.

The host smiles broadly, amused by himself. Then, "Is there room service? Can 'guests' order gruel and thin soup at any hour, day or night?"

Laughs.

Barely waiting. "Does the spa offer services like fifty lashes, thumb screws—"

Suddenly, a shrieking noise fills the studio and a small person covered head to toe in a brown burqa runs onto the stage and begins circling the host.

"Ladies and Gentleman, Mrs. Ayatollah Khomeini—"

She jumps around, screaming gibberish. The audience laughs.

"Mrs. Khomeini, how should we approach your husband to get his help in releasing the hostages?"

A long string of gobbledygook. The host pays close attention.

"Yes, but this is L.A. I don't know how we'd find seventy-two virgins."

Mrs. Khomeini jumps around even more, the nonsense she's spewing increasing in volume.

Giggling.

"Ah, you think he'd settle for thirty-six. Still a tough order. How about three?"

Mrs. Khomeini amps it up even further.

"You hear that folks? Three virgins and the hostage crisis is over."

A smattering of laughter.

"So if you're a virgin in Los Angeles just come on down to the studio. The first three get a free trip to Iran. And Bobby—my producer, Bobby—Bobby send the rest to my dressing room."

Laughter.

Mrs. Khomeini acts up again.

"Oh, you've got to go? Well, thanks for coming by. Ladies and Gentlemen, Mrs. Ayatollah Khomeini!"

Applause.

CHAPTER TWENTY-THREE

I walked into the apartment and called out Wendi's name. She didn't answer. I went down the hall to my bedroom—my mind solely on what I should grab. Wendi's door was open, but the bathroom door was shut. She hated talking to me when she was on the toilet so I didn't call her name again.

In my room, I stripped off my uniform and threw on a pair of jeans and a shirt. Then I grabbed my suitcase, dumped most of my socks and underwear into it, and began pulling clothes out of the closet. Rolling up shirts and jeans, I jammed them into the suitcase.

I wouldn't be able to take much. My one suitcase wasn't that big and I'd managed to pick up a few things in the almost two years I'd been in Washington. Maybe a lot of things.

Wendi was going to hate me. I was dumping the apartment on her. She'd have to get another roommate. Fast. But I didn't have a choice. I had to get away from Washington. She'd understand that. She knew—

"Wendi!" I called out again, ignoring that she hated when I yelled for her.

I was definitely going to have to leave my books. Well, maybe I could take a couple. I grabbed *The Persian Boy*—I was re-reading it and, well, now that I knew David wasn't some evil spy trying to ruin my country it had sentimental value. I tossed it into the suitcase and it fell open. Agent Walker's card fell out. When I picked it up, I realized it was two cards stuck together. One for Walker and one for—

"Wendi!" I called out as I rushed out of the room and down the hall. "Wendi!"

I knocked on the bathroom door. No response. I checked the door; it wasn't locked. I pushed it open slowly. "Wendi, I'm coming in. Are you all—"

She was in the tub. The water was a brilliant red. The tub was only a few feet from the door but it seemed like I walked a mile to get there. As I got closer, I saw that the water was near the top of the bathtub and every so often it would gurgle down an overflow drain. She wore a baby blue camisole that looked sort of violet now that it was soaked in her blood. Her wrists were slashed in deep, violent cuts.

She was dead. That was obvious. Her face floated an inch or so below the water. Eyes open, staring. At me. Waiting for me to do something.

I was still holding the business card. It was also from The Publius Society. It said Leonard Latowski. Lefty. Not truly under-standing what that meant, I ran out to the living room and called 911.

"My roommate's dead," I told the dispatcher.

"Can you tell me what happened?"

"There are big slits in her wrist."

"She killed herself?"

"Yes," I said, though it felt wrong. She couldn't have killed herself. If she had, why would she have put Lefty's business card in my book? That was a message. She was telling me—

Oh my God, her habit of looking through a date's wallet. Lefty must have finally taken a shower. And while he was in there, she looked in his wallet and found the card for The Publius Society. Which meant he was working with Walker. He wasn't her boyfriend. He'd been spying on her, no, on me, just as I'd been spying on David and his father. And Wendi figured all that out.

She must have fought with Lefty. Or he figured out she knew. He killed her, though, that was certain. He killed her and made it look like she'd killed herself.

"I have to go now," I told the dispatcher and hung up.

Then I went into the bathroom and sat on the toilet next to the bathtub. It was a hard thing to do, I wanted to run back to my bedroom, grab my few things and leave. Run as far away as I could. But I couldn't leave her there all alone.

Paramedics came first. I opened the front door for them. They looked at Wendi in the bathtub and said that there wasn't anything they could do, which was not a surprise. They told me the medical examiner would be taking her body. Eventually.

I went back to sit with her again.

Then the police arrived. They looked at Wendi just as the paramedics had, coldly, dispassionately. Then one of them, a black guy of about forty, introduced himself.

"I'm Lieutenant Baxter, do you mind if we look around?"

"No, that's fine," I said, not knowing what else to say.

He nodded at the other officer who went into Wendi's room.

"Tell me what happened?"

"I don't know what happened. I wasn't here."

"Where were you?"

"I was at work."

"Was your roommate depressed?"

"No. She was happy. She had a new boyfriend."

"Maybe they broke up?"

I shrugged. "Like I said, I wasn't here."

"Did she have any emotional issues or any kind?"

"No. She was a very together kind of person."

Baxter gave me a look that suggested he didn't think any woman could be 'very together.'

"What's the boyfriend's name?"

"Lefty Latowski," I said, then wondered if that was even true. Leonard "Lefty" Latowski was the name on his business card but there was no reason it had to be his real name. "He said he worked at a not-for-profit focused on famine in Uganda. I don't think any of that's true, though. I think he was spying on us."

"Spying on you?" He glanced around the apartment. "You have a lot of state secrets around here?"

"No."

"Where did your roommate work?"

"Le Marquis at the Hotel Continental."

"Oh, so this Lefty person was spying on you. Where do you work?"

"I work at Le Marquis, too." But my boyfriend is a prince, I thought to add and then didn't. I could just imagine his face and the snarl that would go with his next question. He'd believe me even less than he did now. This was a disaster.

"I'm sorry, I'm really upset," I said. "I guess I meant, there was something creepy about him. I didn't trust him."

"Do you know where he lives?"

"I think Wendi said he lived at the Watergate. With two roommates. That might not be true either."

Baxter eyed me suspiciously.

"So, were you jealous of her boyfriend? Did you want the girl for yourself?"

"No, I didn't." I had to tell him, though the idea of telling a policeman kind of freaked me out. "I'm gay."

"That was okay with your roommate?"

"Why wouldn't it be?"

He shrugged.

"She wouldn't have killed herself," I said.

"That may not have been her intent. Was she expecting you?"

"I don't know. Maybe."

"Very often attempted suicide is a cry for help. She may not have wanted to kill herself."

"It wasn't a cry for help. She wasn't the kind of girl who needed help. She wouldn't have done this to herself. Someone else did it."

"There are no signs of struggle."

"How do you know?" I asked. "You barely looked at her."

"Signs of a struggle are very obvious. Particularly when there's blood involved. If she fought back there would be blood all over the walls."

"Maybe he drugged her," I suggested.

"He? The boyfriend? Why do you think her boyfriend killed her? What would his motive be?"

I tried to arrange the words in my head so that Detective Baxter would believe me. The Publius Society. Tricked into spying. Hostages. Iran. The Prince. Poison. Crap, they were searching the apartment. What if they found the poison?

Wait. Where was the poison? I thought back. I'd put it into my jean's pocket the night before and then didn't kill Nasim. So that's where it was. In my jeans. I casually slipped my hand into my pocket and felt around. There. It was there. No one was going to find it and question—

I'd been asked a question. 'What would his motive be? What was this Lefty's motive.'

"I'm sorry," I said to Baxter. "I'm, I'm probably wrong about Lefty. I'm upset and confused. I barely know what I'm saying.'

He looked at me for a long moment. I didn't think he liked my sudden reversal any more than he would have liked the truth. Still, he moved on.

"I'll have more questions for you later. What's the number here?"

I gave it to him.

"Do you know how I can reach your roommate's family?"

"Wendi, please call her Wendi."

"How do I reach Wendi's family?" His voice a tiny bit kinder.

"There's an address book on the phone stand."

"Thank you."

They left two hours later. The medical examiner finally came and looked at everything, took pictures, then put Wendi on a gurney and took her way. They drained the tub. For some reason the water was very loud leaving the apartment.

The moment they walked out the door, I took the poison out of my pocket and stared at it. What would happen to me? I'd been instructed to kill Nasim el-din Qajar and I hadn't. I was a failed agent who knew too much. A failed agent of The Publius Society. A group that kills people.

A group that killed Wendi.

When I was in junior high school, a girl no one liked was run over by a car. We wandered the hallways before class that morning, somber-faced, some of us crying, sobbing even. Struggling to remember some memory of her that might be deemed fond. There was no reason for our grief. We didn't care for the poor girl. The nearest I could come to a reason for our over-dramatic behavior was that the death of someone so young filled us with fear. If it happened to her, it could happen to us.

I had no idea how to grieve for Wendi. I had grieved so little in my life I had no language for it. My father died when I was nine or ten. See, I can't even remember how old I was. I barely remembered anything about him.

It was almost dawn when the police left. Sitting in the living room, I looked down and noticed I was shivering. Had I been shivering all along? I had no idea. It was breakfast time and I was hungry, but the idea of food was disgusting. All I really wanted was David, wanted him badly, but how could I tell him the truth? He'd hate me. He'd be right to.

The telephone began ringing again—it had been quiet while the police were there, so it had to be Walker. I was being watched. I didn't answer it.

It was Walker's fault Wendi was dead. Yeah, Lefty had done it, but it was Walker who'd sent him to spy on us. It was Walker who'd tricked me into working for The Publius Society. If he hadn't tricked me, if he'd found some other way to spy on the Qajars, Wendi would be alive. I wanted to pay him back, I wanted to do to him what—And then I had an idea. I knew exactly how I would pay him back.

Under the sink in the kitchen, there was a pair of yellow rubber gloves. Wendi used them when she cleaned, especially if she'd had a recent manicure. Well, she'd always had a recent manicure, she was proud of her nails and kept them up. I grabbed the gloves and brought them with me into my bedroom.

Then I dug around my closet until I found a dark blue handkerchief I'd once bought. It was supposed to mean something sexual depending on which back pocket you put it in, but I was never sure I'd bought the right color and I never worked up the nerve to wear it.

I got my cigarettes and set them on the coffee table. Then I took the poison out of my pocket and laid it next to them. I wrapped the handkerchief around my face and put on the gloves. Agent Walker had said not to touch or inhale the poison.

At first, all I did was accidentally tear two cigarettes to pieces; the rubber gloves were that awkward to work with. They might pick up a dime on TV, but they weren't much good for working the tobacco out of a cigarette. I hadn't even opened the glassine envelope, so why I was wearing the gloves I didn't know. I took them off and then successfully emptied half the tobacco out of a cigarette.

Putting the gloves back on, I opened the envelope of poison and tipped it into the empty paper cylinder. Then I sat there for a few moments. There was no way I'd be able to fill the end with tobacco without taking off the gloves. It might be okay, though, there was paper between me and the poison. I decided to risk it.

After I took the gloves off, I held the cigarette by the filter flush to the table so that I could carefully drop the tobacco into the cigarette. It took a while and it was messy. There were shredded tobacco leaves all over the floor. Eventually, I got enough of the tobacco tapped down in the paper tube that it looked like a normal cigarette. After that I emptied out the pack so that when I put the poisoned cigarette in it was all alone.

Then I waited.

Ten minutes later, the phone rang again. This time I answered it. I picked up, but didn't say hello.

"Is Sylvia there?"

"Can you meet me in ten minutes?"

"It will take twenty for me to get there."

"Twenty then."

"You're not going to run away from me again, are you?"

"No. I'll do it."

"Do what?"

"What you want. We just have to talk about how."

Then I hung up. Of course, the last was a lie. I wasn't going to kill Nasīm. I had to stay on my toes. I had to assume Agent Walker would be suspicious and at some point he'd want to kill me. I had to make him think I was valuable for a little while longer.

It was cold and drizzling as I walked over to Dupont Circle, completely uncertain what would happen. I had on a jean jacket with my cigarettes in the front pocket, the pocket had a flap protecting my weapon from the rain. There was no one else in the park. It was empty.

When I got to our usual spot, Agent Walker wasn't there yet. I sat down on the wet bench knowing that, no matter what, this was the last time we'd meet. I didn't think I'd ever come to the Circle again. It would always be the place where I met Walker. And then I wondered if I was even going to get out of this alive, no less come back to Dupont Circle. It was entirely possible Walker wasn't coming, instead a—

And then he was standing there, wearing his raincoat and galoshes. He sat down and said, "Why did you run from me?"

"That was Barrett Copeland. He got the wrong idea about what was going on. I couldn't explain—"

"That's bullshit."

And it was.

"You're not a CIA agent."

"What makes you say that?"

"And Nasim is trying to get the hostages out of Iran. He's not trying to keep them there like you said. He's trying to help our government."

He remained quiet. I reached into my jacket pocket and took out the cigarette I'd slipped in behind the pack. I lit it and inhaled.

"I love this country," he said. "But I hate what it's becoming. We need to get back to what we were. We need to turn back the clock." He nodded at the cigarette I was holding. "Can I have one of those?"

He'd asked. Just like I knew he would. I was numb. Dry-mouthed. Afraid I'd start shaking again.

"Are you sure?" I asked. "It's not the best way to quit."

"It's the last one. I promise."

I took the squashed pack of Salem cigarettes out of my shirt pocket, bounced the pack until the single remaining cigarette popped up. Agent Walker reached over and took it. It looked sad and a little bent.

"Sorry. I sat on the pack."

He took the cigarette. I held out the lighter but didn't flick it on.

"You killed my roommate, didn't you? Lefty couldn't have done it alone."

I could see him mentally scrambling for an answer.

"Don't lie," I said. "I'm tired of lies."

He studied me a moment and then said the most truthful thing he'd ever said to me. "I wouldn't say I killed her, and I wouldn't say Lefty did; I'd say you did. I told you to keep our little project secret. If you'd listened your friend would be alive." He glanced at the lighter in my hand. "Could you—?"

Numbly, I flicked my lighter on and held it for him. I watched him inhale.

"The question is, can I ever trust you again? It would be a shame to lose you. There's a particular senator who likes young men of your sort. Controlling his vote would be—"

"My sort? Aren't you also that sort?"

"No. Not at all."

"So that was a trick too."

He smiled. Took another drag off his cigarette. He coughed. Just a tiny little cough. Almost a clearing of his throat. Then he paled.

I breathed a sigh of relief. I'd been worrying the filter might have blocked the poison, but that was silly. The filter couldn't save you from cancer so it couldn't save you from poison.

"Why are you looking—"

Something was happening. He gasped and struggled to inhale. He looked at me in surprise, trying to say more but unable to do more than gurgle. The cigarette fell to the ground and his hands grasped his throat. He gasped for breath, his eyes on me the whole time.

"I thought I should return the poison you gave me," I said simply.

Pain and anger flushed cross his face. He reached toward me and I slid down the bench. He fell onto the ground, his body bucked a bit, he might have been having a seizure, I don't know, and then he went completely still.

I got up and walked away.

CHAPTER TWENTY-FOUR

It takes so little to ruin a life. That's what I thought about as I walked away from Agent Walker, that a life is easily ruined. And I wasn't thinking about his life, I was thinking about my own. How had I gotten here? How had I reached the point where I'd kill a man? How did that make sense?

I'd been a college student, an ordinary student, and then I'd given the wrong person my homework. That led to my being thrown out of school, which led to my coming to Washington, which led to my meeting a prince, which led to my meeting a fake CIA agent, which led to my killing a man. That was what had happened. Except even that didn't make sense.

I was a murderer and I felt ruined. I'd never be what I was, and I'd never be what I might have been. The rest of my life would be shaped by the fact that I'd killed a man, perhaps only subtly if I got away with it—something that seemed entirely possible since it would appear Walker had a heart attack—or hugely if I was caught.

But I wasn't sorry.

Wendi was dead; my friend was dead, and now at least one of the people who'd killed her was dead too. That was justice and it was murder. It was both at once.

I'd gone a couple of blocks before I realized I wasn't walking home. I was walking to David's house. Why? Why was I going there? I couldn't actually articulate an answer. Was that because murder was so primal? I'd killed a man and slipped into some deep preverbal part of myself. I was on my way to David's. It felt right, though I couldn't say why. It was time to tell the truth before my lies hurt anyone else. That was as close as I could come to an answer.

When he saw me, David took one look and said, "You're breaking up with me again, aren't you?"

I shook my head. "I've done something awful."

He waited for me to continue. We stood in the living room where the ancient butler had led me after he let me in. I didn't know where Nasim was. He might not even be there.

"Remember when we broke up?" I started. "Well, the next day I met a man."

"And you're in love with him."

"No, no, that would be so much easier."

David frowned. For a moment, he was simply a guy who was afraid his boyfriend might be cheating on him. I wished it could be that simple.

"Easier? How would—"

"A CIA agent. I met a man who said he was a CIA agent. He told me your father was trying to prevent the hostages from being released, that he was trying to influence the election. But that wasn't true and he—"

"No, it's not true, Father— Wait, I don't think I understand what you're saying."

"I've been spying on you. I've been giving information about your father to an organization called The Publius Society. He, the CIA agent, he told me it was his cover but he was lying. That's who he really worked for. They don't want the hostages released until after Reagan is elected. They want to find a way to stop your father."

"Stop him how?"

"They don't want him to go to Paris. They wanted me to kill him so he—"

David stepped out into the hallway and called out, "Father! Father come here, please."

When he stepped back into the room he glared at me in a way that made me afraid to speak, and then afraid not to. "I know you'll never be able to forgive me. But I hope someday you'll understand how sorry I am."

"Shut up."

There was venom in his voice. He was angry. Well, he should be angry. What did I expect? I'd betrayed him. It didn't matter that I'd also been betrayed.

Nasim came into the room. He must have just been in his study. His eyes flicked back and forth between us. "What is it, Davoud?"

"He's the spy. Not Ebrahim." And that told me the conversation I'd overheard had not been about me, it had been about Ebrahim.

"Why do you say that?" Nasim said much more calmly than I'd have expected.

"He just told me. He's working for something called Publius."

"Was, I *was* working for them and I didn't—"

"I told you to shut up. I don't want to hear your excuses."

Nasim seemed to weigh the situation then asked, "Patrick, why did you confess to Davoud?"

"The man who approached me said he was a CIA agent. I believed him. I just found out he wasn't. I just found out what The Publius Society is."

"Do you know who these people are, Father?"

"Yes, I've heard of them. I know what they do."

"They don't want you to go to Paris. They wanted Patrick to kill you."

"But I couldn't. I couldn't do it," I rushed to say.

"This man who said he was a CIA agent," Nasim asked. "Does he know you've learned his true identity?"

"Yes."

"That's unfortunate. We might have been able to give them incorrect information through you. That could have been useful."

I was surprised by how quickly Nasim absorbed the information and then tried to turn it to his advantage. Meanwhile my mind was moving like sludge.

"I killed him. I killed Agent Walker."

Nasim said, "Oh. I see."

David visibly softened. "Did you kill him for us?"

I shook my head. "He killed Wendi."

"Wendi? Wendi's dead?" David asked. He was visibly shaken.

"I told you she had a new boyfriend. He was from Publius too. I think she figured it out and he killed her."

"Is this the girl you brought to the party?" Nasim asked.

"Yes."

"How unfortunate. Such a charming girl. Tell us what happened, Patrick," Nasim said.

"I found her in the bathtub with her wrists slit."

"So, she killed herself?" David guessed. Obviously, that would be an easier explanation.

"That's what the police think, but they're wrong."

"Why? Why are they wrong?" David was disturbed by all of this. Of course, it was actually disturbing. "Why do you think you know better?"

"Walker admitted they'd killed her before he died. Before I killed him."

"How did you kill him?" Nasim asked.

"He gave me poison to put into your tea. It was going to look like a heart attack. He always bummed a cigarette from me, so I put the poison into his cigarette."

"Clever boy. Patrick, why didn't you kill me? You would be much safer if you had."

"I couldn't."

"But you've just killed a man, why not me?"

I didn't know the answer at first. I could have said I didn't kill Nasim because I loved David, but that would have only been partly true. Finally, I said, "You haven't hurt anyone."

"You don't know that for certain," Nasim said.

"Father—"

"You haven't hurt *me*. It felt wrong to hurt you."

The doorbell rang. The ancient butler appeared and answered the door. After a moment, Fred and Ebrahim walked into the room.

"Are you ready, Nasim?" Fred asked. "Where are your bags? Ebrahim will take them to the car."

Ebrahim frowned at his enforced servitude.

"I'll not go today, Fred. It's good that you're here though."

"Father, what are you doing? You have to leave. Your flight. You have to be in Paris."

"They've tried to kill me once. Best to assume they'll try again. I imagine they know what flight I'm on. I'll go to the airport tomorrow and buy a ticket there. Or perhaps I should go to New York. That might be a better idea."

"What are you talking about?" Ebrahim asked.

Quickly, I told him I'd been spying on the Qajars and that—

before I could finish Ebrahim turned to David and said, "You see, it is just as I've told you, these people have no loyalty, no decency."

"Shut up Ebrahim," David said, turning to Nasim. "Father, what about calling the White House? They'd help us."

"There's a problem with that," Nasim said. "No one will suspect Patrick of killing Walker because there's no reason to connect him. But, if I call the White House I have to connect him."

"So what?" Ebrahim said. "Let him go to prison. He deserves—"

"No. If it wasn't him, it would be someone else. Someone who might not have told us the truth."

"I am sorry for what I did," I said.

Nasim shook his head. "You have brought us luck, my friend."

It didn't feel that way.

"You don't really believe him," Ebrahim said. "He's just a little boy telling stories."

"Ebrahim be quiet," Fred said.

"You should call the White House and ask for help," I said. "It doesn't matter what happens to me."

David glanced at me. Clearly, I was coming up in his estimation. Actually, I was coming up in my own too. I waited for Nasim to decide my fate.

"The greatest risk in any conflict is becoming the enemy you hate. If we stop caring what happens to you, Patrick, we are no better than Publius."

"Then maybe I should leave. If they follow me—"

"No," David interjected. "Aren't you listening? We need to make sure you're okay. It is the right thing to do."

"It's time to pack your things, Davoud. It's time to go."

With nothing else to do, I followed David upstairs to his room. I paused at his door, unsure whether to enter. He glanced over his shoulder and looked at me. "Well, come in if you're coming."

I walked in and sat on his bed. He took a couple of pieces of Louis Vuitton luggage out of the closet and began packing his clothes. He was silent as he folded his clothes and laid them carefully into the suitcase. When he was nearly finished, I reached out and put my hand on the back of his as he smoothed out a folded shirt.

He stopped and stared at our hands. "I don't know if I can move forward, Patrick. I don't know who you are."

"You do know who I am. I never lied about that."

"You're the kind of person who would spy on us. I didn't know that about you."

"I thought you were doing something awful."

"You see, you don't know me anymore than I know you," he said.

"You're wrong. I didn't know you, not when we began. But I know you now. And you know me."

He closed his suitcase, pushed it aside and sat down next to me. "But I'm not sure if I like the things I know about you."

"I don't know what to say to that. I'm trying to be as honest as I can be."

"Now."

"Yell at me."

"What?"

"I said, 'yell at me.' You're angry. You have good reasons to be angry, so go ahead and yell at me."

"I can't do that. It wouldn't be appropriate."

"Because you're a prince?" I asked.

"I suppose. Is it so terrible to have a code of conduct?"

"I wish we could just be two guys in love."

"I wish that too."

"Then why can't we be? Why can't we put everything else aside and be two guys in love?"

He stared at me for a long moment then said, "We need to go back downstairs."

I used to believe that politicians were all the same, that there were no differences between parties. Now I think that, while there might be little distance between the parties, there can actually be great distances between politicians. And great distances within parties. There are politicians, on both sides, who believe in what our country stands for and others who care little for that and instead believe in flags and geographies. Or perhaps they believe in nothing at all and only want to gorge at the public trough.

A country should stand for the freedom of its people, their happiness, their safety. And, yet, I've also learned that freedom is dangerous since at its most extreme it allows people to plot its destruction. And there are those who *do* want to destroy it, who are constantly working to bring that about. They do not see that a freedom that allows them to steal from others is not a freedom at all. They do not see that freedom carries with it the responsibility to see that all are free; because when you steal another's freedom you must remember that the wheel will turn and your freedom will be taken next.

We left just after the sunset. Our bags were brought down to the foyer. When we were ready, David pulled the Lincoln around to the front of the house and we dashed down the steps to quickly fill the trunk. Fred and Ebrahim stayed to the last. As we were saying goodbye to them, Samira hurried out of the house with a bag full of snacks for the road. There were tears in her eyes and she stood at the edge of our little group saying things in Persian, probably curses and blessings by turns. Cursing us for leaving and blessing us with a safe return.

And then we were pulling away from the house. David driving, Nasim in the passenger seat and me in the back. We took Rhode Island out of the city, having to cut across P street. That took us by my apartment and I got to see it one last time. The light was on in the living room, making it seem warm and inviting, as though Wendi was sitting there reading a book and sipping a cup of chamomile tea.

But then I wondered why the light was on? I'd left in the morning. I wouldn't have left any lights on, and I certainly didn't remember leaving one on. Maybe Wendi's parents had come by earlier. Or maybe Lefty was in there waiting for me. No, he wouldn't turn on a light. He'd sit in the dark waiting to kill me.

We drove out of the city and into the suburbs which seemed to never end. The night was bright with streetlights and glowing signs. I'd just seen one telling us we'd crossed into Maryland when David said, "There is someone following us."

I spun around in my seat. A thousand feet behind us there was a set of headlights.

"How do you know, Davoud?"

"They've been there since just after we left. They don't get any closer and they don't get any further away."

"What should we do?" I asked.

"We need to find a gas station," Nasim said.

"We don't need gas, Father, I filled it up yesterday."

"We need maps. And when we stop, I think they'll go by us and wait further down the road," Nasim guessed.

"What if they come into the gas station and try to kill us?" I asked.

"It's not their way," Nasim said. "They'll always want murder to look like something else. It is what they did to your friend, making it look like a suicide. The poison they gave you would have looked like a heart attack."

"They could try to make it look like a robbery?" I suggested.

"Do you think they're prepared for that?" Nasim asked.

"You mean, do I think they have guns? I don't know. I don't think Walker carried a gun. I know Lefty never brought one into the apartment, Wendi would have noticed. He might have one now, though."

"There's a Texaco station up there on the right," David said.

"Pull in, but don't get out of the car," Nasim said. "Let them pass first."

We were silent as David pulled into the gas station. None of us moved. After a long twenty seconds, a brown sedan drove by the gas station. We breathed a sigh of relief.

"Quickly, run in and get maps," Nasim said to David.

David jumped out of the car and ran into the gas station.

After a short silence, I asked Nasim, "Do you think it might have been a coincidence? Do you think the car wasn't from Publius?"

"No. I think they want to run us off the road."

"Then, why haven't they?"

"They're waiting for a good spot."

He was right, of course. We weren't on the highway yet. We were on a route, a basic street through residential areas. There were two lanes on each side and a median in between, buildings everywhere, no abutments to steer us into, no deep canyons or gorges or ravines to send us over, no oncoming traffic to nudge us in front of. The best they'd have been able to manage would have been a minor fender bender. No one dies in minor fender benders.

"You have been good for my son," Nasim said abruptly. "He is not so arrogant."

"I doubt I'll be around much longer."

"Oh? You have tired of Davoud?"

"I don't think he'll ever forgive me."

"He will. And that will be good for him too. And it will be good for you. To be forgiven."

"Do you? Forgive me?"

"You are very young. The young make terrible mistakes."

David jumped back into the car. In his hands were half a dozen maps. He handed them to his father and then put the car into gear and started to pull out of the gas station.

"Make a left turn," Nasim said.

"We're going back to D.C.?"

"No. We're trying to lose these people." The dome light came on and there was a rustling sound, which told me Nasim had spread open one of the maps.

"Take the next left."

He did. After a long moment he said, "It looks like you can cut through this neighborhood and get to Blandensburg Road. When we get there turn left and stay on it until it turns into Annapolis Road. That will connect to the Baltimore-Washington Expressway."

Nasim turned off the dome light. I looked over my shoulder out the back window. There were no headlights, nothing but blackness behind us. When we reached Blandensburg there was occasionally a car coming toward us as we passed a car wash, a McDonald's, a used car dealership, a supermarket, a hot dog stand. And then a sign that told us to veer right for the waterfront park. What waterfront, I wondered? Were we already at the Chesapeake Bay? I didn't think so. The road in front of us began to rise and I wondered if we were about to cross—

The interior of the car lit up. I looked out the back window and saw that there was a car very close to us. It had been there all along. They just hadn't turned their lights on.

"Hang on," David said.

The sedan got into the inside lane and sped up, trying to go around us as we approached—a bridge. We were about to cross a bridge. They were going to drive us into the river. David hit the brakes and swerved sharply to the left, slamming into the brown sedan. It made a tremendous sound as metal ground together. Then, the sedan hopped the median, wiggling as it tried to right itself. The driver hit the brakes too hard and the car's front bumper hit the pavement before it flipped over, landing on the bank of the river.

CHAPTER TWENTY-FIVE

We crossed the bridge. Silently. It was as though none of us wanted to say anything about what had just happened. Finally, I said, "Should we stop and see if the car is alright?"

"No. We can't take that chance."

"Father, how long will we be in Maryland?"

Nasim turned on the dome light. Rustling. "It looks like we're around ninety miles from the Delaware border."

"About an hour and a half," David said. "Faster if—"

"Don't speed. We don't want to explain the damage on your side of the car."

The ride across Maryland was calm and tense at once. Nothing happened, that was the calm part. We were terrified the police might have found the accident quickly and been looking out for a white car with brown paint scraped across one side.

Of course, whoever was in the brown sedan might have survived. I doubt they'd have called the police, though. Not right away at least. They might have just gotten a tow truck to pull them out of the river and then gone on their way. So, no one would be looking for us.

Still, we drove in silence. It felt like we weren't saying anything because that would somehow make everything that had happened much too real. I closed my eyes and tried to sleep, but it didn't take. Soon enough we were approaching Baltimore and Nasim navigated us through the harbor tunnel. Then we fell back to silence.

Well, not silence. There was the rhythmic sound of the tires on the road, the whoosh of the occasional passing car, the click of the digital clock in the dashboard, our breathing—particularly Nasim's which was heavier and sometimes whistled—and the rustling sound I made as I tried to get more comfortable.

And then I wondered something, something I should have wondered long before now. "Where are we going?"

"We're dropping Father off at LaGuardia, and then you and I are going on to Montreal."

"Canada?"

"For about a week. Then we'll meet Father at our flat in London."

"I don't have a passport."

"It's taken care of," Nasim said.

I didn't know what that meant but decided not to ask anything else. The whole exchange felt wrong somehow, forced, as though silence was now more natural.

We had just gotten onto the New Jersey Turnpike when Nasim opened the bag of snacks. I heard him say something like "Oh, nanny-no-she."

I slipped into the middle of the backseat and peeked around the headrest. Nasim was taking out one of the apple-shaped cookies that Samira left him every night before bed. I wanted one, wanted to see what they tasted like, they looked so exotic. I was about to ask for one when Nasim said, "Oh no."

"Father? What's wrong?"

Nasim's hand clutched his throat as he struggled to breathe. He tried to say something but could only make a guttural sound.

"Father?"

"David, he's been poisoned. The cookies."

"What? No."

David slowed the car, turned on the hazards and pulled over onto the shoulder. Traffic was light. It was the middle of the night.

"Baba? Baba!" David called out before saying something else in Persian.

Just as Walker had, Nasim went into a kind of seizure. A tightening and then release. He was gone.

David wailed. I was trapped in the backseat. I could reach between the seats and touch him, but I couldn't hold him, couldn't take him in my arms as I ached to. Poor David. Poor Nasim.

As David wept, I wondered who had done this. Was it Samira? She was displeased with many of Nasim's choices, but would she kill him? And if she would, why didn't they simply have her kill Nasim two days ago when they'd wanted me to do it?

It could have been Ebrahim. That made more sense. In the chaos of our preparing to leave, he could have slipped into the kitchen and dribbled poison onto the cookies just as I had been told to. And they wouldn't have chosen him to kill Nasim in the first place since he didn't have the access to Nasim that I'd had.

"David, let me out of the backseat."

Still crying, David pushed the heavy door open and folded down the seat. I climbed out of the car and into his arms. We stood there in front of the open door and I held him while he sobbed. Occasionally a car sped past.

After a long while, I untangled myself, stuck my head in the car and threw the bag of snacks into the back seat. We should handle it as little as possible. The look on Nasim's face was disturbing. He was frowning slightly, as though someone had made an inappropriate joke.

"Should we bring him to a hospital?"

"He's dead, David."

"What should we do?"

"Get back in the car. I'll drive." I had a license, though it might have lapsed. Still, David was in no condition to continue driving. He crawled back into the front seat and sat close to his father. I climbed in behind the wheel.

I pulled back onto the turnpike, pressing hard on the gas so that the powerful car yanked us forward.

"He must be buried before sunset tomorrow," David said, then he began to pray in Persian.

How would we bury Nasim? We couldn't go back to Washington. How would we get a death certificate? How would we find a funeral home? What if people began to ask questions about how he died?

"David, people are trying to kill us."

"He must be buried."

At first, I didn't know what to do, but then I saw that we were approaching Trenton so I got off the turnpike and found an Esso station. On the side of the gas station was a pay phone. Luckily, the phone book that went with it was new enough to still be there. I got out of the car and hurried over.

I found the address for a mosque on State Street, which I hoped was a fairly big street. I got back in the car and said to David, "Could you look at the maps and see if you can find State Street in Trenton? We're looking for East State Street."

Fifteen minutes later, we were parked in front of a toffee-colored building with chocolate trim. It was a mix of brick and wood, was two-stories and had a subtle sign on the second floor in Arabic. Next to the mosque was a row of three brick houses with boarded up windows. The front door was on the corner and had two low cement steps painted brown.

"Where are we?" David asked.

"This is a mosque."

He squinted at it for a moment before he mumbled, "This is a horrible place."

"No, it's just a poor place."

"There's no one here."

I took a deep breath before I said this, "We have to leave him."

"What? No."

"He would want us to," I said, though I couldn't say for sure that was true. "They will find him and take care of him."

I could see him working to understand what I was saying. I felt very bad for him. He was having to absorb so much so quickly. Getting out of the car, I went around to the passenger side, opened the door and, after taking a deep breath, wrapped my arms around Nasim and pulled him out of the car. David began to help and solemnly we carried his father over to the mosque and left him on the stoop.

We stood there looking down at him and David said a few things in Persian. Then I asked, "What are you saying? Is that a prayer?"

"No. It is customary to speak to the dead. I am telling him he was a good father and not to worry; someone will be here soon. You say something nice to him."

"You were a good man, Nasim. You tried to help people. You raised a good son." My eyes were beginning to water and I wiped them before I could cry. "We should go, David."

He nodded. "I would like to call Fred. I want to tell him where Father is."

And then I told him I was sure it was Ebrahim who'd poisoned the cookies.

———

The sun had just risen when we pulled up to the Canadian Border. A short line of cars waited in front of us. The ride had been difficult, several times David had been so overcome by his emotions that we had to find a place to stop so that I could hold him. I couldn't blame him. The things that had happened were terrible.

There was a big billboard next to us that said, BORDER INSPECTION in English and French. In front of us, a low structure that looked more like a tollbooth than a border crossing. When it was our turn, we pulled forward.

The attendant in the booth looked us over and then came out. Right away, I was nervous about that. He hadn't come out for the two cars in front of us. He stood in front of us, holding a clipboard in one hand.

He came over next to the car. I opened the window.

"Passports."

I didn't know what to do. Nasim had said it was taken care of. But what did that mean? Did David know what that meant? David reached over me and handed the agent his.

"I don't have a passport," I said, looking over at David. Did this mean we'd have to separate? Did this mean we'd never see each other again?

"We can accept your license," the agent said.

"Oh, okay." Blushing, I took it out of my wallet and handed it to him. I hoped the fact that it was out of date wouldn't matter.

The agent seemed to glance at our names and then stop. "Can you pull the car over there?" He pointed at a parking lot in front of a low-slung building.

Numbly, I did as he asked. I closed the window and asked, "What's happening, David?"

"I don't know."

My mind was racing. Publius had found a way to stop us and we weren't going to be able to leave the country. I was sure of it. I'd killed a man, after all. It wouldn't be surprising if they decided to put me in prison.

The border agent had walked over to the parking lot with us. We got out of the car and he led us into the Border Services office.

"You're Patrick Henry Burke?" he asked.

"Yes."

"And Davoud el-din Qajar?"

"Yes."

"Good."

Once we were inside, he told us to take a seat in the waiting room and he left. I was beginning to sweat. "David, what's happening?"

"I don't know."

A few minutes later, the border agent came back and said, "Welcome to Canada, Mr. Burke. I have your passport right here." He handed me a white passport. Then he handed one to David.

I opened mine and saw that my name was wrong, or rather almost correct. They'd flipped it so I was now Patrick Burke Henry. The photograph was my senior class picture in which I wore a polyester green jacket and a cream-colored mock turtleneck. Most surprising was that the passport said Temporary Passport/Passeport Provisoire on the cover below an elaborate seal and the word CANADA.

"I'm Canadian?" I asked, surprised that that had somehow come to pass.

"There's a note for you," the border agent said, handing me a folded piece of paper.

It said, "Best of luck. Don't come back – Barrett Copeland."

I looked at David and said, "Barrett did this."

"Father must have asked him to." He handed me his passport. It said, "David Eldon Carter." He, too, was Canadian.

We checked into the first motel after the border, about three hundred feet away. A long one-story, beige wooden building with red doors every fifteen feet. It was called Hôtel Bernard and smelled of fish, though I didn't think we were close to any bodies of water.

David clung to me all that night. We made love in ways that surprised me. I thought I had learned him, had explored every inch of him and knew how he'd react. Now he seemed different, vulnerable, exposed. I was on top of him, deep in him, and he whispered into my ear, "You're all I have left."

"I love you. I'll never leave," I told him. It was the kind of thing that lovers say in a moment like that, but I meant it. I would never leave him. I couldn't.

Afterward, I lay there, sweaty, sticky, holding him tight wondering what it would be like to just be a regular guy with him. If he weren't a prince and I had never been a spy. I'd have to teach him a lot. I knew a lot more about being a regular guy than he did. We'd get an apartment somewhere and I'd teach him how to cook — not that I knew how to cook, but I could make bagels and scrambled eggs, I could teach him that. We'd both get really awful not-very-glamorous jobs and come home and watch TV every single night. It sounded glorious and I didn't believe for a minute it could happen.

"Will you go to Paris and take your father's place?" I asked, tucking my head under his chin. I'd been dreading the question. Hadn't been able to think about it, no less ask it.

"It's too late. The people Father was dealing with, they wouldn't trust me. It takes time to develop that kind of trust. No, I'm done with politics."

"You are?"

"Father told me what he wanted most in the world was for me to be happy whatever that would mean."

"When did he say that?"

"In Delaware, I think. You'd fallen asleep."

"No, I didn't fall asleep at all. The whole way."

"You were snoring."

"I don't snore."

"You were breathing very loud, like a buzz saw."

"You're lying."

"I think I am done being a prince."

"Really?"

"Yes." He lifted my head off his chest and kissed me, sweet and gentle. Then he said, "Now you may tell your friends you have kissed a simple man named David."

Smiling, I said, "I will. I will tell them."

LE BOURGET

Paris, France
October 19, 1980

The Gulfstream II could carry up to twelve passengers, but that night it carried only two. The passenger and a Secret Service agent. It was nearly light when the jet began its descent.

"Buck, did you know that Le Bourget is the airport where Lindberg landed after his transatlantic flight?" the passenger asked, his voice famously nasal.

"No sir, I did not know that."

"Controversial figure, Lindberg."

"Yes, sir."

The passenger shifted in the wide leather seat. The seat had seemed so comfortable when they took off, but any seat begins to wear if you sit in it long enough. Ah, but the flight was almost over. It had been longer than anticipated, since the pilot wanted to avoid the tail end of a tropical depression.

He looked out the window at the lights of Paris, which were becoming easier to see.

"There will be a car waiting?"

"Yes, sir."

"How long will it take to get to the hotel?"

"About forty minutes."

"What time is it in Paris?"

"About four a.m."

They'd left just after lunch the day before. He'd have only a few hours to sleep before the first meeting.

"What time is it in D.C.?"

"About ten."

And that was why he was hardly sleepy. It was still last night in Washington. The jet took a turn around the airport and then started its landing routine. There was no stewardess on the flight, per the passenger's request. The pilot and the co-pilot were carefully vetted.

The jet came to a stop on the tarmac. The passenger gathered his few things: a light overcoat, a copy of *War and Peace*, a brown leather briefcase. As he walked down the short aisle to the exit door, the captain came out of the cockpit and tipped his hat. "Enjoy your stay in Paris, Mr. Vice President."

"Now, let's not put the cart before the horse," the passenger replied in a nasal New England twang. "It's not Mr. Vice President yet."

"It will be, sir."

"You can be sure I'm doing everything I can to make that happen."

ACKNOWLEDGMENTS

First and foremost, I should mention my debt to the *Washington Blade* archives. The archives currently cover 1969 through 1982 and were enormously helpful in recreating the bits of Washington's gay community in late 1980 used here. I'd also like to thank Lemise Rory, Randy and Val Trumbull, Danielle Wolfe, Joan Martinelli, Nathan Bay, Kevin E. Davis, Dolorianne Morris, and Jeanie Williams.

END NOTE

I spent a year at the University of Louisville in 1979. For some reason, there were a lot of Iranian students on campus. I remember very clearly the beautiful Iranian girls running around with their glimmering, straight black hair, heavy makeup, designer jeans and tiny, wooden Candies. One afternoon, after the hostages had been taken, I walked along the edge of campus past a group of four or five of those pretty girls. Suddenly, a pickup truck covered in anti-Iranian signs and full of white guys careened by and the boys yelled at the girls to go home. I remember thinking, they don't want to go home, they'll have to spend the rest of their lives in a gunnysack. The incident has stuck with me all these years, I think because the Iranian girls and the Kentucky good ol' boys really believed in most of the same things, but events that had little to do with any of them put them on opposite sides. On some level, that incident was part of the reason I wanted to write this book.

While there was a Qajar dynasty in Iran that ended in the 1920s, Nasim and Davoud are from an imaginary branch of the family. I chose not to research the actual Qajar dynasty descendants and have no idea if their feelings and/or beliefs might be similar to Nasim and Davoud's. They are entirely fictional characters of my own creation. None of this is meant to reflect on any members of the Qajar family living or dead.

There is, of course, a famous conspiracy theory about the 1980 election called The October Surprise. Basically, there is speculation that George H.W. Bush or William Casey negotiated with the Iranians before the election to keep the hostages captive in order to bring down President Carter. To date, there is no definitive proof that the Reagan campaign was in touch with the Iranians. My fictional conjecture is that others may have attempted to influence the election—one way or the other—and that the conspiracy theory is true, but with different participants. Whether that is true or not, what is true is that by refusing to release the hostages until the first day of the Reagan administration, forces in Iran and the Ayatollah Khomeini influenced an American presidential election.

There are currently groups similar to The Publius Society with similar aims, though the ones I am aware of were not active in 1980. I have no idea if these groups have their own covert operations; again, that is fictional conjecture.

My primary aim has been to write a fun, sexy thriller. I do hope, though, that the events depicted are close enough to reality to provide some food for thought, not only about our past but also our present and future.

If you'd like more information about this period I suggest the following as a starting point:

An Enduring Love: My Life With the Shah: A Memoir, Empress Farah Phalavi
> *Guests of the Ayatollah,* Mark Bowden
> *All Fall Down,* Gary Sick
> *White House Diary,* Jimmy Carter

ALSO BY MARSHALL THORNTON

Praline Goes to Washington

Aunt Belle's Time Travel & Collectibles

Masc

Never Rest

ABOUT THE AUTHOR

Marshall Thornton writes two popular mystery series, the *Boystown Mysteries* and the *Pinx Video Mysteries*. He has won the Lambda Award for Gay Mystery three times. His romantic comedy, *Femme* was also a 2016 Lambda finalist for Best Gay Romance. Other books include *My Favorite Uncle*, *The Ghost Slept Over* and *Masc*, the sequel to *Femme*. He is a member of Mystery Writers of America.

CPSIA information can be obtained
at www.ICGtesting.com
Printed in the USA
LVHW021625120320
649865LV00002B/267